TEEN ANGELS

A Novel by Joey Bauer

Copyright 2020 by Joey Bauer

Email: Joeybauer1967@gmail.com

Published by Amazon - Nov. 20, 2020

CONTENT

PROLOGUE

How to start? Well, first of all, full disclosure, I get real sleepy when I talk about this stuff. My shrink of the day, she tells me it's called Conflict Narcolepsy. I sleep so much that I could get the gold in the Olympic sleeping marathon competition. The best time of my life is when my head hits the pillow at night, and the Sandman pays me a visit. The worst time of my life, it's whenever I open up my eyes in the morning. Well, enough about me for now. We'll see what you think of me soon enough.

This story comes in sweet and sour, too, much like pickles or my ex wife, Tiffany. You'll see for yourself. Okay, here it goes. Bottom line: truth is stranger than fiction. What is there to say about my Wild Bunch, the cast of characters in this story: that there's no sinner alive, nor has there ever been, without a bright future ahead of them; that there's never been a saint yet that didn't have an ugly past; or that God's most favored angels have dirty faces? Proof? I've got your proof right here, undisputable.

Those children that you spit on, so immune to your venom, are the subject of this morality tale, and tell it from the mountain I will till I no longer draw breath. I beseech you, do not to let it die with me.

Why didn't you tell them that the world applies to them, too? God only knows that I tried every trick in book to do that, to win them over to the light side; I tried wooing and shaming and abracadabra and nothing seemed to work, nothing; I failed, and, in my failure, there was a triumph of the spirit. It's better to have loved and lost than to never have love at all. I loved those kids of mine to death with every beat of my heart and every breath I took.

Yes, there is that, but I loved and lost; let's talk about the journey. I'm ready to go public now; I've made progress from bitter sour puss to joyful happy face. And so, let us begin to connect the dots and do the math. This is my story. You wanted it; I had it; you got it.

CHAPTER ONE

ENTER THE DRAGON

To know them was to love them. Cue the young rascals. There were seven, count them seven in all: the sullied Beverly Hills princess; the famous hip-hop/big screen starlet; the faux psychotic arsonist; the method actor doing street theater; the classic East Los Angeles Whittier Boulevard Cruise Night crawler, who drove slow and low; the pay-for-play party boy; and even a baby's proud "uncle-daddy."

There was common ground, too. They had all flipped polite society the bird and told it to bug off and stick its moral code where the sun doesn't shine; they were wounded in action; they were drowning in a sea of deep trouble; they were scared to death; they were gladiator cocky; they were aged seventeen, each of them entitled with all of the self-proclaimed freedoms and privileges that go with their exclusive teen tribal affiliation; they want the world; and they want it now.

What they wind up with, though, is a 9 ft. X 12 ft. cell at Juvenile Hall with its three hots and a cot, just as advertised, bare bones. They were society's ill children in for the Cure by all means necessary.

While the exact circumstances leading them here to have their wings clipped might've been radically different, the people weren't; they were all of them stuck to the sole of Society's shoe. These kids were no more than glorified lab rats, and they knew it, too. They were movable props for a movie to be called "Dysfunction American Style." I was Prop Master by default; I badly needed the check. Mc Donald's wasn't hiring. So, there's that.

It was my job to somehow some way use the carrot and stick to finesse them into a socially-acceptable lifestyle. Theirs was to throw it back in my face. It made for good drama.

Together, we'd go to hell and back, seeking the stairway to heaven through forgiving ourselves for being human; it proved to be easier said than done.

Listener, both they and myself, we have gifted you with our most precious possession, which is simply these scribbled pages; they are to be considered a rare and priceless map. Follow it closely for it leads to our respective deeply buried "treasure chests" in which are to be found our very own precious unique life stories. Take what you will from them and treat it well. When all is said and done, it's all that we've ever had to offer anyone of any real value.

I only knew my Gang of Seven, this Juvie posse, aka the "Teen Angels," merely for a single hour's time window, but, in that brief sixty-minute interlude of hilarity, grief, confession, bravado, seduction and mind-blowing testimony with all of the requisite shock and awe, they became the best and most colorful friends that I'd ever had in my entire twenty-six-year roller coaster lifespan with its extremes of thrill and spill.

I was playing the role of a rebel without a cause, a latterday Robin Hood, in this melodrama and doing it well to rave reviews, I must say, until I no longer could handle the weight and caved. Looking back, I fought the good fight against Destiny, an undefeated and untied foe. Giving up wasn't an option because I didn't do surrender. The color yellow wasn't in my crayon box; you'll see. I took it to the limit and fought like my life hung in the balance, which it actually did, and like my hair was on fire, too, which it was.

Knowing those kids was my choicest blessing and an eleventh-hour reprieve from my own final judgement, smothering by the hands of a merciless and relentlessly dogged monster from hell, Guilt, the Big Bad G-dog. I couldn't stop it; I could only hope to contain it. When the race was run, it had its way with me and left me decimated.

So, Listener, here is my memoir. Who could make this stuff up? Its message? Well, try out this one on for size: fear not the door; it's Fate. Nobody is there.

Go on, now meet the kids who might, but for the fickle finger of Chance itself, just as well might have been you or, perhaps, even yours. Tarry not because this Rat Pack's scant patience trends thin on the very best of days, and today was to be no walk in the park. It was best not to mess with this, the Platoon of Doom, but, hey, why the hell not?

The hour in question here was spent in a room at East L.A.'s Central Juvenile Hall called the "Animal House." The only furniture on the scene was eight industry-standard folding chairs arranged in a half-circle formation to facilitate their coming usage. There was nothing else there, just the seats and their occupants' butts.

I worked like that, bare bones and otherwise prop-free, because this was only to be a talk show, anyhow. It turned into a pitched full-blown brawl, though, and nobody escaped unscathed, including myself, the last man left standing. Ah, but I digress. Sometimes, the truth hurts like hell, such as like right now. Fight on!

To the Gang of Seven, I might just as well have been the eighth chair in the room and nothing more because they were totally ignoring me; oblivious to my very presence. My most earnest pleas for silence fell on deaf ears, futile. With every "Hush!" coming from my mouth, they ratcheted up the white noise's decibels merely because that's what they did, and they were world-class contrarians on their A game. Me as myself, I was a stranger in a strange land, and they let me know just that with every breath they took.

They had their own set of rules carved in stone, and they meted out rewards and punishments strictly according to that. I could barely keep up with them; they played the game of one upmanship at warp speed, as though it was their last hour on earth. For me, that was both my fondest hope and worst fear. What they were saying was: "Turn blue! You can't touch this," and they were spot on correct. The joke was on me. I could lead them to the water, which I did, but I could not make them drink, which they did not.

Like the other four-hundred-eighty-nine Los Angeles County adolescents making up the Hall's inmate population roster that day, they were down by law by virtue of having been collared right in the act or not too long thereafter for their alleged crimes ranging from shoplifting to murder one and being unable to post their bail or having been denied such by an unsympathetic heavy-handed killer shark hanging judge they called "King Kong on Crack."

To them, anybody over the age of thirty ate their own children just for sport, meaning that my days were numbered. I'd just about come to the end of the road, and what a long strange trip it had been. It was my twilight of the gods now.

There at Club Juvie, surrounded by barbed razor-wire fences, locked away like the dangerous animals that our society in general branded them as, they would remain until such time as they would no longer be labeled as persona non grata everywhere else.

For some, that player's time out in lockup would be just a matter of a day or two. For others, however, it meant that they would be held until they stood trial or turned the legal age of majority, eighteen, remanded to the adult court and shuttled off to become a certified "new booty" at Central Jail for the guys or Cybil Brand for the girls. These chatty kids acted like they couldn't care less. The truth was that, down deep in their heart of hearts, they couldn't have cared more, though. Actors act. They were good, too. They had to be; their very lives hung in the balance.

Take it or leave it, in my humble opinion, anyhow, you can say that I was dressed for another day at the office if my name was Roy Rogers or Gene Autry or Hopalong Cassidy or, God should only be so gracious unto me, the Lone Ranger, and this was the Dodge City Long Branch Saloon circa 1860 movie set of a melodramatic morality tale depicted in a black and white film to be released for mid 20th Century kids to feast on at a Saturday matinee for a dime.

For yours truly, those flicks were tasty mana, angel food. At heart, you see, I was one of those '50's kids for better or for worse. I'm wired like that. Go figure! I was to be found in the bin labeled "strange fruit."

My costume was basically the latest in vintage movie cowboy gear, consisting of destressed Levi's, snakeskin boots, an ornate shirt with a rose covering my heart, a bandana tied around my neck and even the standard good guy trademark, a spotless white cowboy hat. The outfit was my security blanket of sorts. You might even say that it was my life-preserver in a churning sea of burning funk, too.

Ah, my good listener by choice, I digress again basically because I'm opening an infected wound over here, and it's hard. Well, spoiler alert: there will be blood spilt soon, lots of it. Beaucoup cans of whoop ass would be opened. So, get out the mops and elbow grease.

Inside this manly stud-muffin visage still beat the heart of a twelve-year-old boy. You see, my natural maturation and age-appropriate socialization had been stunted by virtue of tragic catastrophes for which I was yet stuck in a state of denial.

Three strikes and I was out of Club Juvie and on the street without a clue; I doubted that I was ever to be a happy dude. Sure, joy exists, yes. It's just that it's for other people. Some life! I'm still trying to find myself. If you should see me around, phone it in, won't you please? I'd be ever so very grateful.

I'd been down so doggone long that it looked like up to me. It was a wonder that I could even tie my shoes right; I was treading water over here. As for how much longer I would stay afloat, only Time would tell, and I'd been granted an hour of it. That was my mandate, to sink or swim, survive or perish. I was as good as dead in the water, as I saw it, a bad bet to even finish the race. I would though, crawling across the line in the end; watch me do it. Then, do talk about me when I'm gone. I bet my life that you would do just that.

Well, these kids clad in institutional uniforms, orange jumpsuits with "prisoner" stenciled on the backside, who were making enough racket to outdo a dozen high-torque jackhammers, were drowning in that same ocean of woe, as well. So, we had that going for us.

They say that you can only go down three times until it's over and you get an endless sleep. They and I were all on our third bobs with the weight of the world pulling us down hard. We had each other to cling to; that's about it. We'd all been traumatized. It takes a victim to know a victim; I wasn't hardly alone, as we sniffed out each other's identities like a newly formed pack of dogs.

"What'll it be already, 20th Century relic schizoid man in the gay butch gear?" Inmate Jimmy said. "Speak up, time warp!"

On cue, I shot back with a stock answer from the many many cowboy flicks that I'd seen on TV: "Whisky for my men and water for their horses."

They didn't get it; they didn't know from saddles and cowboy boots, which was just about all I had in my entire storehouse of knowledge, other than a killer recipe for marijuana-laced muffins. So, we had that going for us, too; we were all strangers in a strange land, every last one of us.

Channeling Gen. Custer at the ill-fated Last Stand and all the noteworthy embattled defenders of the faith against insurmountable odds, I gave this my best shot, standing tall and belting out: "It's a beautiful day in the neighborhood. OMG! Just check you twenty-four-hour party people out, styling the very latest thing in suave slammer designer-wear; must be L.A. Fashion Week up in here. Orange so becomes you; it matches your skin tone. All right, all right, all right, you beautiful inside and out yet just a tad rough around the edges people, from here on out, it's just the big three: you, me and Hepatitis C." No reaction. "Announcement, now hear this: the Incest Survivors Club's pancake and sausage breakfast has been cancelled." No sign of life. I was dead to them. This was one tough crowd all right. I had a hard row to hoe, and I didn't know shit from Shinola.

I resorted to the age-old art of pleading and begging; it was the only arrow left in my quiver: "Be more chill because I'm dying up here," I said. "What am I talking here, Yiddish? Oy, Gutenyu! Ganug. What do I have to do, speak in tongues?"

Bingo! It worked like a charm. There is something about watching a train wreck in progress that appeals to the great unwashed masses, I guess. I saw an opening, and I took it. Note to self: "You go, Cowboy! Ride 'em. Man up."

"Here's the deal, ya misfits by nature ya," I continued; I was now on a roll. "Those smug Personnel Department cheap suit and Shoes for Less wearing Nazis downtown at headquarters gave me this very absolutely last chance to jam my peg into their hole, namely a one-hour conscience-cleansing emotions purge session led by yours truly, turning your misspent lives around in the opinion of this correctional institution's esteemed director, our resident tyrant, Dr. Crabtree, who's expected here momentarily to lead me in the singing of the company song and then lobotomize me."

The stunning, nubile natural blond knockout in our midst, Panda, wasn't encouraging in the least bit. She was a practical girl, who had been around the block a few times too many by now for her own good. Evidently, she didn't lay it on the line and go all in for long shots. She hurled two barbed words at me: "Mission impossible!" Ouch.

Jimmy, under siege by an encroaching war party of attack-acne and losing the battle badly, threw his log on the fire with: "Abandon all hope! You're going down hard." He wasn't a starry-eyed optimist, either. The rest of the renegades chirped up that they didn't like my chances for success, as well, not the least bit. A loser by any other name is still a loser or, if you will, a pig with lipstick is still a pig. Oink.

"Where is my bridge over troubled water?" I wondered. If ever there was a time for the Lone Ranger to make an intervention, it was right now. Who's a desperate guy got to do to get a message out to him in this place, huh?

You can't keep a good man down, though. With that worn out adage in mind, I tacked on: "Okay, the aforementioned dominatrix, Dr. Crabtree, aka 'Snaggletooth' ... Give it up for her! Raise the frigging roof off this sucker!" That evoked a resounding chorus of window-rattling booing. BOOOOOOO! "Either she tells those evil back-stabbing Personnel Department devil's disciples that I'm acceptable in these parts or else."

The mouthy brash girl wonder in our midst, known from coast-to-coast as "Baby Girl," had something to add to that: "Or else what?" She was the prototype fly in the ointment and proud of it. Her claim to fame was being inappropriate and loving it to death. Such was her creative muse. Rude, to her, was just a four-letter word.

"Funny you should ask me that, oh, ye of little faith," I said. "Or else means that I get the axe today for beating off to the cadence of a different drummer. They say I never saw a rule that I wouldn't break." The kids nodded their heads because they like me just a little bit, see. So, there's that. "Or saw an authority figure that I wouldn't defy."

They nodded more vigorously. They liked me even more now. You go, boy! I'm on thin ice over here, but holding my own.

If I was seeking sympathy, though, it was to be found in the dictionary after shit and sorry; I was looking for love in the wrong place: the story of my life. What I needed now was a friend, but in this town without pity, all of the friends were already taken up, and even the damaged ones went fast.

Baby Girl, weight-challenged but carrying it well, rubbed salt in my wound with: "Call when ya find work."

Then it was Ronnie's turn to pipe up. He was not one to bite his tongue, either. His mouth was literally a tool of his trade: we'll get to that. He said: "Don't let the door hit you in the butt on the way out."

Jimmy, not to be out done, let loose with: "See ya; wouldn't want to be ya!"

Strange thing, though, none of us would want to be Jimmy, either, not on a bet. That's just me, though. If you want to hang out with Jimmy the Burner, get life insurance, a must have; you'll see. He had a diagnosed personality disorder, or in other words the shrinks had declared him to be a hopeless card-carrying psychopath, but every vote counts, right? Actually, he was a charming kid, acne facemask and all, and he totally worshipped at the altar of the late great martyr, Kurt Cobain. So, what's not to like?

I had their collective ear now; I was the only diversion available to them at the time, other than ranting and raving about deprivation at Club Juvie and patting down their respective private parts to see if the authorities hadn't taken those away from them, too.

I was known to be inappropriate, myself. So, I went with what I do best: I rolled like that; I wasn't about to change horses in mid-stream. Mine was not to question why. Mine was just to do or die a death by a thousand cuts. That, Listener, was in the cards.

Today at Club Juvie, this test by fire was the Personnel Department jokers' sordid idea of giving me my last rites. I would forgo the blindfold and cigarette and look the executioners right in the eye. I'm from the Bronx, see; that's where the *shtarkers* come from. I was a hard nut to crack for sure, ask around. Bring it on!

I continued with: "Tell ya what; everybody leaves here a happier and lighter you; promise you that. If I'm lyin', I'm dyin'. Kid stuff; I can do this standing on my head." They laughed loudly. It could've been with me or it could've been at me. Either way, I 'd take it; I wasn't afraid of them. That was a good thing, too, because they could smell it on me if I was, and that would bring out the dreaded savage beast in them.

They flipped that switch with ease, too, and without the slightest warning; killers kill.

I had a choice between fight or flight; I went all in on fight. That's what Roy Rogers and the fellas did. Running away was not an option. It was for cowards: that ain't me, babe. I'm a stand-up throw down kind of guy with a "Kick me" sign on the seat of his pants.

I reloaded quickly and blazed away with: "You're going to strip off that Band-Aid called 'denial and shame' and clean up that infected sore left by horrible trauma by admitting the damage done to you and by you and diffusing it. No guts, no glory. No pain, no gain. No tickee, no washee."

Baby Girl was never at a loss for words. "Preach!" she shouted. So, I did just that: "This is your healing. Welcome to Happy Hour, one and all!"

Well, that went well. I was offering them a natural high and a Get your Mind out of Jail Free card in this, the only unrigged game of chance in town open to the likes of them. They just might play ball with me or not. The smart money was on "Or Not." It was a tough crowd in the house, until it wasn't. Time wasn't on my side, though, in this countdown to kickoff. I do my best work like that; I'm a gamer: ask around.

Panda rode that pony named Negativity hard. "What's so damn happy about it?" she said.

Baby Girl didn't particularly like Panda, registering with a strong one for "not at all" on a popularity scale of ten. Actually, our Baby Girl, or call her BG if you prefer to be one of the cool kids, she was green with envy, despite her star's featured spot in the cosmos. She was a true point of light; just ask her. She knew her worth; she could buy anybody in the room and keep them as her pet: that was a given.

Nonetheless, BG would soon get on board with me, but it was a tug of war. "You straight trippin' now, Chalky White," she threw in my face. "We don't do happy here. This is a lockup, not the damn Love Boat, shit!"

Healing is sure a challenge. I happened to have a tempting one of those for them and could only hope that they would bite on the dangling worm. Otherwise, I was dead in the water. The relief pitcher was already warming up in the bullpen just waiting for me to be yanked. The circling sharks smelled blood on the water, mine.

The Lone Ranger shot his way out of Box Canyon when outgunned by a hundred to one by ruthless outlaws, bitter Indians with a bug up their butt and greedy cattlemen. Roy Rogers made his bones by cleaning up more bad news saloons than there are Chins in the Chinese phone book and Gene Autry and Hopalong Cassidy muscled up on any faith-traitors who refused to salute our flag or escort ladies across the street.

I felt their presence with me here and now; they were truly a bridge over troubled water. I had their scent in my nostrils, and it smelled like victory. Maybe, I'm just stunted, though. Ignorance is bliss. I wore rose-colored glasses, too.

So, I got in my exiled brood's faces like this: "Take my hand and come fire walk with me, Angel Choir. Yes, you'll go barefoot over burning coals. You can do this, and you will, one bold step at a time. Be advised: There will be no half-stepping or looking back, though. Expect a miracle today!"

De Andre asked me what there was about him that makes me think he gives a fuck, and I wanted so badly to tell him that, well, for one it has to be the scar running down his cheek, but I didn't. It was a trick question or maybe a bad joke on me with a dangerous punchline soon to follow.

That dude was one intimidating brother to put it mildly. Standing tall at well over 6' 5" and going about 250 lbs. of solid muscle, he could sure sell a convincing scowl and a piercing death stare to set it off. It was like he was a rattle snake shaking its tail, which was code for his mantra of: "I'm bad; I know it; and now I'm gonna show it." His biceps were so big that it was if they had thoughts of their own. I swear that I could hear them speaking to me in unison, just two words: "or else."

I could easily have been intimidated, but I kept it in check, fully knowing that he could snap and mop up the floor with me. The handwriting was on the wall. He had a presence that could ice a volcano, and he used it well. After all, he had lived to see seventeen candles on his cake. In his own neighborhood of Sweet Home Compton, seventeen was the new seventy.

"Try reality, man!" he said. I was up to that challenge, but I didn't know what the R word meant, though, actually. I must have been absent from class on the day it was explained; I much preferred fantasy, anyhow; it was my regular bedfellow, albeit a strange one. I like it like that; I'm bazar.

"If you do this today, like right now," I added, "then I can say that I beat the system, and then you, you guys can say that you beat the odds. Go on, shoes and socks off and take my hand. I haven't lost one kid, yet, not a single one, not even close. You are about to catch a break in your exact size today! There is just one left; so, claim it."

Panda, God bless her and give her a professional discount on high-grade ribbed condoms and organic lube, tacked on a doubt: "You just never know." She had been burned before and often. To her, money talked, and promises walked. Somehow, she had made it through the rain to see this day. Amazing! She had been at Death's door before and often; she wore it well, too, an old soul.

I once knew a boy who'd memorized the whole Gettysburg Address. Then, there are stage actors who could spout ninety plus pages of dialogue on one leg. That said, I knew by heart the entire introduction to the Lone Ranger's '50's TV series. My father taught it to me, among other survival skills, such as hiding from the White Knights of the Ku Klux Klan and knowing when and where I wasn't wanted. I begin and end every day of my life with it; it's my ritual. It sure hands down beats out: "Fuck the world!" or "Up your hole with a Tootsie Roll!"

Hasidic scholars know the Talmud by rote; Moslem holy men can spout the Koran verbatim; and us Lone Ranger disciples, we all have this intro and the firm belief that Good trumps Evil every time; there will be a happy ending no matter how perilous the journey may be; and there's a sunny place somewhere out there in the universe for us all, be it only Neverland.

Spoiler alert: Here it is and don't take it lightly: "A fiery horse with the speed of light, a cloud of dust and a hearty hi yo, Silver ... The Lone Ranger! With his faithful Indian companion, Tonto, the Masked Rider of the Plain led the fight for law and order in the early West. Return with us now to those thrilling days of yesteryear. The Lone Ranger rides again!"

That, my friends, is my audition piece for when the Hollywood Dream Factory calls out my name at long last, and

I can blow this lemonade stand on my own terms. I revealed it to them, and now I do so to you, too, valued Listener. So, call me Weirdo, but just don't call me late for supper. Ha Ha Ha … It's often said about me: "He needs watching, that guy." You think? Well, DUH, I know, right?

Panda, steeped in the oral arts, particularly putting her lips where your money is, as you will soon hear about straight from the horse's mouth, put ending punctuation on my ever so moving rendition of the beloved Masked Rider of the Plains' intro by telling me: "Don't quit your day job, man-child."

And why don't I just pack up and high tail it for greener pastures, anyhow, if I'm so deep in the proverbial hot water and indefinitely confined to Life's doghouse, you wonder?

Hey, it's like this, me in a nutshell: A guy goes to a shrink and says: "Doc, I'm just as fine as a good wine, but not so my best friend; he thinks that he's a chicken. What can I possibly do about it?" So, the empathetic shrink says back: "Simple solution here, my friend! Tell him the truth and put him on the straight and narrow path once and for all." To which the puzzled guy replies: "Sure, Doc, I'd so like to do just that, but, you see, I really need the eggs."

When the President of the United States enters a room, he is greeted by a band playing "Hail to the Chief." Our omnipotent director, the much-maligned Dr. Crabtree, now swaggered into the dayroom, and the L.A. Seven took her to their bosoms with a deluge of shrill cries, such as "Bust!" and "Blacula's here!"

Clad in a black business suit and shod in red pumps, she was indeed hefty, yes, but she carried it with confidence. Black and proud, Dr. Crabtree played social hardball like a champ. She was no one to trifle with and nobody's fool. Her reputation preceded her, and she was just as advertised. Two words tell it all: street fighter. In her eyes, I was a problem, and she was going to solve it. This was not a rehearsal; it was doomsday.

B.B. King crooned: "I have a right to sing the blues." Well, so did the good doctor. She threw a mean knockdown pitch at you if you crowded the plate on her; she'd dusted me before and often; she was to be the designated hitman for the cold-blooded Personnel Department Mafia. We both knew it. It wasn't a question of if I'd get fired, only a question of when, and this was my final hour of grace, passing me by like a blur.

The Director just stood her ground, glaring; awaiting my greeting and my putting yet another bullet in my foot. "S' up, Black Queen!" wasn't even an option. Nor were "What's crackalackin'!" or "What's the big haps, home girl!" So, I went with: "Wow, I'm so very delighted to see you again; talk about a cute meet!" And I was off to the races. Yes, I said it; I meant it; I'm here to represent it.

"Aren't you just the ultimate fashionista today," I rocked my monologue. "You look seven kinds of fabulous. Big air kiss, both cheeks. And, oh, that good hair. Look out, Beyoncé! Who are you wearing? I know … I know … Vitamin E and Botox, right? You go, girl! Work it, Miss Universe. You have the face to carry it off; you have a smile like a jack-O-lantern. WOW! I love that perfume, too. What's it called: 'Maid's Night out?'"

She took a pause to process that, which was a good thing. Then came the barrage of stinging buckshot: "You a wise guy or something?" she said. "Because I can deal with you and talk about you after. You're a strange guy, aren't you? Lots of locked doors in your house. Get real, Portnoy!"

"Yeah," I said back, "me and reality, that'll sure work."

I found my groove and the words just flowed; I was just the conduit: "No, I'm not a wise guy, I'm a farmer; I came here to sell some eggs, Drama Queen."

With that said, the kids erupted in laughter, the Director glaring at them all the while, too. They heckled her mercilessly, and she scowled even harder. If looks could kill, there would've been a bloody massacre in there. I'm here to tell you: it was no laughing matter, not even close.

"In deference to your mature age, I'll show all due respect," I went on. "After all, Dr. C., you are in the book of records as the only living witness to the parting of the Red Sea."

This was a business trip, and she wasn't about to tolerate a fool. "It's Dr. Crabtree to you, Mr. Congeniality," she scolded me with her finger in my face. "You were late coming in this morning once again!"

"Well, I said, "I got pulled over and gang raped by a girls basketball team from China, but, hey, I don't hold a grudge, so why should you?"

Crabby was really pissed off now. "Who do you think you are!" she said.

"I'm Mother Goose," I popped. "What? Are you doing my chart?"

"We have a smart mouth in our midst, I see," she said. "You're a dime a dozen. I could throw a rock and hit ten of you."

"No, don't stop now," I said, "because I think I love you. Does your mother know about me? And how about your dad?"

"Just what are you rebelling against, anyhow, Toxic Avenger?" she pressed.

"What've you got?" I shot back. I'm fast on my feet like that and light in my loafers, too.

Then the beat went on with her telling me in no uncertain terms: "These rebellious minors here are in dire need of structure and discipline. You will provide it for them, and that is not a request, either, no, sir. Why this big chip on your shoulder? Tell me, Bitter Bob. Well? Well!"

Dr. C. was big with the metaphors. I could hang tough with her, though. "What is this, Mother may I?" I fired back. Bull's eye! Score one for the fabulous rhinestone cowboy.

It was time for my next warning. There would be many more to follow. She didn't think that I knew my place in the pecking order; I begged to differ. She advised me to proceed with the utmost caution because big fish eat little fish, and I was but a tiny guppy in this fishbowl.

The kids, thinking that the Big Fish was nothing but a big bully, didn't exactly hold their tongues. More with the heckling, which meant even more with her glaring. It was a textbook Mexican standoff. Who would blink first? Not this guy. Not today. I would go down fighting with flying fists of fire.

I didn't take that guppy slur lying down, though. "Thank you for sharing, Orca," I said. "Like now, I'm supposed to roll over and go fetch? It's like I'm supposed to wear a MAGA hat and tap dance to Yankee Doodle. I don't play that; it's not in my job description. You're not dealing with Chuck E. Cheese over here, lady!"

The prelims were now declared "officially over," and Dr. C. cut to the chase: "This is to be their group therapy day, not a free-style rap fest. Rapapalooza is cancelled; I have spoken. Period. Case closed."

Not one to skip a chance for a punchline, Panda complained: "Bummer! I was so misinformed."

"And you are, Miss Thing?" asked the Big Tuna.

"Cinderella, I'm here for the ball," Panda said. "Mam, does this stupid jump suit make me look porky? Tell me the truth."

BG saw her opening. "No, girl, fat makes you look fat, heifer," she told Panda.

"Well," Panda shot back, "just listen to Miss Piggy over there."

I laughed hard, which pulled my nemesis' attention back to me. Did I per chance look neglected to her? "And you, sir, you are to be their social worker, not a homeboy," she went on. "There are boundaries. How do you say that in the Malcontent tongue?"

Who died and left her the boss of me, anyhow? Do you know what I always say whenever somebody asks me to do their bidding? I say no. I'm a man of few words. It's how I do.

See, I question Authority, yes. Maybe, it's me; I'm usually playing the part of the odd man out in a hot game of Musical Chairs like the one being played out here and now. This was to be a fight to the finish and the beginning of a beautiful friendship, until death did us part.

She went on to explain that should she place one solitary complaint call, but one to the Personnel Department hatchet men about me, I would be well advised to practice saying: "Welcome to Mc Donald's! Try the fries with that order."

The kids started booing again. They were totally on my side. Dr. C.'s silence was deafening, though. The booing was like blood on the water for a shark, and one of the Director's more popular nicknames in these parts was "Jaws."

I told the kids to quickly light a torch. Perhaps, fire would scare her off. They unanimously recommended that, since I was getting paid, I should stop her my own self. Sure, with what, a frigging harpoon?

The stuff had hit the fan, and Dr. C. went into Marine Corps drill instructor mode with a direct order: "Give me your undivided attention, oh, you children of the night, you self-entitled standard-bearers for the Me Generation," she began, "because I will be saying this once and once only. You people take what you want to take, say what you want to say, break the law, numb your brains with drugs and fornicate like horny rabbits. Nonetheless, the good citizens of the City of Los Angeles have made you my charges, while you are freeloading here at Sweet Home Juvenile Hall, the five-star resort known as "Club Juvie" in your native street banter, awaiting the Judge's disposition of your horrifying cases. Therefore, from this moment on, you will not speak out of turn; you will not touch anyone, including yourselves; and you will do exactly what you are told to do when you are told to do it because you sure don't want any of me! Questions? There are no such things as stupid questions; there are only stupid people."

Panda was now feeling her oats. She popped off with: "Hey, Auntie Sugar, you gettin' any?" The kids were loving it and hard, too. This was the most fun they could have with their clothes on, and they knew it, too.

"I will entertain serious questions only!" the Doc said, playing the straight man in the comedy act.

"Grandma Moses, can I interest you in a big-ass dildo with all kinds of neat bumps and ridges on it? It takes two hands to handle a whopper," said Ronnie.

"Say, Happy Meal, can I touch your butt?" Jimmy said. The other kids ate that up. Laughter is good for whatever ails you, and they were very sick and tired of being sick and tired.

"Ignore her," Panda told the group. "She barks at everything."

"Don't press your luck, Missy," Dr. C. said, "because I'm ruthless; I'm so ruthless that I'm diabolical."

I was on the clock now for all of sixty minutes and not a nano-second more, which was the standard counseling session's time frame. The heat was on. It was "balls to the wall" time, and I had best not be a choker if I knew what was good for me. It was clearly going to be either the Doc's way or the highway for me. I had packed a lunch; I was ready to fight the power hard and to the finish. Bring it on!

I explained to the errant boys and wayward girls that it's called "group therapy." They explained to me that it was more precisely called "group bullshit" and that I could bite them because I was a poser and a frustrated wannabe Dr. Phil of feelgood right after the commercial time out ends TV fame.

Not to be denied, I played out my hand. "It's your time to celebrate being a Teen Angel, someone who cares about his fellow man and does no intentional harm," I said. That was met with glassy eyes and loud dramatic yawns for effect. I was boring them to death faster than a speeding bullet. So, there is that. Guilty!

"Speak freely," I added, "because anything goes in here, anything, no limits, no filters, no censorship. Everything's on the discussion table. Tell it like you feel it. Don't hold back on me, people. Go ahead on, shock me and win yourself a priceless prize; I double dog dare ya to. Okay, time to let your freak flag fly. Hello! Is this thing on?"

Panda wanted to know if sex and drugs were in play, too, and I said: "Yes, of course." She then wanted to know if I was buying or selling or just holding.

Who were these people; so defiant, yet so vulnerable? I hadn't a clue. In the Land of the Blind, the one-eyed man is king, though. I had the one good eye going for me in here. So, m crown me!

We were all strangers to each other on this journey from the Land of the Lost to the safe house of our dreams, where we could be ourselves and not fear the consequences thereof.

Apropos, I invited the players in this dark comedy to introduce themselves to the group to ?hich BG asked: "Any more brilliant ideas, Lone Ranger?" I took that for a maybe. Tyrone flat out said: "Fuck you," which I took for a doubtful. It ain't over till it's over, though.

Jimmy, probably the most secure in his own pimply skin, volunteered to lead off. He was a flamboyant exhibitionist and not a humble one, either.

"I'm your guy," he said. "I'm Jimmy; they call me 'Jimmy Juice' because I was doing a twelve-step program for getting my drink on. Alcohol, a friend of yours and a friend of mine. In Jack Daniels there is truth. My problem isn't that I drink too much. It's that I need to drink more. I've been sober, and I've been drunk. Know what? Drunk is better. Now here I am at the rock bottom, drinking jailhouse pruno, and that stuff takes rust off."

"It's not all bad, though," he continued. "The glass is half full too. I'm blessed; I'm an Italian stallion; I have a dick to be reckoned with; I'd whip my stuff out to show you, but it would get dark in here."

Dr. C. brought Jimmy's file up on her iPad, as she would do with all of the others assembled there for their beheading, as well, and told modest Jimmy that he would have to excuse her from his next backyard barbecue for personal reasons, and she truly hoped that he would understand. We'll connect the dots soon enough. Where's the fire!

"This is my second vacation here at the Club," Jimmy, Teen Juicer went on. "I broke my cherry three years ago in 2017 at age fourteen candles next week, when they popped me for stealing a car and leading the cops on a high-speed chase all over L.A., just so you know. It was so cool! I almost got away with it, too, but almost don't cut it, though. My rookie card goes real high."

I asked Jimmy if he had any heroes; it's what I do. It was a talking point.

"Kurt Cobain, big big fan," he said. "He could sing his ass off and play guitar like Jimi Hendrix, too. He's my special guy! Kurt Cobain is rock 'n' roll Jesus."

Then Jimmy came out of the closet for us, saying he would so go down on Kurt Cobain. "I'm here; I'm queer; get used to it. I'm loud and proud. Don't hate me because I'm beautiful," he went on.

"Freaky!" Ronnie shouted. "Ain't nothin' wrong with some snaps, Jimmy-dog," Ty added. "Big limp-wrist salute, boy!" Dee chipped in.

It was unanimous that there were no true player-haters in the group that day, regardless of anyone's pronouns by nature or persuasions by choice. So, we had that going for us.

Jimmy's popular support would soon dwindle significantly, though; watch it unfold. His story untold was sure one for the book.

Eye-candy Panda went next with a cheerful greeting: "S' up, my fellow criminals for Christ! I'm simply too marvelous for words. It's just me and the truth: I'm this year's girl. To know me is to love me, and you can take me anywhere; I have mad skills; and I'm a hands-on kind of person, too," she added, "totally touchy feely." She went on to say that if they had the money, then she had the time; she was a material girl that one.

Tyrone was smitten with Panda. He begged to be her stocking stuffer. "Let's me 'n' you knock boots in the bathroom right quick," he offered. "I got a heavy hammer, and I really put it down." He tacked on that he was down for the freaky deaky and that he aimed to please. The kids cheered him on, but Panda, the object of his affection, was a veritable ice carving. Ty brought the heat, but she didn't melt, though, not a single drop.

Second verse: "I'm a be your mailman," he told her. "I'm a drop it where you want it, and I'm a always come again. They call me Candyman. You can't tell me nothin'!" A truer poet there never was, he added: "I can do you on the table like homework."

Panda yawned hard and long. She'd heard it all before. Different player; same old song. She was a working girl, that one, and it was all about the Benjamins. Ty was officially S.O.L.: shit out of luck. The mighty Babe Ruth of booty had struck out. Cue the lamentations.

Frustrated led to agitated now, and Ty got in her face with an admonishment: "That's all I get? You just gonna sit there like a damn porch monkey or what? The lights are on, but it ain't nobody home, girl, shit! Hey, you ain't the brightest bulb on the Christmas tree, now are ya?"

The kids roared with laughter. They took their chuckles wherever they found them, and those were few and far between here at Club Juvie. The Comedy Store it wasn't.

Panda went back to talking about herself. Did she ever have a story to tell! She was from the rare air of Beverly Hills no less with a big swimming pool and lit tennis courts. She even had herself an Arabian riding horse, she revealed.

BG found that to be impressive. "Whoa! You bought yourself a riding horse?" she asked. "I didn't buy a horse, though," Panda said. "It followed you home?" BG went on.

Panda told us more. At last count, she had a grand total of six parents and counting, and none of them wanted any parts of her in the least. "Parents are so overrated," she said. "Dogs screw, too." I thanked her for that visual.

Dr. C. observed that this was Panda's third arrest this year for, as she put it, "whoring with the devil's children."

According to Panda, that was the bad news. The good news was that she gave an absolutely amazing world-class blowjob with all the bells and whistles. "I bet you do," said the Doc. "I bet you don't," Panda counterpunched. The kids shook with laughter at that and put their backs into it. This was as good as it gets around here. Comic relief from the eager hangman; gallows humor at its best. Who knew? Funny is as funny does.

In essence, pretty Panda was a threat to Baby Girl's status in the group as reigning queen bee, and BG lashed out at her rival with: "Yo, Snow White, what ya been doin' lately, throwin' up with your anorexic little spoiled brat self?"

No slouch in a cat fight herself, Panda, who had many notches on her pistol grip, replied that she'd been busy growing a penis, which ended round one.

"You look like nothing's ever happened to you," BG continued. "Well, trust me, vanilla girl, that's about to change, shit! Count the number of times I go upside year head."

Panda parried and lunged with the flippant observation that saying it wasn't doing it.

Then BG came out for the next round with a headshot: "I'm rockin' 36 double D's. Can you touch that?"

Panda's retort was a classic. "No, bitch," she said, "but I know my father!"

The rest of the group started chanting: "Fight! Fight! Fight!" And the two eager combatants jumped to their feet and charged each other, breathing hard, faces flushed and fists clenched. So much for putting a happy face in the Happy Hour logo. Welcome to the Terror Dome in the Hour of Chaos.

Dr. C. put out this fire quickly. "Cease and desist!" she shouted loudly enough to be heard a mile away. "Squash it," she continued. "I'm not having this in here. Remember where you are, people. Big Mama doesn't bluff! Who wants to make that next mistake?" There were no takers. It was her ball, and she made the game rules up as we went along.

BG advised that Panda had best restrain her ass because she would kill Panda's whole family and her secret Santa, too. She tacked on that she was just about to go ballistic white boy crazy on her then and there and be on be on the evening news.

"Ever been in anger management before?" went Panda.

"Ever been in a coma before?" spit BG, which was followed by a hug and laughter. Girls will be girls. The sisters united and all of that good stuff.

BG said that she didn't mean to come at Panda like that, all belligerent 'n' shit, but a bitch tries a bitch sometimes. "Girlfriend, we ain't nothin' but some big-ticket high-end tricks," she added.

Panda agreed. She said that they both were smoking hot, too, the real deal, top shelf right up there with the Dom Perignon champagne and Russian caviar.

"That's just so touching," I told them. "By the power vested in me, I now declare you to be besties. Go on, girls, you may now bitch-slap each other."

The other kids, they declared that it was a disappointing draw much like kissing their sister and moved on, as did I and the lurking controlling head umpire among us. It wasn't to be the end of the hour's hostilities in this arena by a long shot; it had only just begun, actually. Call it the prelim on the card. It was to be blood-sport, a free-for-all, ultimate fighting cage match here. For this I went to college? Somebody, please!

"Hey, y'all, you know me," Baby Girl announced. "I'm BG, straight outta the big bad South Central. WHOOP WHOOP ... I sock trifilin' bitches up just 'cause that's how I do. Take note: It's a new diva in the show now, y'all, me," she added, "and I'm finna take names and tap that ass. You best recognize. Now what!"

Dr. C. shot right back at her, saying that, on the contrary, she, the Doc, was herself the one playing Diva in this epic episode of "The Young and Restless" and that BG was cast as Bad Guy by virtue of something in BG's recent past about a battered homeless man, now on life support, she believed, and that BG's ballroom days were over.

Referencing Dr. C.'s bulk, BG, not to be denied, said: "See that, y'all! A elephant never forgets."

The kids started to heckle the Director again, which was code for she still wasn't to expect a Christmas card or a valentine or even a solitary love note, either, for that matter. The dropped jaw look of shock on her face told us that she got the message, as it was loud and clear. So, score one for the home team; fighters fight. They were gladiators ready to battle hard and until the finish. Death before dishonor.

Dr. C. was down but by no means about to be counted out, though. She had much heart. Confrontation made her love come down and got her nose wide open. We hadn't seen her A game, yet. She hadn't even broken a sweat.

Next up in the Rogue's Gallery Variety Show was our Ronnie, who had a gripe. He'd had a '64 Chevy Impala with $10,000 each Dayton ("Dana Dane") wheel rims, until some after-hours kleptomaniac hijacked his stuff. Ronnie swore that Mr. Slippery Fingers would most definitely pay hard and that he was dead on the case, too. He added that he'd cut the fool's hands off and offer him ice cream afterward.

"Don't mess with me," he warned. "I'm the first one they call and the last guy you'd ever wanna meet; I'd kick a three-legged blind kitten down a flight of stairs and not give a damn. Play nice, children!"

Dr. C. asked him what he was getting his old man for Father's Day. No one but Ronnie got the bad in-joke, and he took a pass. All things will be revealed in time; this right here and now is still just your player introductions as they take their positions on the field of play.

Ronnie parried and lunged back with a suggestion that Dr. C. tell Jenny Craig to give her all of her money back because she cast a wide shadow. That one the kids got, and the heckling was merciless. Dr. C. was totally unfazed, though. The barbs and slurs bounced right off of her, and the kids packed no Kryptonite to drop our Super Woman with.

"What it do! What it do! I'm Tyrone; last name's Badass," the next player off the bench fired at us. He added that we could call him Ty, and that the homies back in the hood called him "Cool T," but we weren't any of them, though.

Then, just for the record, he revealed that his African name was Mobutu and that in the Mandingo dialect it meant "doggie style." The kids laughed at that, and so did I. Old Stone Face, Dr. C., took a hard pass. She was the poster child for sour grapes.

Well, it was like this: she had a veto on levity. To her, Club Juvie was no laughing matter; she was a serious woman, and she packed a punch. I was a happy-go-lucky fella. When we went toe-to-toe, I went down swinging every time out. It was her game to lose, and she called the shots. I couldn't stop her; I could just hope to slow her down. She was playing the abominable snowman to my snowflake in this blizzard.

It was mano e mano for sure. The Club Juvie street was on my side; whole lot of good that did me, though. I was going down slow on the killing floor.

Ty, about whom my unenlightened father would say that he was black as the ace of spades, went on to tell us that he was made in Bed-Stuy, which is in Brooklyn for all of the all-Cali-all-the-time claiming fools.

"Be cool *wit me*, I'm a be cool *wit chew*," he continued. "I'm true blue, ya know what I'm sayin', Cuz? Don't cross my line; I'll erase a motherfucker and bone his sister after." I was in no mood to call his bluff. Lions bite lion tamers all the time in this cage.

After quickly referencing her iPad, Dr. C. told Ty that she saw that he likes riding motor scooters and doing drive-by shootings. "Nothing like multi-tasking," she tacked on. To which, Ty instructed her to kiss his caramel booty and called her a "chowhound." It was not a term of endearment, thusly moving his name way up on her hit list. Ty was officially in play now; he had made the cut.

The kids, a veritable Greek chorus, reacted with a unanimous cry of: "Ooooooo!" Jimmy shouted: "And she took it!" He had turned heckling into an art form. Big props!

De Andre, Black and proud himself, introduced himself to us next. We could call him Dee if we were so inclined. "That's Dee, as in don't ask me for shit!" he said. "I got three, yep, it's three baby mamas in play," he added. "They're all of 'em crazy pretty, except for one. Hey, I like to fuck, shit! What more can I add on that, feel me? I fuck white thighs; I fuck black thighs; I fuck mine; I fuck yours; I'd fuck fuck if it could be fucked. Okay, there are at least 200 interludes that I can remember, and that's not counting the ones I forgot about cause I was higher than Ned the wino on substances that I would best not discuss up in here. And that brings me to whacking off, ah-ight. Figure a average of four times a day over a period of five years. That's four times 365 or some 1,500 times multiplied by five, which comes out to 7,500 hand jobs, yo. That's a whole lotta elbow grease, shit! I'm just a hopeless sinner, too. I'd take yours just to save my own. Yep, I'd steal your shit, and then ask to help you find it. The commandment is you should not ever never steal your homeboy's bitches. To be brutally honest with you, I'm crazy fast running outta homeboys, ya feel me? And that's all I'm a say about that, too." Period.

He'd never been out of L.A. proper, no cruise to the Bahamas, but he did cruise Crenshaw Boulevard, though. "Don't burn the spot!" he warned. I wouldn't be the one to take that lightly. Crenshaw Boulevard was Mecca for night crawlers, especially on Cruise Night.

Dr. C. looked Dee up on the iPad and told him that the best-case scenario for him would be getting a suspended driver's license for his crime, to which she tacked on: "Jumper cables, indeed!" Dee said that a Boy Scout was always prepared for contingencies. "Sometimes, a fool need a jump," he added. "If not me, then who?" Each one teach one.

Next man up was our goodwill ambassador from south of the border, spouting off: "Que pasa! Yo soy el Ricky, brown and down. Some a you don't understand me, but it ain't for you no way because this is for la Raza; my social club, suntanned cholos in those creased-down pantalones, white tees and firme Chuck Taylors for members only!"

He also said that we can be cool with him or we can roll in the dirt; it made him no difference which. He hated all teachers, all cops, all priests and, especially, especially, all people drawing breath on westside L.A. for reasons soon to be revealed.

Not one to be easily taken aback, Dr. C. accessed Ricky's file on the iPad and told him that it appears that he is real handy with a crowbar. "Blood stains are a stubborn out, aren't they?" she asked him. Ricky chose to take the Fifth on that one. He held his cards close to the vest; he never bluffed. What you saw is what you got.

There you have it, Listener: your starting seven in today's lineup, the Club Juvie Rat Pack. Jimmy took it upon his self to call for closure, telling Dr. C. to make like a magician and totally disappear. "Yeah," Ronnie added, "be like a hockey player and get the puck outta here!" The kids were loving it. They laughed so hard that it was difficult to believe that they were facing a harsh Comeuppance, which was to pounce on them soon enough, cut to the chase and go for the jugular.

About to take her leave, Dr. C. fired off the kill shot at me with the news that she actually had a life-altering phone call to make right about then about my future, anyway, and Love wouldn't let her wait.

"Don't call us; we'll call you," I ran off at the mouth with. Wrong time. Right message. You can't kill a vampire with kindness; they don't play fair.

She then informed me that there would be no more warnings and that her playing Mr. Nice Guy in this stage play was over, too. "Drop the gloves, Portnoy!" she ordered. "It's bare knuckles time," she tacked on. "Okay, where do you want it?"

The kids harassed her even more. They said that she was a bully and her breath stank. Well, if it walks like a duck and quacks like a duck, then chances are good that it's a duck, right?

"And you," she said to me, "you think you're such hot stuff, all that and a bag of chips, with your Robin Hood/leader of the pack act here, biting the hand that feeds you. Well, sir, you are banal in my book, very boring, just another generic rebel without a cause. What makes you think that you're not like everybody else on Oprah? Social worker, heal thyself," she added.

Ty, not one to bite his tongue, told her to go fuck herself, and she said back that all options are on the tale, as Jimmy suggested that she try a juice cleanse and lots of yoga. Then, the Doc, our Daisy Duck, departed in a huff without as much as a quack quack for me.

My kids didn't play fair, either, nor did I. There were no rules in this madness, no tapping out allowed, either. Winner takes all. Losers weep.

Hi ho, hi ho, the wicked witch is dead! Well, not really, just pulling your chain. It was more like she was gone, but not to be even close to forgotten. You take what breaks you can get at Club Juvie; they were few and far between.

This was just an intermission and nothing more, the calm before the terrible storm hits and brings its total havoc down on us with a vengeance. Soon enough would come the tsunami and the deluge. She'd lower the boom and bring the thunder, lightning and hailstones, the storied apocalypse was closing in fast, watch. There would be no afterglow, no rainbow and no rapture here this day.

She'd just been toying with us, playing a game of Cat and Mouse until she got her rocks off. That woman was no joke; she was acting out the leading part in this show, the role of "Elsa, She Wolf of the SS," just as written, and she was sure doing it to death. Respect! They got a big bad wolf to play a big bad wolf. Now, Listener, that's what I call casting. Kudos!

I told the group that I felt a pause was needed for us to tune our instruments. Got to marinate before we grill, right? On the subject of pleasing the palate, BG suggested to me that I should eat her ass. I replied that I was trying to quit. The kids laughed, and I liked it. Look at me, the second coming of Richard Pryor over here. I was waiting for the other shoe to drop, though. It was coming soon enough. Bombs away!

"No better way to launch this therapeutic set than you pouring out your unique ready-for-prime-time saga of mayhem and victimization," I said, "all the while inhaling the sweet scent of your peers' praise. Let's do this!"

That was greeted by glassy-eyed stares. Their bodies were here, but their minds were in a galaxy far far away. Reality bites! They avoided that devil dog at all cost, and so did I because it sure ruins the best of natural highs. Call me Mr. Fantasy.

Undaunted, I continued, trying to ratchet up the energy level: "Raise the roof off this sucker!"

That elicited an awesome wave of yawns. Well, whatever doesn't kill me, makes me stronger. Stick and move, baby. It was on!

Ronnie demanded to know the rules of engagement. "Yeah, all the do's and don'ts up front and no surprises," he said. Never trust the Man, and that's what I came dressed as to the party, Sheriff John Law at your service.

I replied that the only house rule was just this one: "Don't hate, congratulate." It's the singer, not the song. Jimmy told me that I rocked, and BG told Jimmy to quit sucking up. The

Club Juvie street went with BG; it wasn't to be Jimmy's day at the races, just wait. You haven't seen anything, not yet.

Panda went with the flow, asking me what the "reach around" was. "Want to hear the music, you have to pay off the band and do it proper," she said. She was a mercenary; strictly pay for play, a 21st Century fox that girl. She always landed on her feet, always. She'd been bloodied, but never bowed; battered but still standing.

I got down to the real nitty gritty now, announcing that, after they share their sob-story with us totally raw dog, harsh and drastic, they'll pocket a tasty and strictly forbidden in these parts contraband Snickers, complements of yours truly, as simple as that. Tit for tat. "What you give is what you'll get," I said.

Jimmy yelled out: "Groovy!" The others were conspicuous by virtue of their silence, which spoke volumes. That's when I played the trump card and pulled a big bag of the aforementioned chocolate currency from a desk drawer and waved it high in the air for all to see that I wasn't just selling wolf tickets. That was greeted by a resounding "Oooooooo!" I had scored. Put down one for the chique underdog in butch cowboy drag. BOOYA! This is me, preening like a veritable peacock.

Always the contrarian, Panda burst my party balloon with: "We look like rescue dogs to you, man? Like here's your treat, Frisky!"

"WOOF WOOF WOOF!" The kids all started barking like dogs, followed by laughter. Well, you find your chuckles where and when you can. They were scarce in jail, especially now because the good ship Titanic was going down slow, and only the strong and the lucky would survive to tell the tale.

I informed them that, before moving on, we needed a safe word or phrase, code for cease and desist when the probing hit a raw nerve. I asked for suggestions. "How about fellatio?" Panda popped. "How's your mama?" Ty shot back, setting off a roar of laughter. Where was I, the Comedy Store?

This was a crying game. It was on their home field, too. I didn't have a snowball's chance in hell of a win; that was a given. Bottom line: I'd made a sucker's bet. The show went on, though. I had a rabbit or two to pull out of my hat, yet. So, call me Houdini.

Cue the toxic duo of Negativity and Skepticism: Dee chirped up that he just wasn't feeling this "touchy feely Teen Angels hype." Ricky matched that bet and raised him one with: "I smell a rat, and I think it's got two legs!"

Then BG joined the whine fest, informing me that what I had in store for them, a chocolate tease/mind game, was cruel and unusual punishment and that she knew her rights.

"I didn't sign up for a part in an afterschool special, Mr. P.," Panda said, shooting straight from the hip as gunslingers will do. "So, count America's Sweetheart, the phenomenal porn starlet known as 'Panda the Huggy Bear' out of the picture."

The momentum had shifted for the worse. Ty wanted us to play some dominoes, instead, and Dee invited his bedfellows to play Bid Whist for mail stamps. "Forget this Happy Hour circle jerk!" Ronnie chipped in.

Bad enough? Not hardly! The Angel Choir started a loud chant of: "Who bang! Who bang! Who bang!" At Club Juvie, that was the inmates' preferred way of collectively relieving stress, while driving Authority out of its mind. It sure worked for me. Who bang, indeed! When the chips are down and all else fails, try it out; it's a game-changer.

Buddhists have "Nam Myoho Renge Kyo." Us certified Members of the Tribe of Abraham, we have the all-purpose lament of "Oy vayzmeer!" Now you, too, share the amazing healing power of "Who bang!" Don't thank me; it's my job. Tell a friend. This one is on me.

Jimmy, the Kiss Up Kid, trying out for undisputed Teacher's Pet, told me that, if I talked to them about my own pain first, then he would talk about his; take it or leave it, this being his last best offer. Liking what he was hearing, Ronnie went with the flow, adding: "Yeah, man, you hit that shit first. This is equal opportunity sorrow up in here; you feel me? I'm just sayin'."

Panda popped off to me with: "How can you even talk to Jimmy; he's so gay?" I smacked her right back, pointing out that she wasn't exactly associated with the royal family, herself. "Besides, I'm just a little bit stoned and holding," I added. "Hopefully, you won't find that to be a shocker." "Hell," she said, "I whack off to Goofy. Hopefully, you won't find that to be a shocker."

Well, my heart was like: "Yes, yes, sure, I'll so do this; I can eat," but my brain was going all: "Cannot do it, just can't is all there is to it. So, that's that. Forget about it!" As they all could easily see, I was just a wise ass on a real short leash over here.

Jimmy was persistent, though. "Black Mamba has Portnoy by the balls, and he's about to get juiced," he piped up. BG wanted to know if I was a man or a mouse, and I had to think about it. I did like cheese a lot, though.

They were seducing me with appeals to my manhood and group loyalty; it smelled strongly like teen spirit. I wished that I could bottle the stuff.

"Life spit on us real bad from the get go," Ty said, "and we spit right back and hard, too. It's a war, and we in it, all of us and you, too, Mr. P. You might be old, but you ain't dead, not yet, no how. When they come for us, they'll be comin' for you, too. Fight the Power! They have the guns, but we have the numbers. Game on, motherfucker!"

The consensus was that I could take the heat if I was really all cowboy from nose to toes, right? So, I should grow a set and fast; they, my *cojones*, come in handy for both work and play.

I needed to put my big boy pants on and show these skeptical adolescents in the hopper just how to ride the wild horse right. No one would know anything about what I said in there, either. No way would any of them rat me out to Crabby Crabtree, either; that was the #1 house rule right there. Snitches get stiches, and there would be blood.

Dr. C. was their Public Enemy #1. The floor was open for good and welfare now.

"Crab Cake plays for keeps, though," BG said. "She's evil, and she has cop's eyes in her big head." Panda added that Dr. C.'s kind eats their young and that that back-in-the-day scarecrow is stone scary to her. "Who's in the field keeping the crows away from the crops if she's up in here with us, anyhow?" the Princess asked.

Ty wasn't intimidated by the hefty boss in basic black, either. "Fuck that chunky monkey, Cuz! Big shit talkin', swole up hippopotamus-lookin' parade float, she got a "wait problem"; she can't wait to eat, and she's on a "see food" diet; she sees food, she eats it. I found out something about the heifer: her African name is Lamumba; it means 'stank pussy.' She's evil and vindictive, and you can kiss your badass goodbye when she gets that big head of hers on a swivel, shit! She need to have her ass basted. Her days are numbered, just you wait and see. It's on! The Club ain't big enough for the two of us."

This was not a pro-Crabtree crowd even if this was her home court. "She keeps me awake nights," BG commented, "and I need my beauty winks, too, like a police need a donut." Panda told BG that she was obviously falling way behind in the beauty winks department. Cats will be cats.

"What's she going to do to you, anyhow, Mr. P., shoot you?" said our royal Panda, repping the big bad Beverly Hills 90210.

That was the straw that broke the camel's back. I decided that okay, they should from that moment on consider me to be their player-coach. "Tee it up, Fire Walkers! This is how we do it," I declared. "Follow me!"

"Portnoy! Portnoy! Portnoy!" they shouted. I was popular again. This I could learn to like in a hurry; I felt good all over.

"I'm Jerry Portnoy and you're not," I said. It was a start.

"Hi, Jerry!" responded the captive audience.

"I'm way hotter than Brad Pitt, and I'd go see him in anything," I added. "I light up a room, and, need I really state the very obvious, I get on my knees for free to no one in particular, regardless of their pronouns by nature or persuasions by choice."

Their patience waning fast, I was now hearing: "You're a deadbeat, and you work a dead end job." "You're divorced and hate your wife and kid." "You're depressed and can't get laid." "You're slowing down, and the only thing that still runs is your mouth." "So, worst thing ever happened to you is what?" "Go for it, shit!" "Time is money."

And so, I served them up the juicy tender dark stuff, the choice cut. My own personal prison was walking through this world all alone. My life almost ended three times. Once in the Bronx, when my best friend took a bullet for me. Another time in Cleveland, when my dear auntie was brutally murdered by family right before my eyes. But my first time dodging a bullet though, it was in Biloxi, Mississippi, and that was the one that let the dogs out. It's also where I was born; a Southern man. These jaded kids want drama; I'll give them so much drama that they will have the overflow coming out of their very ears. Try this one on for size, oh, you restless A.D.H.D. riddled hormone-explosive malcontents you.

"Listen up, acne warriors! Storytime: Sweet Home Biloxi is famous for its catfish, hushpuppies and good ol' country boys up to no good in the name of Jesus," I began. "They lived life by the numbers: drink, fight, fish, repeat."

BG, our resident cynic, snapped: "So, what d'ya want from us, a cookie?" Little Miss Sunshine over there; go figure.

"Papa had a bar down there, The Silver Dollar Café," I continued, "and he was one rough tough Jew by nature, took mess from absolutely no man born to woman! Bar tender was a jovial dimwitted local fella, Gomer, with a huge beer belly and a decided limp that they called "Tilt," who kept reciting a little ditty from the ' 50's that went like this: 'What's the word? Thunder Bird! What's the price? Thirty twice! How's it nice? On ice! Who drinks the most? Colored folks!' Tilt claimed to be the house authority on all things Dixie and could go on and on for hours on end about the healing benefits of oxtail, black-eyed peas, Jack Daniels and, especially, 'nigger pussy.'

"One night, when I was just ten," I continued, "Papa, he went and tossed a red neck called Crackerjack out of his place for being very drunk and rather disorderly. Said very drunk and rather disorderly red neck Crackerjack just so happens to be the police chief, his day job, and the standing Grand Wizard of the Biloxi Ku Klux Klan franchise, the night gig, and he had no love lost for his Hebrew American neighbors whatsoever. We weren't exactly hard to find, either. So, there's that.

"Well, around 3 a.m. when me and my family were all of us sound asleep, we were jolted awake by somebody in the yard yelling: 'Hey, you hook-nosed bastard, I'm callin' you out!' Yep, it was him, CJ, the good ol' country boy from earlier, all right. I look out the window, and I see them, some twenty or so, all of them carrying shotguns. Their faces were lit up by the glow of the burning cross on our lawn.

"Papa, he then proceeds to open a window wide, and he's all: 'Kiss my ass, Cracker!' Then he orders my stepmom, my little brother and me into the basement, where we run and hide in a locker. Stepmom's got my poor little two-year-old baby sister, Ruthie, in her arms.

"We can hear the bad actors ransacking the house, just shredding it room by room. 'Goddamned Jews are hidin' somewhere! Check the basement!' goes the Head Klansman in Charge. Then there are footsteps closing in on our hideout, but they don't find the locker; too dark down there, I guess. Luck of the Irish!

"In a minute or so, the coast is clear; we can finally exhale. We all didn't make it through the horrible thunderstorm unscathed, though. To muffle Ruthie's screams, Papa holds his hand over her little face, much too tightly and for far far too long, and she suffocates to death. I hardly knew her; she was still new to me.

"I was scared out of my wits, you know, much too scared to tell Papa to loosen up his grip when I saw Ruthie's face go purple. She could've made it. All my fault, every bit of it! I have her blood on my hands still and can't no way get it off of me. I've tried and tried ever since, everything from talk therapy to LSD, but, hey, enough of my crying over spilled milk for one day. Now, you open a vein, and you can bleed all over me. I'm open for business. Come on, talk to me!"

What I was now hearing was the likes of: "Tough break, dude!" "Life's a bitch, and then you die." "That's a really uplifting story, which kind of makes me want to just run right out and shoot myself in the head." "Her in a better place." "That was then; this is now." "That's fucked up!"

BG chipped in with an astute chirp: "A guilt trip like that leave you constipated like a motherfucker. I was in a bad brouhaha, my own self, and they had to call in Roto Rooter for my inactive volcano butt."

Panda switched gears. She now wanted to know why I'd become a social worker in the first place, and, trust me, it wasn't just because those that can do, and those that can't do social work, either. Look at me, I had twenty years of schooling, and they put me on the chain gang.

Well, I told the misfits by choice that I do social work mainly because it's a hell of a lot better than selling insurance, but not as good as being born rich. Besides, doing something better than anybody else makes me higher on life than I've ever been before.

So, there's that, and I'm such a huge Cubs fan. There once was this very pregnant mama lion, okay, and she gave birth to a litter of five cubs, which sapped every ounce of her strength. However, her maternal instinct kicked in, and she was now able to start licking those gooey cubs clean as the Board of Health.

Well, she got through the first four of them, burned out, hit the deck and kicked the bucket. The four squeaky-clean cubs, they skipped off into the jungle with their glistening coats of fur to lead totally joyous lives, but, ah, not so poor Cubby #5, the pathetic leftover; he was to wind up wandering through life all alone, a shunned outcast, unwanted and unloved till the day he too died.

"And you, ya slime balls ya, you're that gooey fifth cub to me," I said. "Just one difference, though: you have a friend; he answers to the name of Battling Jerry; and he holds a bar of soap and a water hose in his hands. Step right up! It's officially your designated Clean Day."

They were on my side now; not a discouraging word from any of them was heard; I was in a zone and feeling it; I was the cock of the walk and all that. Try this sampling of the good stuff I was hearing now: "We're here for you, too, mighty Jerry dog; it's what we do." "Us gooey cubs take care of our own, Cuz; goo is good. God don't make ugly." "Lean on us 'cause Life make you dizzy." "Ya gotta reach out; it's just too many enemies out there to handle by your own self, and they've got back up, too. The motherfuckers are deep!"

And then, live on that very stage, it was time to heal or die trying. I asked Jimmy to lead off and help us help him to run off a haunting memory of ghosts and goblins and what was truly the mother of all cookouts gone wrong.

"Bible's the truth! The devil is a liar," I told him." The group backed me up. The consensus was that Jimmy should go hard or not go at all. So, he delivered the goods, and the boy was no slouch as a storyteller, either. I'll give him props for that.

"Don't shoot the messenger," I told the group because they could snap and kill without even a hint of mal intent; I wouldn't be their first to be classified as "Killed in Action." Case in point, take Jimmy dog. All he was missing was an apron and a chef's hat, no joke. You'll see.

Jimmy, our own resident culinary artist, spilled the beans like this: "This is about the so-called 'loving parents' out there, especially the ones that care about their own health and welfare. So, listen good with both ears; it's my true story, and I'm sticking to it, too."

He added that those breeders that made us shouldn't no way beat us down or insult us; it's not the loving thing to do, and, like they say: "Kick a dog, get ass tore up." He added that, in the end, the love you take is equal to the love you give.

What goes around comes around, and that was why he was at here at Club Juvie awaiting the arrival of his personal destiny, and said Destiny was always on time.

"I'm the designated hitman in this drama," he went on. He explained that he had seen some very sick stuff in his life and times and life at the Club was a piece of cake for him because he'd already literally been to the pit of hell and had had a baptism by fire. Then he got down to the real nitty gritty. Buckle up! The road gets bumpy fast. Memory lane isn't for wimps.

Emotionless, he said that his parents were ruthless, and he just couldn't stand it any longer. So, he burned the house down with them in it. That's the way it's done in his book. Payback is a motherfucker!

I said that surely my lying ears had deceived me here, and Jimmy fired back that he didn't slur or stutter.

The hornet's nest had been jolted and all hell had broken loose. There would be no going back now. This was to be the new normal. Ronnie had an observant take to share: "That's really some messed up shit, dog!" Panda added that Jimmy was one of those "at risk children" that we were hearing so much about these days; that girl had a head on her shoulders.

In self-defense, Jimmy continued with the funeral dirge and explained his side of it. This was his requiem: bad things happen when parents treat their kids like animals, which is why he became a mad attack-dog. He tacked on "Grrrrrrrrrr!" for emphasis: performance art live. It's tight like that.

BG was obviously moved by it all, telling us that killing your parents is the new masturbation, and it doesn't get sticky, either: no muss, no fuss. Then she asked our Jimmy if he could say: "Spread your cheeks?" and tacked on that he was so screwed now and his bad self would never again see the light of day.

The now-confessed remorseless parent-killer went on with the horrifying details; you could literally hear a pin drop in there, as the hits kept right on coming. Jimmy went on with his blast from the past and brought the heat.

"You guys just don't know how many times I sat in my bedroom at home bleeding out tears," he said. "I even cut my wrists down to the bone. SLASH ... SLASH ... GUSH ... I think about it sometimes, yeah, and like I ask myself: 'Hey, dude, how could you just broil your very own parents in their very own juice?' Can still hear them screaming for help. I scream; you scream; we all scream for ice cream!"

As they say, Jimmy had gone seven kinds of crazy on their butts. Coming soon, "Fried Folks," starring Jimmy Juice as X-Man Pyro. Sick is as sick does.

Jimmy tried his level best to win the day. He had no feelings left for his victims, the people formerly known as "Dad" and "Mom," who, the last time he'd seen them, were cooked medium-rare, the "Chef's Special" according to him.

Tyrone was totally unsympathetic. "That's some satanic cult on crack shit right there," he said, pointing an accusing finger in Jimmy's face. "Your basic every day run-of-the-mill street brother wouldn't be burnin' down no populated domicile, though, flamboyant Flame Thrower. Hey, Mad Dog, got a light?" he added.

I made a decision right there and then, but kept it to myself: "The heck with therapy! Forget that noise. From now on, I can do Jimmy and myself a whole heck of a lot more good as his theatrical agent; I knew a guy."

Then I asked him if he had any advice for other kids with parental issues. He replied: "Use gasoline, baby! POOF!"

For the time being, at least, Jimmy was the Man of the Hour. He had the following share for us: "While I was bravely stepping up to do my desperate deed, I bumped up some Jim Morrison and The Doors on the sound system real loud; it's my jam, ya see. *'The killer awoke before dawn; he put his boots on, and he took a face from the ancient gallery and he walked on down the hall. He came to a room where his sister lived, and he paid her a visit. Then he stopped by to see about his brother and moved on down the hall. He came to a* door, and he looked inside. 'Father?' 'Yes, son.' 'Hey, you old fool, I want to kill you.' 'Mother? Woman, I want to ...'"

He screamed shrilly and laughed the laugh of a very deranged and demonically-possessed certified card-carrying psychopath, reserved for serial killers and neo Nazis. Something about it was fishy, though. You'll see why so when the time is right. I'm playing Guide; you're playing Tourist. Suck it up, Listener, because it's about to get many flavors of shocking on this journey through the past: you've been told.

Ricky advised Jimmy that Jimmy would be a guest of the State of California forever and a day and that he would be well-advised not to bend over for the soap. "Watch your donut," he suggested.

In a perverse way, Jimmy was having himself so much fun now. Apropos, he came up with a joke that only he appreciated: "Knock Knock! Who's there? They are; they're dead; I'm not; let's keep it that way."

I sang a lighter note, myself, when I told the group that in a hundred years there would be all new people. Panda ran with that by informing me that in a hundred years my "gay apparel" just might be in style. "Trick or treat, old dude!" she said. "You're not in West Hollywood anymore, and I see that you dress from the left."

The refreshing shower of good humor was intoxicating and the ensuing laughter was contagious. Ty got on board, saying to Panda that that wasn't a banana in his pocket; he was just happy to see her. "I wanna reach out, pull you real close and bite ya!" he continued. Panda shot back with: "Oh, Romeo, that is just so frigging original. I'm using that."

But the jovial interlude was to be short lived. We went back to the regularly scheduled program of shock and awe. There was so little time left in our healing hour and so many tears yet to be shed. Time flies when you're having fun. It was just now getting good to us.

"Talk to us, Ty," I said. "Nothing's sacred. What's said in here stays in here; count on it." The group wanted to hear Ty's story, as well. Their shouts filled the air: "Go for your guns and blaze like a motherfucker!" "Don't come in here with no weak stuff, neither; kill it, homeboy!" "Handle your business, Ty; bring it!" "Say it like you feel it, Cuz!"

He caught their drift; he wasn't stupid; stupid ghetto kids don't make it to seventeen. Actually, he held an advanced degree in Street Science, and he gave as good as he got; he was a Street Brother with portfolio and proud of it, too. If he could make it there, he could make it anywhere.

Ty eyeballed the group carefully and suspiciously, before he shared his take on Thug Life: "If you in a gang, don't stop, don't quit. Live the Life to the fullest, y'all, 'cause you, you the one that's gonna die when it's your turn to die. Be down or be dead, bitches!"

Then he shared these pearls of wisdom with yours truly, assuming that his peers already knew them well enough by now. "It's a Gee thing, Portnoy; for true soldiers only. What you know about that? No wannabes or posers need apply for the position, and it's a height requirement, too, Shortstop."

I invited Ty to water the bush; he was next man up. "Say it like you mean it," I said, as if a fish needs encouragement to swim. "You're a registered guest here at the luxurious 'Hotel California' because just why? I asked him.

He told me that he was the Angel of Death. His real name was Lucifer, our tour guide to the Dark Side, known to naïve suburban white boys like me as "hell," but popularly known to him and his peers as the "hood."

Well, everybody had to be something at this masquerade ball, and cowboy was already taken, just room for one: Two-Gun Jerry P., the legendary L.A. Kid, is the name; ride, rope, shoot, sing, repeat is the game. Ah, but I digress.

"Where you from, Cuz?" Ronnie asked the Man of the Moment. In Thug Speak that meant which gang he was claiming. They were often the last words that a gangster would ever hear before he met his maker.

Ty could play that, too: "The big bad insane to the motherfuckin' brain Dead End Crips," he boasted, "and that's since peewee, Cuz, feel me?" he went on. He tacked on that he'd been shot, stabbed and beaten down so many times that he'd lost count. "Man, it's hard out here for a pimp!" he said.

Sister Baby Girl, an O.G., original gangster for the uninitiated, punctuated it with: "Crippin' ain't easy, Cuz, but it's sure fun, though."

According to Panda, sometimes things just have to play out hard. It's the life that they had all long ago chosen or been assigned to by default. So, fly high now; pay whatever price later.

Sage Ricky piggybacked with a take that sometimes, you eat the bear, and sometimes, Mr. Bear, he snacks on you. Deep!

Dee was all in: "It be just like that, too, shit!" he said, which set off a wave of affirmations from the Amen Corner. For most of them in the choir box, Club Juvie was the only church they had ever known. All of them had been frequent visitors here, and they knew the ropes by now and quite well, too. They were second nature: 1. Never rat. 2. Never back down. 3. Never it up the booty unless it's good to you.

Ty was guest reverend at the pulpit, and he referenced scripture when he told them that his mortal enemies, from this point on to be known as the "Slobs," had caught him slipping and popped him in both of his legs and put a bullet in his back to remember them by. "I ain't forgot shit, Cuz," he assured us. "Can I get a witness?" he asked.

He got just that, too, and it was unanimous; they had all been wounded in action, both physically and emotionally. They had dodged their share of bullets, but were sure that one of those yet to come had their name on it for sure. Soon enough their silhouette would be chalked up on the street. That's how it ends, branded "D.O.A. R.I.P."

"That tends to smart some," Jimmy threw like gasoline on the fire. He was ignored. The Italian Stallion, our Mr. Cook Off, was not Mr. Popularity by a long shot, make no mistake. Either he was really derranged or he was a world-class method actor. All things will be revealed soon enough.

"Gangster kills rival," that was the logline. Here's the treatment according to Ty, the aforementioned killer, straight from the horse's mouth: "I got the equalizer from the big homie," he said, "and went on a mission to get back at the punks that lit me up. Caught up to one of 'em slippin' as he came outta Micky D's, and I served his. BOOM! I shot the fool just to see him die; it made me nut up like Planters peanuts, y'all! I'm just livin' the dream large; hope I die before I get old and get my ticket punched, too, Cuz. I did what I hadda do. It's in my job description. Kill or be killed. Ride or die, bitches!"

Dee was totally on board. He piped up that, if he was president, he'd make a law that, if you take a "punk-ass sucker" like that off the map, all you can get is a warning ticket.

The home team showed their high esteem with a chant of: "TYRONE! TYRONE! TYRONE!" He could do no wrong; he had passed the taste test. In the Game, he was a Player for Life, which here at Club Juvie, anyhow, is our nation's highest civilian honor and a medal to be polished and worn with the utmost pride.

The accolades poured out: "You the man, Ty!" "Your story will be told in song, and children will study about you in school, watch!" "You a O.G. All Star, Cuz." "I want your rookie card." "Autograph my breast!" BG said; that being the ultimate compliment. "Just one?" Ty asked her.

"Hey, I know," she added, "how about a blowjob? Let me wet your whistle for you. Don't that just make you pucker up?"

"You'd suck my dick?" Ty said.

"Well, something tells me that it won't suck itself," she said. "I'll suck that dick like it's never been sucked before," she went on. To which Ty said: "Cool! What's in it for me?"

"BANG! ZOOM! To the moon," she promised him. "And myself, I get to be Ty's #1 lady. Get ready for this, Doggie Daddy, because a big-legged woman takes what she wants."

"Thank you! I'm using that one, too," Panda said. "You, you're good."

"Hold on, baby!" BG went on working the seduction. "I'm comin'; I need a man so bad I can taste it!"

"Ooh-la-la! A Hall Mark moment," Panda teased. "I'm all misty-eyed. Dust off the Johnny Mathis music. Life's so beautiful when you're young and in love."

Final thought, for the cops, Ty said that he had three little words. He maxed out the volume when he yelled his terse message meant for the ears of L.A.'s finest, the boys in blue, cops cruising in a black and white: "FUCK YOU, PUNK!" He added that the cops could protect and serve his rich black ass, too, and that he wouldn't piss on them if they were on fire.

The cheering was interrupted by Jimmy's announcement of: "Surf's up!" That was code for the wicked witch of the West, Dr. C., had returned with a vengeance. Much like Santa Claus and the Easter Bunny, you never knew for sure when she'd pop up, and she liked it just like that. She sprang many the ambush that one.

She as herself was not of good cheer; she made it clear that she was not to be mistaken for Bobo the Clown, nor was the circus in town. Her tidings were not in the least bit glad, either. To be quite blunt about it, she really jumped in our shit. Got the graphic?

"WHOA! Be still my heart!" I said to her. "It's the second coming as foretold in scripture. Oh, do forgive me, it's just the weed talking. Don't bring me down; I'm already late for the sky."

She read them the Riot Act, thusly. She had been in her office next-door and couldn't help but hear Ty's F-bomb go off and loudly, too. "Who has the potty-mouth in here?" she demanded to know in no uncertain terms. "Tell me or so wish that you had. Once again and for the very last time, who fouled out and needs to be benched in the penalty box for a time out?" She was, of course, referring to solitary confinement, aka the hole, in the kids' eyes a fate far far worse than death, itself.

The kids laughed and pointed their accusing fingers at each other. So, the undaunted Dr. C. shifted gears and waxed biblical for us. She said that when Moses received the Ten Commandments, he started down the mountainside beaming with joy and singing "Oh Happy Day." "However, what did he then see?" she asked me. Again the Jews!

I replied that she had me but good right there because I'd called in sick on that very same day. Who knew? The kids thought that that was choice humor and fell out. She wasn't buying it, though. "You're not even close to funny!" she scolded me, as she pointed a finger in my face, so that there would be no doubt as to the identity of the designated target of her ire.

Witty me, I shot back with my own take on the matter. "Maybe so, but I'm movie star handsome and hung like a bull moose."

Dr. C. was not to be denied. "Moses saw the Hebrew children dancing the Boogaloo like the wild jungle orangutans, much like you delinquents assembled here do," she said, "and I suspect that they were using that ugly F word, too, as is your primitive tribal custom."

The kids' booing filled the air, but Dr. C. was on her high horse now and rode on with a salvo of even more venom of the worst kind: "So, Moses smashed the holy tablets. Likewise, I will be smashing your fondest desire to leave here with a positive performance evaluation."

Jaws dropped and heads hung low over that news. It was a low blow to say the very least. She reloaded fast; she totally ate this stuff up, which showed. She was now on a roll and loving it, too. Ah, behold the thrill of victory! She then put the pedal to the metal.

"There will be a notation in your case file regarding your utter lack of self-control and decorum," the Queen Bee went on. "Lots of good luck to you with that black mark following you wherever you go from here on out. Have a good life, and, if you hate policemen so darned much, next time you need one, call a gangbanger."

The kids looked at each other because Crabby had missed her mark with that zinger. The next one would score, though.

"I've been listening to the likes of you pour out your pathetic tales of woe," she continued. "You people blame your parents; you blame your teachers; you blame the police and everybody else but the man in the moon, but you left someone out. You need to blame the man in the mirror. You pulled the trigger, baby, and you're now going to pay for it."

You can't keep a true-blue standup gangster female down for long. BG jumped right in Dr. C.'s face with: "Why ya gotta do us poor lost sacrificial lambs like this, Church Lady? We ain't done shit to you, though. The hell!"

The flood gates were open now, and the homies piped up with: "Another chance, Granny!" "Spread the love around." "Have mercy upon us, Sister Bitch." "Por favor, Gorda!" "Give us a frigging break over here, Church Lady." "We're the friends that you never had before."

Dr. C. said that she wasn't impressed and that she wasn't to be confused with their Fairy Godmother, either. The kids howled with laughter over that and caught her flush on the jaw with it, too, their Sunday punch. BOOM!

The force of nature known as "Hurricane Crabby" snapped back. She'd heard it all before. "Laugh, clowns, laugh!" Then she said that the last laugh was the best laugh, and it had her name tag dangling from it.

Ultimate defender of the downtrodden, intrepid yours truly, I informed our alias Dr. Feelgood that there were no clowns here, just these damaged kids, the leaders of tomorrow, and that their pain has a long shelf-life; it demands to be felt!

Dee yelled out that I needed to "smack my bitch up," and so I did just that, so to speak. "You know, you're a whole lot cuter when you turn that frown upside down," I told the big boss lady. "On three, say 'extra cheese.' One … two …"

Dr. C. wasn't having any of that nonsense today. She let me know in no uncertain terms that insubordination was grounds for immediate dismissal and that ignorance was no excuse, either. Case closed. I was now burned toast about to be tossed out on my ear with the rest of the garbage.

"You right, though," BG ran off at the mouth with. "It's a funny clown be up in here for real, Miss Thing." Shifting her focus to the home team now, she added: "I.D. the funny clown for the nice big-boned deep purple lady of the hour over here, y'all!"

The kids unanimously pointed at Dr. C., who reeled in shock, setting off a torrent of loud yuks. It was a real hoot, until it wasn't.

"Now, if the young and restless will excuse me," she said, "reports don't write themselves, now do they? Don't you people go anywhere on me now, you hear? It's not hardly over! The best is yet to come. The Easter Bunny is on the way to the Club Juvie home house, and no one leaves here empty-handed this day. Yours is to receive."

Then the seething administrator stormed out of the dayroom in a tizzy. BG marked the departure by addressing me: "Ouch! That shit sure smarted some. Huh!" Indeed, it had, too. I licked my wounds and led on through the night for day.

CHAPTER TWO

TEEN BEAT

Mr. Tactful, Jimmy with the hot hand, laid out his very own unique version of the game plan for us like this: "Let's listen to Egg Roll Ronnie now! I didn't know that Ronnie was Asian till like today; I thought that he was just really tired is all."

"Ooooo! Ronnie broke wind!" BG accused, holding her nose with one hand and fanning the air with the other. "It smell just like mugu guy pan to me. That stuff does collateral damage."

Panda saw an opening and took it, saying: "She that smelt it dealt it." BG glared at her, and the fuse on the bomb was lit.

"Yep, Chinese food make a motherfucker blow, boy," Dee chipped in. "It comes back to repeat on you and leaves nothing but death and destruction in its wake."

"Tell it fast, Ronnie, almost dinner," Jimmy said. "Speak your truth."

"I can eat! What we having?" Ronnie asked the group.

"Your favorite, cocker spaniel," Ty spat out in Ronnie's face.

At that, the kids roared, maxing out on the laughter meter. Also, at that, Ronnie charged Tyrone and grabbed him by the shirtfront. It was now officially on!

BG, one of the cooler heads, offered her suggestion: "Fuck him up, Ronnie! Lay him out. Kung Fu his purple ass."

The rest of the kids were digging it, too. Shouts of FIGHT! FIGHT! FIGHT! filled the air.

A born leader of men and a guy's guy with the coolest head of all in the crowd, I pulled in on the reins. "Hold your fire, people!" I demanded. We sure didn't need a squadron of ill-mannered shameless hooligan-guards with beer guts and also with a bug up their butt and an itchy trigger finger making an uninvited social call on us now when things are just getting good to us at long last. We'd come way too far to stop now. You cannot be friends with those people; they have no shame.

"They don't even bring flowers, those rude goons. The nerve! No home training," I went on. "They'd pepper spray their own mamas on Valentine's Day in a heartbeat. Forget those minimum wage, bloated butt having rent-a-cops. They all think they're auditioning for the part of next comic book superhero anyhow, but they don't have the goods. Busting kids up, that's all they know, and you aren't anybody's damn punching bag, either. You have a much higher calling in life; you have a definite purpose. Don't ask me what that purpose may be, though. I'll get back to you on that one. It's hard; you people are too special for words."

The Teen Angeles Los Angeles chapter got the message, and Ronnie vs. Tyrone moved toward a reconciliation or sorts.

"Keep in your own lane, Jackie Chan!" Ty demanded.

"Jackie Chan? Jackie Chan!" Ronnie shouted. He wasn't about to be easily placated, not now.

"What are you, a parrot?" Ty added. "Turn me loose or we throw down for reals; you heard? It won't be no tappin' out, neither. I throw down, clown! I'm a bust your oriental ass up, watch me, chopped suey for brains havin', wonton soup slurpin' gay yin yang motherfucker!"

Dee wanted to get his beak wet now. "One monkey don't spoil no show, Ronnie-dog," he said. "You're fearless for your size; this we know. And what we're actually having for dinner up in here today is French poodle; her name was Fifi. Yummy ... Yummy ..."

Jimmy shouted: "Save me a leg!" Everybody laughed, except for Ronnie, who reluctantly released Ty to fight another day. The intensity level ebbed for now, but it soon would ratchet up again and go through the roof.

Without the full-tilt drag out brawls, Club Juvie was horribly dull, boredom being the bane of adolescence. This place was a veritable drama school at the very least, though, but this was no dress rehearsal for life; it was the real deal. There were no do-overs allowed.

Ronnie laid it all out for us thusly: he was a storybook kid, totally a straight arrow, too legit to quit. All of that changed the day that he saw his big brother with crazy flash money, a shiny new Caddy Escalade and a ton of bomb-ass gear, all of the freshest labels out now.

So, he got initiated, "jumped," into his brother's fraternal order, the consensus most vicious Asian gang in town. They shot first, asked questions afterward and they knew how to party down.

"Blood in; blood out," read the tattoo on his left forearm. On the right forearm appeared: "Asian pride!" That says it: all you need to know.

"Represent!" Ricky told Ronnie.

"Westside Assassins!" Ronnie piped up, head held high and chin out: that was code for defiance, and, much like his homeboys, he would defend it with his life and, if need be, take it to the grave: death before dishonor.

It was now time for the Great Turf War to begin in earnest. BAM! This was the ongoing land battle that separated the boys from the men and sent many the street soldier to an early grave and made many the poor mother weep.

"Westside!" shouted BG, alerting the faithful. It was a battle cry.

"Blessed side!" responded that turf's locals in unison: BG, Jimmy, Panda and Ronnie. Their honor defend, they'd fight to the end.

"Eastside!" Ricky countered. "Thee side!" yelled that contingent of: Ricky, Ty and Dee. The get down was now jumping off for sure! Forget about diplomacy. We were at Dep

Con four, the cusp of all-out war by all means necessary. Fists, feet and furniture would soon fly. This was an ultimate fighting cage match to the death, anything goes, no holds barred.

BG informed Ricky that people get their feelings hurt bad from playing that "Eastside thee side" mess. "Speedy Gonzalez, what you need to be sayin' is 'Eastside cheese side!' You ain't in Tijuana no more, non-native speakin' chihuahua breath havin' wet-back taco bender," she added.

The other kids ate it up, going with a universal Ooooooo! "Wow, she sure read you," Panda told the targeted Ricky, now in BG's sniper rifle's crosshairs. "And he took it!" agitator Jimmy observed, thusly stirring up the now boiling cauldron of frenzy and fraught.

Ricky informed BG that talk is cheap. "Yo soy un hombre. Cien por ciento!" he added to the tirade. "I'm highly dangerous; make no mistake, hood rat!"

Then he put his foot to the floorboard with: "You outta your league now, Gorda; you can't hang with Big Dog."

The rest of the Westside contingent went totally bonkers with a cacophony of barking: "RUFF RUFF RUFF!" The hell hounds were loose, and they were mad, too.

BG wasn't at all intimidated. She told Ricky that he talks the talk, but does he walk the walk, calling him "Frito Bandito." "Whoever back down now, their mama," she challenged him.

"FIGHT! FIGHT! FIGHT" yelled the hopeful blood-sport aficionados. They wanted action so badly that they could taste it, and they wouldn't be denied. This fight had all the earmarkings of a classic brawl; two heavy weights going for broke. No quarter was asked for because none would be given.

The verbal exchange was impressive enough just by itself, though; just listen to it; a veritable poetry slam, two pros on their game.

"We can get down right here right now; it makes me no difference," BG continued, totally in combat mode and prepared to throw blows by times of ten. She gave as good as she got, telling Ricky: "I'll cut a bitch! Mama said knock you out, and today, today is my 'Socko de Mayo' party. I don't give a fuck! You're ugly; your breath stink; and your mother dresses you funny."

Ricky put BG in check, saying that he didn't tussle with "no females"; he didn't roll like that.

BG counterpunched and ramped it up by telling him: "Step up, Macho Man! Come get to this. Well, you gonna bark all damn day, you stray mutt, or do you bite, too, because that's what I came for? Your panties in a bunch or what? Wedgies happen. Ask your drippin' wet mama!"

They now closed in on each other, fists clenched, breathing hard, about to start a serious go-for-broke epic Club Juvie punch out for all the marbles from which no prisoner would be taken. This is the stuff of which legends are made, the mother lode had been struck.

Meanwhile the kids egged them on, impatient to see delivery on the promise of violence and lots of it, too. This was such great fun for them. They appreciated the performance art because Club Juvie didn't offer them cable TV, a heavy cross to bear for sure.

BG explained in vivid detail that there were going to be just two hits coming up soon on the agenda: her hitting Ricky and Ricky hitting the floor.

Ricky fired right back at her with a body blow: "You're gonna walk outta here with three shoes: two on your feet and one in your ass."

"DO IT! DO IT! DO IT!" the kids chanted anxiously. Talk was for chumps. This was an all-action all-the-time crowd, and they were ready to rock.

Ricky got in one last lick. "You mess with el Toro, you get the horns, cabrona."

"What are you, a matador now?" she taunted him. BG had no parts of quit in her. She would take it to the limit for sure. "Boy, have you lost your damn mind in real life? It's no need for you to buck up like the gorilla you are," she said. "You need to put that crack pipe down!"

"Yeah," Panda said, "put that crack pipe down, Ricky."

"Bitch, is your damn name Echo!" BG snapped at Panda, adding: "You ain't the only one up in this motherfucker with a GED, you know? You need to have your ass beat! Who you tryin' to be cute for, anyhow?" Then she returned to Ricky, saying: "Now what?"

The confrontation exploded when I told them: "All right, you two, what'll it be already: cop or rock?"

Push led to shove. They swang from north. They swang from south. Then they locked horns. BG smacked the taste out of Ricky's mouth. He retaliated by grabbing onto her hair and pulling off a handful of extensions. This was blood sport for sure, and the ringside fans howled their approval. Both fighters were going for broke and bragging rights.

Soon enough, though, their higher power prevailed, fearing that Dr. C. would be on them like white on rice. "Forget about it," they agreed, inserting a bookmark. Tenderly massaging his bruised jawbone, Ricky told BG that she wasn't no punk. BG smiled at that. Truce. So much for the epic Battle of the Sexes. It was too little and too late, much like my marriage. Ah, but I digress. That was then, and this was now. The smack down was over for the present, but, at Club Juvie, grudges die hard.

Ronnie picked up where he had left off. "So, I was real deep into the whole big bad mad drama now," he said, "and the next week my brother's ace homeboy, he takes a shot to the head, and that shit was fatal, too. BAM! Some fool, Bandit from Asian Boys, tagged him. So, that dude, he was now standing on shaky ground.

"And like all of us," Ronnie went on, "we caravan out East on a scout for our payback; me all strapped with the Glock, shaved-headed and sagged-down, too, thinking that I was Westside Gangster of the Month, which is as good as it gets. I cannot tell a lie: I wanted my stripes and a combat medal. The chicks would dig it; that shit is a chick magnet; and certified-pure untapped virgin Asian booty is a terrible thing to waste."

BG pointed out that Westside Assassins don't be pussy footing around; they were known to be trigger happy; they fired no warning shots and shot to kill. The handwriting was on the graffiti wall now. Blood would be spilled. The God of

Carnage would be pleased. The devil would soon get his due. All hell would break loose. Game time! The players took the field. Play ball!

"So, we blasted on everything that moved in our enemy's house," Ronnie continued. "Then my homeboy, Sniper, he gets out of the gee ride for mop up duty in there: no come back to bite you in the ass later loose ends were needed, feel me? That is how we do; you know us."

What I was now hearing was that they were all in play in that house; every man, woman and child gets their fair share of a lead lunch. Dead people don't idly chit chat with the bulls, and a big game has a big-ticket price attached.

"Jaden Smith just has to play Ronnie if there's ever a movie about this shit," Jimmy said. "Justin Bieber's a must get, too."

"Plus you and Smokey the Bear, too," taunted Tyrone.

The kids shouted Jimmy down, just not his day at the races, I guess. It would only get worse for him, though, soon enough. The time bomb had been activated.

Ronnie got back on the lead horse. "So, we went to my house to watch the News, and they said that a little girl like age six had got got in that place, and Sniper, he's all: 'Oh, hell no! I killed her; I killed her!' Then he all of a sudden bolted on us. It was to be his last live performance on the Payback Tour. His name was headed for the wall to be followed by the tribute letters: D.T.D., standing for 'down to die.'"

Ronnie was overcome with grief after that, sobbing and pouring out his tears. I told him that he could stop now; we got it, but he insisted on forging ahead. "No," he said, "I need to tell this; it's choking me to death; I can't breathe."

"So, the pigs, they raided up on the house, and, yo, there's Sniper with a face that only a mother with bad eyesight can love," Ronnie went on. "He caught the whole drama on smart phone video, and his mom, she turned it over to us to screen."

"We seen Sniper stacking chips in a suitcase," he added, "and then he's looking dead into the camera; he's all like: 'I know that the money won't bring your child back home to you, but, maybe, just maybe, it can help you out in some small way.' He next goes and points a .357 Magnum at his head."

BG got into the act by tacking on an ending sound effect: "BOOM! It's his check out time, y'all."

That was Ronnie's breaking point. He began sobbing harder and rocking back and forth with grief, his head held in his hands. Then he rallied and said: "For my gang, I cry; for my gang, I die!"

In deference, I stood with my water bottle in my hand. "For the soldiers that didn't make it home from battle," I went, "till we all meet again in heaven proper. They're gone, but they're not forgotten. It's so hard to say goodbye to yesterday."

That being said, I spilled water on the floor in the dead homies' honor. They might have been criminals and reviled outsiders, but they were still our brothers and sisters. We, all of us, we are the family of man. Enough of that sop, though. The teen beat goes on; it will never die.

The critics' reviews came in, all good. "Much respect! Big props, man, mean it," Ronnie offered up to me, add on to it with: "Good looking out." Panda said: "That so says 'huge heart,' Mr. P. You rock! You're young Mick Jagger. I'd so do you right now. Voice your choice. Anything goes with me, but just stay away from my asshole."

"Funny you should mention it, I have the same policy," I said back. Then I told Ronnie that he looked so upset to me and informed him that sometimes, we forget about the simple pleasures in life, like smiling for instance. I read that it takes all of nineteen tiny muscles just to put a frown on your face when some schmuck pushes all of your buttons and gets on your last nerve, but it only takes like three muscles to raise up your arm and pimp slap that annoying jerkoff, though.

The kids laughed loudly at that, Ronnie included. I was a funny guy; I could've been somebody, a contender, not just another stumble bum with a heavy monkey on his back, which, Listener, is what I basically am.

Panda shared that you can either cry like a bitch or smack a bitch, and she wasn't about to cry anymore. "Fear the Panda bear!" she added. The kids agreed with her, and so did I. It's a warrior's world, and girls can play, too. Panda was our very own Shera the Jungle Queen.

It was still Ronnie's time to shine, and he let the cat out of the bag now. He revealed that he was a hard-trade hustler and wasn't in any way ashamed of that pursuit, either. He straight needed food money, okay, and his old man was scarce.

When his pop did climb out of his hole on monthly Welfare Check Day, which is called "Mother's Day" in ghetto-speak, his tardy self was steady falling down crazy mean drunk.

Ronnie added that his father chewed him up and spit him out like day-old bubble gum. For all intents and purposes, Ronnie had been emasculated long ago. He did what he had to do to survive. He was cute; that was all he needed to get over on the Man.

"That's his old man's code for loser," Panda chipped in. "I have six of those fools, myself. So many blessings for just one young girl; I'm just saying."

Ronnie explained that he used to go to this porn movie theater that showed that niche hardcore dog and pony act XXX-rated stuff like "Boys in the Sand" and, in the dark, he would get with grown men, and he'd be all like: "Touch it over the pants, pay me ten bucks cash, no loose change or I.O.U.'s taken. Pay up front or get no play date."

"Been there, done that, got the tee shirt," Panda admitted to us. "I was a movie house hoochie coming up: cop a bare feel for a fifty."

I told her: "By all means necessary. Only the strong survive."

Our ragin' Asian went on to reveal that one time, this guy behind him at the Raw Hide Theatre goes: "You get a easy twenty, I touch skin." And that voice was really familiar to him too, okay? Should've been, though, because it was his old man in the flesh on a bender, holding a bottle of "Old English" brew in one hand and his dick in the other.

Jimmy was quick to call Ronnie's father a "putrid piece of garbage."

Panda was even quicker to tell Jimmy: "Fry cook, please! Like you're the new poster boy for normal, right? Mr. Roasty Toasty over there."

"I'm all: 'Dad, the fuck!'" Ronnie continued. "Then Pops, he runs out and goes in the street, me right behind him, and I … I see it coming on real fast. 'Look out!' 'Look out!' Too late, though; he gets faced down by a city bus, and that's all it was to it, till I go to sleep tonight and see it all over again one more once on the instant replay."

Distraught Ronnie collected his Snickers and sat. Head down and trembling, he was visibly shaken to his very core. The postmortem then began.

"Forget that sleazy perv," BG chipped in. "There are rules: #1: Kids get a pass," said the Panda bear. "Just hope he had a slow death, but hey that's just me, though," Ty added. Then he doubled down with: "Hopefully, Old Dude suffered with every dyin' breath he took, too." And Dee made an astute observation, telling Ronnie that there was a special place in hell for his old man to park his disappointing ass in, and it was a fiery furnace.

The kids were unanimous in their disgust for only a New York minute, though. Then they were ready to move on; they had bigger fish to fry. It was like a reality TV show in there, way better than "Keeping up with the Kardashians," and the stories kept churning out. The train kept rolling with no end in sight. It was all good.

The sideshow known as "Tyrone vs. Panda" went on unabated, as well. It was much like a "Punch and Judy show" in which two puppets smack each other upside the noggin with clubs. Well, different strokes for different folks, right? Call it tough love to be politically correct.

"Hey, Panda!" Ty opened this round with.

Panda responded with a low blow: "Uh oh, the mailman's here again. How's that working out for you so far?"

"I ain't a player," Ty swore to her. "I just crush a lot."

Panda scored with: "Eat shit and die, Horn Dog," which was effective, as attested to by the other kids' resounding chorus of "Oooooo!" The street approved. Panda's cred was now firmly established; she could really hold her own. The girl packed a wicked punch, too.

Stoic Ty shifted into begging mode next. "Help a sufferin' brother in need," he said, "anything would be appreciated. Every little bit counts."

"Sounds like a personal problem to me," the target of Ty's affection said. Ty took it like a champ, ending the exchange of haymakers with: "Cool then, put 'baby' on it."

Since Dr. C.'s admonition, my precious Teen Angels seemed up tight. So, I advised them not to fear the Head Witch in Charge because her bark is worse than her bite, and that's a bite that I've got to take, nobody but me. It's not a question of if, just a question of when, and Happy Hour was quickly winding down. Crabby had chewed my butt up so many times already that it looked like the track after the track meet had been run on it. Trust me; I'm a cowboy. I know things.

I was then cautioned by more than one of my assembled malcontents that I could still get myself totally fired off this dark-secrets for smuggled-in chocolates scam, though. The message was that this was nothing but a rerun episode of "NCSI–LA" up in here. They added that the ruthless Personnel Department anal-retentive fascists will pull my license too, and I'll be old news so fast it will make my pretty little head spin.

"Bring it on!" I replied, and, that said, it was Dee's turn at bat to dazzle and amaze the home fans, as he spoke his truth. You just cannot make this stuff up.

So, responding to the group's entreaties that he should go for the gusto, come correct and otherwise make shit happen, Dee swung for the fences.

"For the rest of my life," he said, "I'm a be hated by a whole lotta fools, feel me?"

"Ain't by yourself, homie," Ronnie assured him. The kids were unanimous that they too had a ton of enemies hot on their trail and a bullet or a razor-sharp blade awaited them. Listener, it broke my heart in two.

Dee added that he didn't give a fuck because he'd be a public enemy till the day he died and went to hell. "Just confessin' a feelin' and keepin' it real for y'all," he said.

BG had something to say about that, herself. "Cold slap: everybody dies sooner or later. Nobody gets outta this life alive. In the Game, we just croak younger, and we fall harder, too. We sure do leave a pretty corpse, though. I'm goin' out all dressed in red with diamonds on my every finger just to set it off right; it's hot like that."

Panda asked her what it was about her made BG think that Panda gave a shit. Obviously, old grudges die slowly. BG scowled at her, no love lost, not even a trace. Panda was our Snow White, fairest of them all, and BG wanted some of that action so bad that she was turning green. Jealous is as jealous does. It didn't look good on her, either.

I next asked Dee why he was laying over here at the no-tell motel known as "Gangsters Paradise," anyhow, and he set the table for me like so: "I dropped this fool from up-to-no-good Inglewood off, ya see. He dissed my sister, so he hadda go down hard. His blue-black field-Negress mama, she had a problem with this, though, 'cause me and my ace homie, Doo Rock, we straight knocked her boy down with our gee ride Lexus, while he was skate boardin' down the street in broad daylight with some Dr. Dre Beats headphones on. He looked happier than a motherfucker. Well, smile now, cry later, dead bitch and fuck all your dead shit, too!"

"We tied his feet with jumper cables," he continued, "and dragged his sister-dissin' self until there was just the blue left on him. No mercy for the wicked, bitches! He didn't need the Dr. Dre Beats headset no more, so I recycled 'em. Waste not, want not. I didn't have none. Now I do."

"The skank known as his mama of record was peekabooin' out of her front window," he added, "and she had her little stroke and dropped outta the stage play's cast of characters. Thug life be harsh like that sometimes, but it's my life by choice; it's all I know, shit!"

Ty informed Dee that at least Dee wasn't a food stamps and chicken change gangster. "Cuz," he said, "that's a fool that puts fifteen cents in change and food stamps on a table and poses with it with a gun in each hand."

Dee was pleased; he was the Man of the Hour for now at least and wore the crown proudly. He accepted his Snickers and sat; he would be a hard act to follow for sure.

Ricky would give it a shot, though. His story was a mindblower, most definitely one for the book and then some. He was a gangster among gangsters and had undisputable street cred. If you don't know, now you know. He was the real deal, brown and down with seven kinds of pride. He cruised low and slow. If you don't know what that means, you'd better ask some damn body?

I cordially invited him to step up to the plate. "You're next, Ricky. Do your duty, Mariachi Man. Stand and deliver!" "Break Ricky off, people," I told the group.

They responded with: "GO RICKY! GO RICKY! GO RICKY!" And the variety show kicked into high gear, just as Happy Hour headed into the home stretch. Hang on, Sloopy! This is the adults' part of the program now; it separates the kids from the grown folks, all pronouns by nature and persuasions by choice. Call this a rite of passage if you will. Be advised: don't try this at home because it will definitely come back to bite you on the ass.

"Yo soy el primo vato loco de Whittier Boulevard Sur Tresse, East Los pandea strong!" our hombre from south of the border bragged. "They call me 'Big Scrappy'; I remember when I first killed somebody. You never forget your first; it lingers on; it leaves a bad stink all up your nose 'n' shit."

"Don't it linger on, though, Jimmy Firebug?" Dee shouted.

"I did something wrong? Me?" Jimmy replied. "Man, please! You obviously have me mistaken for somebody that cares. The Giants beat my beloved Dodgers yesterday. Now, that, that right there is some unjustified bullshit. I'm just a pawn on the chess board of life, and I got played."

"We was three carloads deep that night," Ricky began, "and we was cruisin' the calles, scoutin' for firme rucas, and that's when some loco payaso, he spit a whole lotta pinche pedo at my homeboy, Lil Puppet."

"So," he went on, "I jump outta the ranfla, and I run up on the talkative cabron and go off on my own, poundin' him upside the dome with a fuckin' crowbar. BAM ... Chinga! It went all in his skull and this fool's blood and brains all over me, too, but I didn't give a fuck about him or his family, though, either. My homeboys are me familia for life. Fuck my mom and dad!"

"They skinned my hands on the stove burner when I got caught stealin' candy at the market," he continued. "I didn't get caught no more, though, shit! I got real fast hands; it's a gift."

The kids cheered for Ricky because they hated their parents with a vengeance, too. So, they had that going for them. We were on common ground, trembling though it may have been. They were still standing, never knocked off their feet before, not yet anyhow come what might. Life had thrown some wicked low blows at them oh, for sure. I felt bad for them because they were too hardened for their own good. There, but for the grace of God, went I, too.

"Now, I'm a spill out what made me a monster to be reckoned with," Ricky continued. "It ain't pretty, though. You laugh at me, bitches, we gonna have more than just words up in here, you savvy? I'm just sayin'."

I encouraged him to step off; the burning coals awaited him. "Embrace the pain and so own it," I said.

Ricky bought in. "Hurts so bad!" he said. "Help me out, somebody; I need some backup up in here because it's the scary part of the story. Chinga! It's all been 'Willy Wonka and the fuckin' Chocolate Factory' till now."

The kids were sold and spurred Ricky on with the likes of: "Run it down for us, Jeffe; you'll feel better if you get it off your chest." "Like yo, tell it already, shit!"

And so, he began: "Christmas Eve at Holy Redeemer Iglesias, I was this cute little altar boy, yeah? Age ten anyos. Midnight Mass was over," he said, "and Father O' Sullivan, he was gonna hand deliver me to me casa. So, did he do it? Can you say 'not even!' He hits me up with: 'Ricardo, my sweet sweet child of God, come join me in my office. I have a very special treat waiting there just for you, darling. It's a special time for giving, and I'm your own personal secret Santa.'"

"Red flag!" noted our street-smart distaff sage, BG. "Loco, what were you ever thinking?"

Ricky said: "I'm thinking 'free candies, hopefully chocolate, comin' my way pronto. Oh, boy! Best Navidad ever. Now, I'm all crazy loud singin' 'Jingle Bells' 'n' shit.

"So, we head to his office, hand-in-hand like we're the very best of boys. My heart was beatin' so fast on me, BOOM BOOM BOOM ... just can't wait to get there, already; I'm so excited! We go in, and he ... he pulls out this bottle of red wine, and ..."

"Speed your slowpoke ass up," BG complained. "I got bad A.D.D. workin', shit!"

Panda threw her log on the fire, too, with: "Yeah, dude, you talk like old people fuck! Don't get me started. If an old man comes a drop, he acts like he's cured cancer."

"And he ... he fills up the cup to the top, okay?" Ricky went on. "Father O. is all like: 'Drink it down, laddie; drink to Baby Jesus. Every drop of that sweet Jesus juice, dear innocent, for our lord and savior on his birthday. Huge mortal sin not to do it.' So, I did it like I was a dog right out of doggie obedience school, a fuckin' Chihuahua named Chuey 'n' shit."

"Oh, you poor poor kid," I said, and I had backup from the support group, a real tough crowd to please this one.

"And he … he pours out another one for me," Ricky said. "I drained that one, too, and he was all like: 'Now, Child, you'll give me my special gift.' So, he unzips his fly and … and he goes: 'Pull it out or I'll strangle you right here and now!'

"Then he goes: 'Drop your pants and get on your hands and knees.' I do that pedo also. He's all … he's now all like: 'I find out you told anyone, anyone even one word, one single word, I'll come to your house in the dead of night, and I'll cut your throat from ear to ear.'"

"So, he's raping me, yeah, like he's been there before," Ricky went on, "and he … he's all like: 'Pray the Rosary.' Hail, Mary, full of grace, the Lord is with thee. Where was this almighty God! Somebody tell me, por favor! Where was this superhero, this all-love-all-the-time fairytale God of ours, the big shot?

"Father O., he used to be steady sayin': 'Suffer the children to come unto me.' Bullshit! He needs to be cut short like the vicious animal that he is."

"That evil vulture!" shouted Panda. "He'll get his by times of ten."

Ty added: "I just wanna punch up that disgraceful cocksucker of the cloth so bad I can taste that shit!"

"I got a little somethin' somethin' fierce just for his despicable predatory ass," BG chipped in. "Can you say 'Saturday Night Special?'"

Ricky added that he's tried so hard to move on with his life since then. "Chinga!" he cursed. "Really do try that forgive and forget shit hard, ya know, just don't work out for me, not even a little bit. It's kinda like 'Night of the Living Dead.'"

"Oh, yeah, sure, that nauseous zombie flick," Panda said. "I eat that extreme horror shit up with a spoon and beg for seconds."

"Dude thinks he's like killed the attack-zombie off for good this time. He's all happy and toasting with a $400 bottle of Cristal champagne," Jimmy said.

"Yeah," Panda piggybacked, "but it comes back to stalk him up once more, and this time it's personal."

Jimmy went on: "Yo, Ricky, O' Sullivan, like he's playing your attack-zombie character in it, am I right? This shit rocks the mic like Led Zeppelin, dude. I'm hearing power chords all in my head now!"

"It's two attack-zombies, Juicer," Ricky snapped back. "There's Father O-Dog, he's numero uno, simone, and the other zombie, you're lookin' at him, ese. So, go on, everybody run away and hide from me now because that's exactly what

I'd do, too, if I'm playin' the part of you in this crazy motherfucker.

"I hate that pinche maricon, but I hate myself a whole lot worse, though. Wherever I go, I turn up with the memory wagon. Chinga! Might just as well as quit on my so-called life, shit!"

Ricky was emotionally wasted by now. I tried to revive him with: "It's not about giving up; it's all about letting go. This is your detox. I got your back; we all do."

"You're our brother, dude," Panda added. "We're family; you matter."

"You bleed, we all of us bleed, too," Ronnie told the wounded boy. "We're all battle buddies up in here, dude. We've all of us been used, bruised and abused, every last one."

The kids voiced their unanimous support for Ricky, but then the mood suddenly changed in a complete about face.

Jimmy sucker punched Ricky, catching him totally off guard with: "You should've fought him off, though, man, or died trying to. Kick him in the nuts! That's in the playbook."

Dee tossed his log on the fire, too, with: "Do somethin'; do anything! Don't be no parts of a martyr, Ricky; be a Aztec warrior. You know how they did back in the day. They sacrificed virgins. Try that shit sometime, homie. It will take your mind off your troubles. Works good for me, though. I be steady settin' 'em up and puttin' 'em down. If they're old enough to bleed, they're old enough to breed."

It was Panda's turn to kick the dog when it was down, and she did just that with: "Yep, go full-blown nun-chuck Bruce Lee: that's the hot play right there. Break out some of that old-school Kung Fu cowboy Billy Jack shit, dude, just sayin'. Don't be no body's fool."

Dee was the last to pile on with: "Still kind of your bad, though, Ricky dog. There are

no innocent victims up in Club Juvie, not me and, for sure, not even you. Ya should've screamed out like he just killed your little pet puppy named Smoochie 'n' shit."

The kids, except for Ricky, naturally, laughed at that. It was comic relief and the ticket

price was right. The seating was priority, too. What's not to like?

"I messed up so bad! It's all on me," cried out Ricky, "every bit of it! I just wanna die so bad. All I think about twenty-four-seven, a endless sleep."

I was feeling him, too; I'd been to that dark place often my own self, and so had the rest of the rat pack, every last one of them was born to lose. It's not very pretty what a town without pity can do?

Ricky got down to the real nitty gritty now. He confessed that he was more sorry that he might have let O' Sullivan down than he was scared of him.

"See," he said, "I cared for the malo gavacho even after all of that went down and was sealed in the book."

"I got more love from him than I ever got outta my own dad," he went on. "My pops called me 'shithead' and 'pinche leva' so much I thought that they were like my real given names by birth. Chinga!

"He'd be all: 'Have a very nice day, puto, and here's a very nice swole lip and a very nice blooded nose to start it off good and proper.' He gave me cigar burns on my face to teach me proper respect when I didn't call him 'sir' loud enough to suit his cruel self."

"Basic payback works so good at times such as that," Panda offered up. "Don't get mad, just get even is all; it's tight like that."

Ty told him: "Payback is a scoundrel."

"But only if the gun's loaded up, though," Panda spat, drawing all eyes to her now. She stuck her chest out and looked very healthy. The actress known as Panda was always in character, and she played the wanton vixen role to death.

"Just listen to Cheerleader Barbie doll over there," BG said, "perpetratin' like she all ghetto-centric 'n' shit. Where your pompoms at, Princess Panda from the big bad 90210? What's on special at Saks Fifth Avenue of late, girlie girl? Fuckin' fashionista over there."

"Yeah," agreed Ty, "with the big-ass swimming pool and the lit tennis courts, too."

Not to be denied, Jimmy tossed in: "And a pet riding-horse with all of its shots."

"Twirl on this, envious sour-grapes bitches!" Panda said as she gave the hecklers the finger, adding: "Fuck all y'all!" She didn't get rattled easily and didn't sweat the small stuff; she'd had had a staring contest with Death more than once and didn't even blink, not the once.

Ricky continued: "I did hint at the dirty deed with my parents once, feel me, and they beat me down like a malo stepchild with bad grades for lyin' on our muy bueno amigo, the most righteous reverend, Father O-dog, who even had Christmas dinner with us. I spit in his mashed potatoes,, too.

"They made me confess to him all humble like 'n' shit for talkin' scandalous smack behind his back, and he gave me a penance, too. Yep, it was ten more of his famous Hail Marys."

"What's his penance, somebody please?" Ricky asked the group. "He's still running loose out there on the prowl for young stuff, the Night Stalker on his game. After he raped me, he lit up a cigar and blew smoke rings in the air. Ain't that somethin' about a bitch!"

I said that the despicable back door man, Father O.'s penance was living with his twisted self for the rest of his days; start there. He will for sure get paid back seven kinds of awful because that's the way of the world: you get back what you put in. The love you give is equal to the love you'll get.

"He ain't hard to find," Ricky told us, "Holy Redeemer Iglesias rectory. I got his digits burned way down deep in my memory bank, too, for a rainy day."

Ty had an off-the-cuff observation to share: "It's too depressin' up in here! Makes a motherfucker wanna chug down some Drano 'n' shit. I'm about to lose my religion and act a fool, feel me?" The Amen Corner was in complete agreement.

Dee had a suggestion: "Spit something funny at us, Beverly Hills Panda! This is your moment, girl. Or ya think you too good for us. Well, you ain't in the 90210 shopping on Rodeo Drive no more, and that fucked up jump suit you're sportin', it for sure ain't Gucci, neither, you poor little rich girl princess you.

"Yeah, go on, make us laugh, Snowflake." Sister BG added. "How it feel to be Goldilocks with a supersize boob job? Aren't you afraid you gonna lose your natural balance like that, though, Miss Top Heavy?"

Going with the flow, Panda then said: "I'm so busted for putting in sex work. Girls just want to have fun, and thee Lady Panda here was getting herself laid and paid. Call me, ball me: 800-RENT A COOCHIE. I'm a sex addict; I like to fuck a lot; it's what I do. I have much game. What can I say?"

"What I'm getting is that you are a practicing street corner prostitute, though, young lady," I told her. "A duck by any other name is still a duck. All you're missing are the feathers and a beak."

She snapped that she wasn't any parts of a prostitute, though. "Instead, try a 'sugar baby' with lots of loaded sugar daddies all lined up by wallet size to get some of this pretty young thing's affection. Pay out for put out."

"I enjoy fine dining, elegant travel and mutual spoiling," she added, "and I'm in the pink, too; I don't eat any meat or any sweets, just amphetamines."

I served up the punchline: "And I'm not a social worker; I'm Bubbles the Queer Stripper here to give you a dance. What'll it be: lap or table? Just name it."

I couldn't resist asking her how much she was pulling in for a date and a dip or for the "minivan," which, in other words, was two in the front and five in the rear.

To that one, she retorted that she raked in the big bucks because she was the Prada of pussy. Then she snapped and chewed me out with: "I don't have to explain shit to you!"

"Is it because I'm a cowboy?" I said.

"No, it is because you're a hot mess, and I don't want any part of it," she went on. "You, you're nothing but an infantilized male. I eat guys like you for lunch."

"I said back: "What do you want to do with your life?"

"I'd like to eat a mile of Justin Timberlake's shit just to get close to his asshole," she said.

"Well, cool!" I said. "It's good to set goals for yourself."

She added that I reminded her of someone, Donald Duck's nephew, Baby Hughey, an infant duck the size of a man wearing a diaper.

"You don't have to be a star to be in my show, Mr. P., she tacked on, "just be your strange self; I like myself some strange now and then. You're an original. That's all you get out of the Panda for free. Show me the money!"

Ronnie wasn't going for it. "What's up! I'm not laughing, yet," he complained.

"Me, neither," Panda said. "I'm sad as fuck! Just hate it here with a full-blown vengeance."

The Angel Choir sang that song, too. "The food here reeks, and you get such tiny portions of it," Jimmy piped up. "Concrete beds and sandpaper TP," said Ty, "industrial strength." "That's some drastic shit they give out!" BG added. It was unanimous that life at the fabulous Club Juvie sucks on the best of days. Don't believe the hype. Camp Cupcake it isn't.

Panda insisted in no uncertain terms that her story was sad but true. "Don't cry for me," she told us, "I can hold my own."

It went down like this in Panda's own words: "I was like … like this runaway rich girl, yeah, mainly because my custodial parent of the month, the father unit known to me as Stepdaddy #2, he had a bad case of Wandering Hands Disease, and like his sole mission in life was to finger bang me with all ten digits, consecutively. Mommy Dearest #1, my bio mom from hell, she was much too preoccupied with Duke, her strapped-on butch dyke lover, to be bothered with all that static.

"So, I'm steady thinking to myself: 'Hey, Pan, what ya got going for yourself, beside perky titties and a cute petite derriere with a personality all of its own,' and the answer was like totally nothing else whatsoever, nada. I was shit out of luck.

"I hit the street and soon realized that, if I didn't work, I just didn't eat. Well, this dude I knew at the homeless teens shelter hooked me up to do porn flicks, and I soon popped my actress cherry as Anonymous Topless Girl sucking on a Popsicle in 'Freaking on the Beach,' followed by the once-in-a-lifetime role of Bootycandy in 'Ass-Backward' with a killer cast of: the twins, Oral Annie and Anal Alice; Chuck Raw aka the Rifleman; and introducing Long Dog Johnny Hung Low, who had a dong on him like the frigging Liberty Bell.

"At tender Sweet 16, I looked like a legal piece of Hot 21. No sweat getting into clubs with fake I.D., whatsoever. Men came on to me like … like bees to honey, which made me feel grown with all of the preferred A-listed perks.

"Well, last Halloween, I'm out there getting my club on, you see, Bat Girl in a pushup bra, feel me, and there's this one older than dirt creep there that kept putting his filthy paws on me. So gross!

"Okay, okay, so he's buying me drinks, and he's getting really really sack-pushy. He asks me to dance, and I told him that I only dance with life from my own planet.

"Okay, she went on," I stuck it out till Last Call for Alcohol and then ... then I'm like out there on the street again, waiting on my bus, kind of tipsy like, and doing a balancing act."

"Why do I think something very very tragic's about to happen to you and soon, too?" I asked her.

Jimmy answered that with: "It's because you're the Mad Genius from Old People Land." Nobody laughed because stand-up comedy wasn't Jimmy's strong suit, nor was forest ranger.

"In a hot second, a car pulls up to me," Panda continued, "window goes down and I'm now hearing: 'Hey, movie star, go ahead on, jump in the ride, give ya a lift home; I'm going your way. These streets are much too mean for a pretty young thing like you without on-sight representation; the freaks come out at night."

"Him! Oh, him for sure," BG shouted. "I got five on it!"

"If it's not him, there ain't a Jesus," Dee added.

"Uh huh," Panda continued, "Lester the Molester, the same lecherous chicken hawk from before, and I totally got in there with him, too; not going to lie about it. Danger gets my rocks off. It was a total high high. I told him to excuse me, while I kiss the sky."

Jimmy popped off to Panda, saying: "Girl, you have a body by Mercedes Benz and a mind by Tinker Toy. You need to change your name to Panda Headroom."

Panda continued: "Okay, so Sicko's packing serious heat. He pulls his chrome on me and puts it to my head; he's all like: 'Even think about screaming, I will sell tickets to watch me blow your brains out of your earholes!' He was very very persuasive, too. He had me outnumbered with a .45 to keep him alive and seven bullets on his side.

"Next thing I knew, we're way way up in the Hollywood Hills at this humungous house. It was for sure some 'Nightmare on Elm Street' shit. So, we go inside, and he has this dungeon with whips and chains, everything but a concession stand; he totally handcuffs me, and he pantsed me and …. and he … he raped me with the gun barrel, as he beat off, repeating: 'Am I naughty, Mommy? 'Am I naughty, Mommy? Am I? Am I?'

"When it's all said and done, he undoes the cuffs and offers me the gun. He goes: 'Shoot me up! Shoot me dead! Go ahead on; I'm a bad bad boy.' So, I refuse, and he whips out this thick wad of cash on me, and he's like: 'Take it; take it all!'"

Panda broke down in sobs; the weight was too much for her to bear. I tried to console her, but it was to no avail. The horse was out of the stable, not to return, not ever.

BG wasn't taking this whole scenario lying down. She put it like this: "Me, slow to anger, fast to forgive, the mighty Battlin' BG, I'm cold snatchin' the shootin' piece and the cheese, and then … and then I'm blowin' Naughty Boy to Kingdom Come. BLAM BLAM BLAM BLAM … There it is! I'm a badass motherfucker like '80's Mike Tyson. Catch me if you can, bitches!"

The other Teen Angels cheered BG on, and she was off to the races. It was getting really good to her now; she had her groove back.

"And I'm choppin' off his dick and stickin' it in his mouth, too," she continued, "as a cold-ass warnin' to other rabid mongrel dogs of his kind in the area. "Beat your meat now, no dick havin' kiddie wrangler!"

Her fans started shouting in support: "BG BG BG!" And the famous rapper/movie star was loving it to the fullest, too. It's good to be queen bee in the hive.

She wrapped it all up by saying that she was just a hardcore-feminist-no-mercy-showing-fearless-caped-crusader. "I see trash; I'm a take it out," she added.

Panda, regaining her composure now, went on with an epilogue for her story: "I just wanted to go home and be a happy little girl again because, once you grow up, your heart like it totally dies out on you, and you, you're a real sad sack individual a lot of the time," she explained. "Will that happen to me, too, Mr. P.? Will I be up the creek without a paddle?"

"No way! It will never happen to you, not you," I assured her. "Someday, your prince will come. So, be ready for him."

"So, I picked up my clothes and made the dash," she went on, "but, know what, I just could not seem to find that little girl anywhere, not even a trace of her was left," she said, "and I've looked for her all up and down. Want to know why not? It's because she's dead to me now; her name was Innocence. I miss her so much, now more than ever before.

She was a long long time coming, and she'll be a long long time gone."

Panda's saga had touched the group's collective heart, not an easy thing to do. There wasn't a dry eye in the place. I cried like a motherless child, myself. My heart is on my sleeve and so were theirs, at least for a minute.

Then, they laughed it all off. To them, vulnerability equals weakness, which is something that they couldn't afford to risk; it often proved to be fatal in a dog-eat-dog world. I was a witness; I'd met the enemy, and it was me. Stay tuned.

"I'm totally blown away that you guys made it through the whole horror story without even once trying to off yourselves; you people are truly amazing," she went. "I could take you anywhere; I get around, too. Big uppity ups! There's a place for us, and it isn't this one up in here, either, no way. We were just programmed all wrong. We weren't born to run."

"Too little, too late," BG added. "You play the hand you're dealt. You gotta know when to hold 'em and know when to fold 'em."

I then told Panda to sign up for "Marvelous Jerry's Natural High Talent Showcase," guaranteed to make her feel whole again and less like the second coming of cracked up Humpty Dumpty and that she should celebrate being Super Panda because she was truly one of a kind, unique, and I meant every word of it, too. She had outsmarted Death in a rigged game of chance, no easy feat on the best of days. My hat was off to her; she would be just fine until sore loser Death returned for a rematch. Then, all bets were off.

"And your talents are?" I asked her. To which she told me that she knew "horse and rider" and, of course, there was "bondage for dummies" and "golden showers," too. Plus, she sings some. So, there's that.

"Seize the day!" I said: "Sing for us then, might as well. You might get discovered. I got a guy."

Ricky followed me with: "Hey, girl, why not, que no?"

"You go, Miss Ass for Days! Don't be no tease," Ty chipped in.

"Use it or lose it! Blow out those pipes," BG offered. "It works for me, and my shit is global. Don't even ask."

Panda was visibly moved by the wave of affection coming at her. "Okay," she agreed, "but no booing or throwing harsh shade at me, though. I don't go for that, and, besides, I'm PMS-ing right here and now, which means I can flat out kill all of you bitches dead and walk out of court a free woman and talk about you to Oprah afterward. So, there's that."

"PANDA! PANDA! PANDA!" went the chant. She'd better represent or they'd for certain turn on her; she knew it, too. The heat was on, but she was a gamer that one. She didn't rattle easily; I'll give her that much.

"This song is for all of the scared innocent young girls out there without any trace of hope," she dedicated, as she sang "Girls have feelings, too" by Barbara Mason.

Just because a girl won't cry

After a boy says it's goodbye

Well he don't realize

It's never been denied

That girls have feelings too

Just because in life

Everything went wrong

The people say that the girl

She won't live long

But they don't realize

That it's never been denied

That girls have feelings too

Just because a girl's life

Isn't worthwhile

She doesn't worry

Still wears a smile

Just because in life

Everything went wrong

The people say that the girl

She won't live long

But they don't realize

That it's never been denied

That girls have feelings too

The kids and I cheered heartily for Panda, who flashed us a smile, blew us a kiss, collected her illicit chocolate gold reward and sat again. This universal joy I could get used to real fast, but it was over in a flash.

You can't keep a horny man down, I guess, because our resident Romeo, Tyrone the Lover, rallied for another pass at the beaming songstress. "I can't live without you," he swore. "The heart wants what the heart needs. What I'm a do now?"

She put it to him just like this: "You'll find your answer at www.loser.com, Cuz, and do feed that dangling hungry snake of yours a mouse."

"Ooooooo!" went the kids. It meant that, for the time being, at least, it was Panda's house and her game to lose.

Six down and one to go. "BG, you're next fire walker up," I told her. "Best act for last. Represent!"

Ty broke it down even more. "Rock the mic, super star. Burn this motherfucker down! Ball out! This is just a tour stop."

"Where all the Westside riders at?" BG shouted.

"WHOOP WHOOP!" responded Ronnie, Jimmy and Panda in unison.

"Where my Eastside riders at?" Ricky bellowed, not willing to be outdone by a girl on game day by all means necessary.

"WHOOP WHOOP!" shouted Ricky, Dee and Ty.

"I be steady rappin' my ass off on the 'Heartless Records' label," BG stated, beating her chest with a fist and popping her collar. "Who gave you some of her 'Beware of Dog?'"

"BG did!" shouted the gang.

"And who gave you some of her 'Freaky Pussy?'"

"BG did!"

Ty reminded everyone that BG had starred in two bomb-ass killer flicks recently: "Ghetto Fabulous" and "Looking for a Fox."

"Saw 'em both on bootleg about ten times over. That shit be bangin'," he added.

"Welcome to lifestyles of the rich and fly, bitches!" BG greeted. It was her house again. Panda had been evicted; she was old news now. The pretender to the crown is dead. Hail to the Queen!

"What up, BG?" Ronnie asked. "Go ahead, talk to us."

"Just rolllin' with them punches, feel me?" she added. "Like last month, I'm with some other famous MC's, motorin' to do a gig in the San Diego city limits. Know what I'm sayin'?"

"Roll call, girl!" Panda insisted, having rallied from the psycho drama of a moment before.

"Ah-ight," BG agreed, "posse was: Big Apple Playa, Dope Poet, Atomic Dog and Mellow Yellow."

"Ooooooooo!" boomed the fans, intending every decibel.

BG went on with it. "So, we drivin' home now, real tired from performin' and bein' up all damn night long, and we smoked up all our ganja stash and sniffed up enough white powder for a ski trip.

"Yeah, we got fucked up; I ain't gonna lie," she added." I just hate it, hate it so much when make-believe quitters out there, the people on the wagon or in the Program, they say about gettin' high: 'Oh, no! I slipped; I smoked up half of Peru, and I snorted up half of Columbia, and that shit just don't work for me no more.' Then they hand off the ball to Jesus and proselytize 'n' shit of that nature."

"Well, that line of such bullshit is majorly fucked up, Cuz," BG said, " 'cause first off that dope, it works good; it works real good; and it works real good every single motherfuckin' time out, always has and always will. Hell, it just plain feels good gettin' high, shit! I hate, hate all a those self-deluded do good like them get-clean-or-die-tryin' motherfuckers out there with a passion! Me, my problem isn't that I do too much dope; it's that I need to be doing a whole lot more."

"And so," she continued, "the beatbox goes on. The wheelman, our luxury ride's heat-packin' driver, that is also our on-location drug dealer by choice goin' by the name of Dr. John the Night Tripper, he pulls in for coffee, which is when a basic homeless-dumpster-divin'-deadbeat-naughty-by-nature fool with all the kinds of tell-tale dick breath known to mankind starts to pleadin' his sad-ass case to us."

"He was after money?" I asked her, forever the facilitator over here.

"What are you, on the school paper?" she snapped. Pure sass is what she threw in my face, and she was world-class at that, too. From this I make a living? Just call me Sass Face.

"Okay," BG began, "I'm all: 'This ain't no Banco Popular, you raggedy-ass, off-brand, tongue-tied motherfucker, and he gets all agitated and puffs all up way outta his natural proportion like a damn Blowfish.

"So, me and my bodyguards, Bobby Two Tons and Too Bad Jimmy Jam, we tag-teamed up on him and flattened his ass, much like your basic thin-crust pizza, and I then commence to pushin' his shit in with a size ten gym shoe. BOOYA! Felt so nice, I did it twice. Hey now!"

Then, she pointed a finger in my face and added: "And, Hebrew Hammer, you ain't no way gonna speak on this drama to the higher authorities that be and bring the curtain down on my ass 'cause, if ya pull that double-agent narc shit, all these riders assembled up in this room proper right here and now, they'll just spot up and declare you to be a fantasizin', lyin' ass, old sawdust fartin' racist motherfucker and swear that you be steady spittin' out all shapes and plus sizes of N.I.G.G.A., feel me?

"This fine-ass, young, gifted and talented Afro-centric female, BG over here, most definitely ain't your everyday studio gangster, either. I'll drop you like you're a bad habit, shit!"

The rest of the kids whole-heartedly supported that threat. It was them against me now. I was outnumbered and caught in a web of my own design. Go figure!

She went on to say that, sure, I played Goody Two Shoes the Cowboy in this scenario to death, but diabolical shit can happen to the Lone Ranger, too, when his luck runs out on his ass. Don't be no fool and you won't get wounded in action," she added.

Panda was now siding up with the Opposition. "This isn't the Mickey Mouse Club, Mr. P.," she told me. "We're the Street Team, and you'd better recognize!"

BG was on a tear. She tossed this on the fire: "I go down, you'll go down, too, and that's head-first. You can take that shit to the bank."

Dee stuck on that I was cool, yeah, but I'm still the stone-cold enemy. I don't play for the home team; I had aged out. Now, I was part of the Problem, and they were the solution.

Ricky stuck his knife in my back, as well. "You can't be one of us, not today, not tomorrow, not ever, old dude."

I'd been served. Happy Hour at Club Juvie was now all over but the shouting. So much for saving souls; that's for the movies, Hollywood pap, huh! Time was not my friend. Then again, who was? I didn't even like myself very much, anyway. So, there's that.

Who am I supposed to be anyway, frigging Mother Teresa or somebody? Me as myself, I'm just a lowly rental, a poor man's shrink wannabe on a budget and at the end of my rope.

What! You were expecting Dr. Phil here, perhaps? If I was so smart, why wasn't I rich? Well, it ain't over till it's over. Did you want fries with that order or not? I'm waiting over here. Talk to me!

CHAPTER THREE

PAYBACK

Cries of "Your candy or your life!" and "Dig down deep, Cuz!" and "Give till it feels good to you!" filled the dayroom, as I held high my bag of contraband Snickers and waved it in the air for all to see and fantasize over. The circus is in town. Let the good times roll!

"Feed the animals; we're all endangered species, soon to be extinct," Panda said. "We're all frigging mastodons, Mr. Pleistocene Age; you, too. I pronounce us man and wife. Kiss the bride, Cowboy! Now, we'll make lots of little cow babies together."

"This is just too weird for me," I told her. "You need to do the tighten up."

"And just because I'm a loose woman doesn't mean that I'm not a nice person," she said.

"You're freaking me out big time, I continued, "and you need to stop! I'm not easy pickings."

"Will you pretty please for God's sake check your self-hate at the door with my own and fuck me stupid already!" she said, adding: "and I do mean I want you to rock me with a feeling, baby, like your back ain't got no bone. Come get to this. Put your foot in it. I've got your sexual healing right here. You scratch my back; I'll scratch yours, deal? Tit for tat. Go on, Big Papa, dust your broom. Panda wants some of that yummy jelly roll."

"That would be a hard pass," I said. "I'm the resident authority figure in here, no joke. Hey, check yourself before you wreck yourself. People get hurt like that."

"Well," she went on, "why don't you just leave right now if you're going to be so fatiguing? When I get bored, I get ornery, you see. This is me, left hung out to dry. I don't play that! Idle hands are the devil's workshop. Allow me to wax poetic: "Jerry and Panda sitting in a tree, K.I.S.S.I.N.G."

"Wow! Every day is Christmas with you people," I said. Of course, it was, though; they were the special young; it was their world, and I was just living in it. They'd been bloodied, but they were still unbowed. Fight on, Youth Brigade! Fight on.

"Congratulations," I went on, "you have made it to the next round; you are now ready to play the ultimate party game with me, my greedy little beggars, namely 'Full-Tilt Mano e Mano and Toe to Toe Telephone Smack Down' for amazing prizes on me."

The response from the invited guests was less than encouraging, however. "Mr. P., you sure know how to have a fun time, I must say," piped up the Panda bear.

"What's next, a spelling bee or is it square dancing?" Jimmy took a shot at me with. "Scrabble is so big these days. Bet you call a mean-ass game of bingo, too."

That was my cue to whip out my cell phone and tease them with it. Yeah, devious me! Cutting to the chase, I was so electronically enabled; they were so not. Telephone contact with the free world was even more scarce for them in that place than the elusive morsel of candy, the holy grail.

It would be a hard sell, though. They froze stiff, in spite of their bravado, at the mere thought of incurring the wrath of Crabby, which would be swift and no doubt harsh if we were caught with our pants down and a phone to our collective ear. Carpe diem! I threw caution to the wind. You can't win if you don't play, right? This was the Players Club, and it was game day. Players play.

"Meet my little buddy, Mr. Smart Phone," I said, "and I'm packing mass chocolate, too. Yep, I came heavy today. Where's your stash at, huh? I can't see it from here."

Ronnie shouted that I should talk business, already, and Dee asked what the catch was. So, I talked turkey. "Okay, you pink-cheeked innocents, you'll get five, count 'em: the man just said five scrumptious stealthed in just for this special occasion Snickers. WHOOP WHOOP!"

"Oooooooooo!" shouted the gallery, as visions of a sugar high danced in their heads.

"What don't I do for you people?" I added.

"What we gotta do for it," BG asked. "It ain't no free lunch up in here." The rest of the crew backed her up, total sceptics all. Lord, it ain't easy to be a saint in the city!

I laid out the game plan thusly: "Okay, ring up somebody that you've hurt and totally ball out with an apology straight from the very depths of your heart of hearts or ... or jingle somebody that's hurt you oh, so deeply with oh, such evil intent that it makes your head spin, gauge the breeze and hock a loogy right in their eyeball. Take back the night, Teen Angels. Now's the time! Let's get it on. All right, it's game time, oh, ye of little faith. You got this. Chocolate good. Abstinence bad. Bite the forbidden apple, Eve. It'll be good to you all the way down."

"Or not at all," Jimmy spat, the frigging party pooper in a chef's hat over there.

Ty led the Opposition, telling me flat out: "Nope! Cool Tee here ain't no way buyin' it, White Shadow. What you don't know won't hurt you or me, either. What else ya got for us in your little bag of tricks, Portnoy? I smell a rat, and I think it's got two legs and wears a played-out cowboy hat on its head. What that brim be about!"

I was not to be denied, though. I came here to fight the good fight for anarchy, and so I did just that. Our time was almost up. This was to be a go for broke hail Mary pass for all of the marbles. There ain't no stopping us now; we're on the move.

"You'll see," I told Ty and the rest of the Wild Bunch, "you'll all be saying: 'Goodbye forever and ever more, Mr. Guilt; be gone, don't call me, I'll call you, Mr. Anger; and welcome to my world, make yourselves at home and stay for a while, Peace and Love."

Ty let me have it right between the eyes, BING, telling me that he'd never hurt anybody that didn't have it coming to them by times of ten in the first place, and he wasn't sorry for anything, either. He added that I should get out of his face with this silliness because games are for kids, and I should just let them wallow in sorrow and misery if they so choose because after all this is America.

Lo and behold, the rest of the kids were actually disappointed at that. They wanted Ty to reconsider and place a call; my unabashed attempted bribery move was paying off big dividends now. One for me. Yes! Ty buckled, wisely taking the carrot rather than the stick. You see that, faithful Listener, shit happens. Can I get a witness? WHOOP WHOOP!

"Candy talk and bullshit walk," he said, extending his hand palm up. "Pay me; I gangster down for my chocolate; I'm the notorious Candyman Capone. Don't Bogart those Snickers! You've been told. Don't make me repeat myself."

I paid up, too, handed over the phone and Ty placed the first call of the day on the underground hotline. If curiosity killed a cat, I was a dead man walking now. At any minute, the sky could fall, and me, I'd be so kicked out on my ear.

It wouldn't be my first time as bouncee. I'd been tossed from better places than this. I'd go down swinging, though. Quite simply, I liked the action. So call me "thrill junky." Crabby completes me. Bring her on! The bigger they are, the harder they fall. "Big boss lady, you're not big, you're just tall is all."

"Granny? It's Ty. (Pause) How I'm doin'? I'm chilin' like a villain; you know me. Diamond in the back, sunroof top, diggin' the scene with a gangster lean. Ah-ight, I'm in touch with Sis; she in San Francisco with her little baby now. (Pause) She don't call you 'cause you cold kicked her out the house in the wee wee hours for gettin' knocked up! You said she has a fast tail. Huh! (Pause) Granny, I'm the baby daddy, straight up. If you don't know, now you know. (Pause) Yep, I showed her what that hole is for; just the dog in me. WOOF WOOF (Pause) No, she ain't any parts of my blood sister, no; she just a half-way sister, though, and I don't care none, shit! (Pause) I know you don't want me back, neither. Cool, too! I'm a still steady put mad cheddar in your mailbox, though, irregardless. (Pause) I'm so sorry, Granny; I didn't mean to cause you no pain. I'm cryin' as I speak my piece, and I ain't particularly known for my empathy, neither. The devil made me do it on the real. (Pause) Hey, I wish you would tell my no good old man all about this shit, though. Do it, go on: it'll give his bad self a little somethin' somethin' new and different to chat up his cellie with in lockdown, and, after ya tell him what I did now, do tell him that I ain't forgot no parts of those scams he was steady perpetratin' on the local civilians when I was just a peewee comin' up, okay, gettin' his Hollywood hustle on; tell him I so do remember that bogus brand a men's cologne he was pushin' called 'Honeys come Running.' (Pause) Cool, Granny, just me 'n' you then; we tight like that, right? We'll rap. Much love. I'm out."

Ty disconnected and returned Mr. Smart Phone to his rightful custodian, as the others cheered. So far, so good. I'm clever like that. Hold your applause till the end. This is just the overture.

I said: "Your old man is locked up, too, I take it. Small world; the apple doesn't fall far from the apple tree."

"Affirmative," he said back, "Pops, he been Mr. In 'n' Out of Jail, since there was Chinese handball. I'd ask Mama when I was little peewee Ty: 'Where my daddy be at now, Mommy,' feel me? And Moms, she be replyin' right off the script that he was far far away and out of touch with reality in Wyoming bein' a all-around rodeo cowboy. I told her that she a bold-faced cockeyed liar 'cause, before that, she told me he a Jedi knight that's down with Luke Skywalker, Obie 'n' Yoda 'n' them, and she then threatens to blind me in both of my eyes and cut my tongue all out of my head if I ever should ask her again. She was all love, all the time. Mama, you're appreciated.

"So, Pops, he comes home in a New York minute one fine day all unexpected like," Ty went on, "and he find Mama 'sleep in the bed with one of my many rowdy roughneck play-uncles, who steady ran through the crib, some of 'em sexin' me up all kinds a bloody 'n' shit.

"Ya see, crack headed Mama straight pimped me out for rocks, and Pops, well, he just gangstered 'em both in the bed, as they slept tight. I seen it go down with my very own two eyes; he set the bed all a blaze, and he was real loud laughin' about it, too. Who knew? The man was rather excitable; I'm just sayin'.

"He told me: "Son, big ups, now you a true man in my book," which was the nicest thing he ever told me. It was as though I was his judge with the power to pardon him. Maybe, though, it was the weed and wine talkin'.

"I must a missed the funny part, though. Oh, well, I never did tear up, purge and cleanse over that shit; I passed my cryin' time up for y'all. You need it much worser than yours truly. So, step up, needy bitches. Bring your cryin' towel."

I told Ty to go ahead and call me "Charlie Cheerleader" if he must, but I think he should look at the bright side of an otherwise bleak picture: he now had a catchy little title for his memoir, "Gangster of Love." I added that he should be a good "uncle-daddy" for little Junior, while he was at it, too. Then I gave the notorious Candyman Capone a fist bump for hitting leadoff. You go, Ty! Try to keep it in your pants next time. Save it for a rainy day because the fucking you get isn't worth the fucking over that you're going to get. Enough said.

"Don't even think about me, dog!" Dee snapped at me, beating me to the punch. "I ain't down for no true-confessional-gang-star-tells-all bullshit today, no. My business already been in the street. So, be thankful for what you got and get outta my face, shit!"

I reminded him that Snickers don't grow on L.A. palm trees of late, though, and Jimmy backed me up with a cry of:

"Heavy duty, dude!" To that, Panda informed him that her gay cousin just called, and he wanted his expression back.

Ty took a shot at Dee, saying: "I got mines, homeboy; get yours." And Dee took the bait. SNAP!

"Portnoy," he began, "my shit arrive C.O.D." We transacted, the beat went on and Dee's phone chat went like this; a true classic with a capital C:

(Pause) "Well well well, if it ain't the voice of the one and only Mary Mary quite contrary Mc Carthy, herself, as I live and breathe. (Pauses) It's Dee Smith. Yeah, that Dee Smith. Still a teacher? (Pause) Still at Pipe Dreams Middle School are we? (Pause) Ya taught your teacher's pet over here a whole whole lot in the seventh-grade year two, Miss Mack. Ready to go down that road with me? (Pause) Cool! You was all: 'It's your birthday today, young stud muffin. How does it feel to be twelve-years-old? You really do fill out your jeans. Dee, that all you? Thank you, Lord, for your bounty. I have a special treat for you on your special day, and your treat is a hot piece of me with whipped cream and a cherry on top.' So, after school, we go to your crib, okay? (Pause) Bitch, I wish you would be so bold as to hang up on me in midstream now! I ain't said shit, yet. I'm a advise your principal and might even tip off the po po, the 'L.A. Times' and those TV news anchor folks, too. (Pause) Yeah, I'm finna straight seven kinds a slut shame your ass all over social media, too, once I get my wings back and fly this coop. (Pause) So, we at the crib now, right, and out come the bong and then come you ridin' me all cowgirl, reverse cowgirl and downward facin' dog 'n' shit. It was too much, too soon; messed my young mind up so bad I turned straight junky on that white lady shit. Yeah, small world, white lady just like you. (Pause) Well, now you gonna pay me in full for my pain and sufferin', feel me, every cent of it, too! Rehab at 'Promises of Malibu' ain't no way cheap, and I got my little heart set on a feel-better Rolex time piece with a diamond crust all on it, too. (Pause) Shit, well, sell your damn house and car then. Say, how your hubbie doin' of late? Bet he'd take this seven kinds a personal. (Pause) I ain't even close to through with you, yet! I know people that will do their very best to make you bleed out for sport! Now, loud say my name."

With the disconnect, the dayroom shook with the cheers of the gallery, a veritable Greek chorus come to life up in here, right out of the time capsule.

Jimmy told Dee that Dee was his newest role model, right up there in rare air with Kurt Cobain. Panda anointed Dee the Most Valuable Player and said that he was the new Rick James, which is as good as it gets in the gospel according to the princess.

"By the way, how long ya been a junky now, Dee," I inquired. Me, curious; it's how I do it. "Spill the beans," I added.

Dee broke it all down for me, as if I was a naïve child. He explained that he wasn't any parts of a junky whatsoever, not even a hint. It was all a big hoax, a slick ruse, and he was a method actor for Jesus. He called this his "supersize rehab scam, the #1 on the menu with everything on it," and said that he was an H.D.M. or a 'highly devious motherfucker' for the uninitiated. Game recognizes game. That says it all in my book.

He was going to get paid for play, too, he predicted, and we should all watch him do it. I was a believer. He had me at hello.

"Cha-ching! Make that paper. If it don't make dollars, it don't make sense," the kids sang out. They were convinced, as well.

"You're getting an elite wristwatch with crust and cash up the wazoo," I told Dee. "Most victims, they just get a steady diet of anti-depressants and self-affirmations. Not even close, you win; she loses. Stay up, Player! Power to the people. Ride on! You got a lot of nerve for your size, and you also got a whole lot of living to do. So, don't look back. Come see me. I can always use a good man like you."

I was feeling quite generous. The bribery business was popping and so was the catharsis, theirs and, by proxy, my own. Proxy would not satisfy this group for long, however, as you'll see. What's good for the goosed is good for the gooser.

"Eastside flash," I said to Ricky, "like me to break you off a little somethin' somethin'? Let's do this. No fear, street soldier! Knuckle down!"

He actually didn't look the least bit frightened to me, though. These kids held their fear in check, deeply, and hid it behind a madeup game face. Otherwise, an enemy might smell it on them: the kiss of Death. They didn't do any parts of scared, at least not outwardly, anyhow.

Ricky said: "Let's do this!" I thought he would. It was his time.

"You go, dude!" "Go on, Slick Rick!" "One shot, one kill!" "Load up, Senor Taco!" filled the air.

It was highly contagious, and I was very susceptible to it. So, I joined in with the Hallelujah Chorus, shouting out something trite like: "Ricky, Ricky, you're our man. If you can't do it, no one can!" You could do better than that, Listener, go ahead on; don't mind me. The kids looked at me like I was wearing white after Labor Day. What can ya do? I try; God love me. I always did get the participation trophy.

The handoff followed: Snickers and phone. He ran with it and scored. Yeh! Call him Mr. Touchdown.

"Father O' Sullivan there?" (Pause) "Tell him it's Ricky Cruz with a blast from the past. (Pause) Oh, Old Dude will remember his favorite twinkie altar boy no doubt. (Pause) Cool, I'll wait till hell freeze over."

"Now or never, Ricky." "This is no dry hump." "Kick his diseased ass in a most ruthless manner; that's what it's there for." "Leave no doubt, lowrider; do your job, cholo." "The past ain't over; it's not even the past." The peers wanted Father O. to go down hard in flames, and they were letting Ricky know it in no uncertain terms that he now repped the big bad Club Juvie home team. This was the Payback Olympics up in here. Ricky carried the torch for the Light Side. You gotta love it!

"Father O?" (Pause) "Simone, ese, really me, still up 'n' runnin'. (Pause) Uh huh, uh huh, been a long-ass time fo' sho' oh, fo' sho'. (Pause) Yup, those were sure the good old days, no question. (Pause) Why this call? I'm collectin' for African Americans without Dr. Dre Beats headphones. (Pause) Oh, ya think that I made a funny. Then you'll mos' def' get a big chuckle over this item just now in then: GROWN FOLKS NEED TO PROTECT CHILDREN, NOT FUCK THEM! Remember that the next time your sickly twisted little mind tells you: 'Stick your pinga in another helpless young child's cherry pie.'"

"RICKY! RICKY! RICKY!" went the bench players.

"Watch your back," he went on. "Your day will come and real soon, too. I'm a go barbarian, slice your dick off and take that shit on tour all over this great land of ours. (Pause) You can run, but ya cannot hide. (Pause) Yeah, that's right: cry;

cry ya big baby! Ya got mass buckets of tears to drop off yet to catch up to me, though. PRAY THE ROSARY! My face will be the last thing you'll ever see. I'm the Terminator, comin' soon to a theater near you. It's a new sheriff in town now, motherfucker! Recognize!"

Ricky ended the call, sobbing hard. I approached the distraught boy and put an arm around him to ebb the flow and console him.

He went through my Kleenex box like it was cannoli at an Italian wedding. He had the makings of a fine actor and played the stew out of grief. The Crowbar Killer was human, after all. I knew it going in. Now, we all did. Tears don't lie.

Ricky's new-found friends, even BG, supported him with shouts of encouragement: "Get it all out, Rick!" "Way to be, dog!" "Give us your sadness, homie!" "Cry us a river!" "Empty the tank, boy!" "Wash away the pain!" "You're so cool!" "You let the dogs out!" "You're the shit, Big Scrappy!"

"BAM! That happened," Ricky blasted out; it was a rallying cry. He had slain the terrible dragon at long last. and it was obvious that the rush was good to him as it surged through his very being.

I told him that he needed to take that injured boy, his inner child, into his arms, hold him tightly and speak to him now, brother to brother. "Call for him straight from your heart, Ricky," I added, "and he will come. It works for me all the time, no joke."

His reply was that I watched too much TV for my age, but he would give it a shot instead of repaying me for the now spent stash box of Kleenex.

"I can do this!" he said, and so he pulled it off without a glitch and beamed like a proud champion should. He'd taken a gold medal in the Grief Olympics.

"Little man, it's just me, Big Scrappy," he began. "No, I never, not even once, stopped thinkin' about you; you can come out and play again; the big bad storm blew over, and it's a pretty rainbow up in the sky now. From now on, it's just us two firme vato locos, the brothers, and that's always and forever."

I was there, making the big bucks to spread the news to these kids that they were the author of their own destiny, and it's a completely new chapter. Today, they've been writing page one, and it's the first day of the rest of their life and all of that good stuff.

The Book of Gangster is so out of print now. They needed to go legit because all of the really cool kids are doing it lately. Crime bad; Teen Angels good. Take that to the bank and cash it.

Ricky was not to be denied. "I ain't no sell out, ese!" he insisted. "It ain't the Disney Channel you watchin' now. Take that Teen Angels mess and your strange white ass with you back to the Valley, Encino Man."

Win some. Lose some. Sometimes, you get rained out.

The kids supported Ricky. This was no easy sell. They had all been burned by putting their trust in the hands of false prophets before and often, many of whom looked much like me. Once bitten, twice shy. They didn't believe in me or my message. Most times, neither did I. So, we had that going for us. I kept a smile on my face, though. Laugh, clown, laugh! When you laugh, the whole world laughs with you. When you cry, you cry alone.

If I could save just one of them from a lifetime of addiction, poverty and incarceration, then this all would've been worth it, but I hadn't yet figured out how to save my own self. It was the blind leading the blind, I feared. I was dancing as fast as I could.

Time was fleeting fast; it was a blur. Happy Hour had just about been shot to hell, no ah ha teachable moment, no come to Jesus breakthrough and not a single hint of one on the horizon, either. How could I turn a tragic conclusion into a joyous Hollywod ending with fireworks and a marching band or, at least, a covered dish or two? I didn't have a clue. Who was I, Steven Spielberg or somebody? This is reality, Listener, and it truly bites. Don't even ask.

Having decided that if this leaky ship was going to sink, then I'd go down with it like a good captain should, I told Panda to roll the dice. "Take the big leap of faith, Princess," I said, adding that the darkest hour comes just before the dawn, words of wisdom. In the Land of the Blind, the one-eyed man is king. I had the only good eye in here. King me, baby!

"Know any more played-out clichés?" Panda snapped at me. Only the strong survive a life like hers, though, and she was one tough cookie not about to crumble for me or anyone else. She had often surrendered the pink, but never her dignity, not even once.

One thing was for sure, though, if Dr. C. was to just stroll in and catch us en flagrant, in the act of playing Phone Tag au natural, it's definitely going to be lights out for yours truly, and my name would truly be mud, heretofore to filed under "Persona Non Grata" like so fast it would make your noggin rotate. "Here today and gone tomorrow": I'd probably put that on my cemetery headstone, instead of "finally got laid."

As the kids bantered about whether or not to fear the wrath of Dr. C. and tremble in her wake, Panda advised me that I needed to wrap myself in a kimono, tie my head up in a turban, gaze into my crystal ball and predict myself a happy Hollywood ending because I was as good as kicked to the curb. She'd see me at the drive through window, muttering something about fries. "This is you going out the door," she added: "WOOSH!"

What more damage could Crab Legs do to us here, though. The kids were already locked up, and I was dead in the water.

"I'm ready for my close up now, Mr. P. and fans," Jimmy announced. I have unfinished business with my brother. If you want my ass on a platter, give up the Snickers. Your candy or your life."

So, I forked it over and Jimmy rocked the mic thusly, short and sweet and mind boggling.

"Hello, Richie, it's Jimmy Glitter still at Club Juvie, coming at you live. Greetings from the underground. I just got this hot minute to speak on the fire. (Pause) Yes, bitch, that fire, shoot! Well, here's the how and why, all right? That night while you were out and about, Dad found your coke stash in the closet. Yep, the cash and the gun, too. So, me, I'm like: 'You gonna call the cops on him or what?' And the old man says back to me something along the lines of: 'No! Not yet. Richie is a common criminal to me now, so I'm about to do the right thing and knock some sense into his thick head with a golf club; this calls for a nine iron.' What was I, his caddy? Well, okay okay okay, I did it for you, Richie. (Pause) What do you mean you would've took the beat down and did the time? That's some unacceptable bullshit right there. Do you know what they do to pretty boys like you in jail? Try death by cock! It's just us now, brother. me and you, us versus the whole world. Up against the wall, motherfuckers! The shrink up in here, he thinks that I'm stone crazy. I guess it's because I stick Cheerios up my butt and sing 'La Bamba' all day, that and flick boogers. I made up a story about being abused like a motherfucker and the shit worked out, too. Well, we all make it all up, anyhow, don't we? All right, I got to go see a man about a horse now. Put a few dollars on my book if you know what's good for you. Kurt Cobain lives! Rock out with your cock out, dude. It's good like that. Feel the breeze. See ya when I see ya."

Fancy this, the sun was breaking through the dark clouds. Panda announced that she was so owning those burning coals now: girl power! She was going in and wanted me to cover her. This I could learn to like: man on top, the natural order of things.

When asked by me who she was about to call on the Love Line, she said it was to be her amazing boyfriend, Woody aka Footlong. "Owe him one big time," she went on. "We had this epic fight; very hurtful words were fired off; and small household appliances, they were launched with much gusto. It was really some eye-popping shit, total shock and awe. You should have been there to see it, man. I mean, we really really threw down!"

She then placed her call. There was total silence, as everyone anticipated the combat's revival. Round two of the slugfest was now on. It was as advertised, too.

"Oh, no!" Panda shouted. "Voicemail ... Message still count for the big payoff or what?"

"Me, holding my breath," I replied.

"Hey, babe, ... Just me, thee one and only, the original huggie bear, Panda, Queen of the Nile! Only called to say that the pregnancy, my pregnancy, it wasn't any parts of your fault, okay? Yeah, I told you it was, but I flat out lied on you, sorry, babe. It was either the accountant's or, just maybe, the stockbroker's. Although, come to think about it, perhaps, it was the architect's; he put his two cents in the kitty, too. Forgive me for this; I just felt so bad, and I didn't want you thinking I was a slut by choice; I'm just a girl that can't say no. It's just me and you, Woody. My saddle is waiting; come on and jump on it! I want you to kiss me all up and down with your lollipop lips and ride me north. I've got an itch, and I need you to scratch it. Yeah, I caught another case. I beat this weak-ass petty fly-by-night rap they got me on, I'll come back home to you and be your hot-to-trot little vixen bed-warmer once again, I swear it, and that's on everything. We can even open a brand new can of worms and make us a sex tape for the ages with all kinds of cool shit like a standing sixty-nine with a frog kick. I'll be your naked lunch. Eat me! Oh, yeah, so I ... well, so I ... I like totally had our baby boy swallowed up because I travel light; I'm just sayin'. Note to Little Bit from Mama Panda bear: 'See ya!' He was abortion #3 on my hit list. LOL ... What's the record now? Hey, I think that the Panda bear should be allowed to terminate up until the kid can argue in its own defense. Well, later days, dude, and, hey, skate naked for me. I so want to be your dog. WOOF WOOF!"

The girl who just can't say no then asked me if I thought that she was down to be a baby mama. Then, that pretty rock chick insisted to everyone present that she had a killer party in her, and it just had to come out, and there wasn't enough room up in there for that and a baby, too.

"Hey, la dee da dee, I like to party, and, when I party, I party hearty," she sang and added: "Yeh, Panda! You go, girl! Big shout out to my genetic makeup."

I advised her, the second-coming of '80's Madonna both in mind and body, that that's the thing about our darkest secrets, though, they have a funny way of sneaking out of the closet to dance all over us.

Well, note to Panda: "It's not really all that LMAO drop-dead hilarious this time, though, is it, girlfriend?"

The kids argued that I was just old school and, therefore, I just didn't understand them or, what's more, Teen Beat in general. Maybe, I was old, and I didn't understand: not the crowbar bashing, not the method actor's supersize hoax with everything on it, not the mommy-daddy roast with a soundtrack by Jim Morrison and The Doors and not shooting for the abortion record, either. But, Lord knows, I tried to, and, if this was to be my swan song as a healer and flipping burgers was to be my new normal, I swore to myself there and then that I would go down in a flaming blaze of glory. I'm dramatic like that, I guess. I'm the glamorous Cher of social work.

Hey, maybe flipping paddies was where it was at. For the longest, all I've wanted for myself was to be financially solvent, that and be a beachcomber. What can I possibly say about my life? I'm a character in a farce; all there is to it. I've concluded that there are just two certainties in life: #1 - we all get killed and scalped by the Indians in the end and #2 - I will burn for eternity.

Happy Hour was for all intents and purposes about to be whistled dead now, as would my job security. "Hi! Welcome to Mc Donald's! What'll it be today?"

Comic Relief returned to us just in the nick of time with a new episode of the ongoing Ty and Panda Show; perfect timing for a laugh riot. So far, this had been a very good day, yes, for a murder, maybe. This was the killing floor, and my head was on the chopping block. Got the graphic, yet?

Ty came on with: "Panda baby, I so wanna open up the love gates to my heaven; I'm a give you somethin' that you can feel, so you'll know that my love is real. Girl, be my juicy fruit!"

Panda wasn't even hearing that. "Your juicy fruit? Oh, really? WHOA! That's so cool. We have a love poet."

Smooth-talking Ty was quick on his feet and not to be rebuffed this time around. There was work to do, and he dug in: "You're a girl in need of a boy. I'm a boy in need of a girl. Let's put our needs together, and maybe we'll need each other."

"I don't think so," she said. "You need to quit. What part no don't you understand?"

"I can make you wetter than a border brother at the river," he promised.

The other kids howled with laughter, as did I, as didn't Panda. Sugar babies aren't easy. Show her the money.

"Can a righteous brother that's down with the jungle fever get some love up in here?" Ty prodded. "I got the fire down below, girl."

"Break yourself!" she told him. "Nobody rides in this shiny new top of the line luxury car for free. Repeat after me, oh, you playboy on a budget: "I wish I was taller; I wish I was a baller." Then she added a postscript that her vagina wasn't his walk-in closet.

The home fans sided with Panda now. She floated like a butterfly and stung like a bee. She was playing Ty like he was PlayStation, and she could do it blindfolded, too. The girl had that much game in her; she was a true natural.

"Damn, that's gangster!" Ty swore; he was an excitable boy, that one. "Fuck it then, shit! I don't even want your sloppy seconds ass no more," he tacked on for good measure.

Panda shot him back right between the eyes with: "And here I was sprung like a mousetrap." Bull's eye! Ty's King was now in check.

Ty was working up a sweat. The friendly pickup game had quickly escalated to "Gorilla Ball." No blood, no foul. The only rule on this court was: "Make it. Take it."

He told our Panda bear flat out that she looked deflated like a piñata after all the candy had been beaten out of it.

Then he called her a skin and bones, uneven-chested catcher's mitt, who had been on her back more than the weakest brother at wrestling practice.

"Ooooooooooo!" The crowd shouted. They were engaged now.

He went on that Panda had sucked so much dick that she walked around on her knees and that she probably learned that trick from her mother.

"My mother is a saint!" she emphatically pointed out.

"Saint Suck a Dick," he popped.

"Ouch!" "You go, Ty!" "Read her!" The kids yelled, as the momentum shifted. Game. Set. Match.

BG, though, was abstaining. She didn't play that macho stuff and was conspicuous by virtue of her deafening silence, which had a good beat and you could dance to it, too. She stared hard enough at Ty to bore holes in his head.

"What it be about, BG? What's the big haps?" Ty asked. "You been steady mad doggin' me out like you all pissed off at me 'n' shit. Pound for pound, you ain't no threat to the King or don't you know that I wear the crown? This is a man's world! You, you're just a guest worker in it with a green card. Players up. Ho's down. That's the way of the world."

"Me? Why the Baby Girl, she just be sittin' up, listenin' to you play the role of Mack Daddy the Ghetto Romeo," she said. "I'm tryin' to figure out just what kind a female you be messsin' with on the street, though."

Ty played this game of smash-mouth one upmanship well, himself. BG was good, but he was better. He told BG: "I mess with fat girls with regular people legs like you, feel me?"

"Negro, please!" she snapped back "I'm from South Central. If you were cavortin' with bitches like me, this South Central pussy'd have you shuttin' your ass up!"

"Ooooooooo! And he took it!" the kids yelled out.

Ty came back at her with the knockout punch, though: "Yup, yup, that South Central pussy'd have me barely hangin' on like those uneven raggedy-ass Dollar Store extensions in your hair, Ghetto Pocahontas." POW!

That was all she wrote. Ty was the winner and still champion in the Battle of the Sexes for now, anyhow. You go, boy! He came. He saw. He conquered.

It was now Ronnie time. "Shoot the moon," I told him. How about it? Work with us over here. Take one for the team."

"Another time, another place, maybe," replied the Westside Assassin with a tattooed tear on his cheek. "It's hard for me to express myself because I can't protect myself if I expose myself. I'll probably wreck myself." All of which translated into two words: "Fuck off!"

I asked what the worst thing that could possibly happen to him was, and he tersely explained that his sister wouldn't believe a single word of what he wanted so badly to tell her about.

"Listen to that, Ronnie," I prodded him with. "It's Opportunity whispering in your ear, saying: 'Seize this moment and work it hard.' Go ahead on, young blood, I'm throwing you a bone up in here. Do the dog!"

Ty flipped the script when he added: "Chocolate don't lie, neither, Cuz." Ronnie now went from absolutely not in to all in in nothing flat.

"Hey, girl," he said, "guess who! (Pause) Just called to holler at ya right quick about Pop, something ya don't know anything about. (Pause) So, Pop, he wasn't, was not at that porno theater that time to get his freak on or nothing scandalous like that, no. Was me all the way, girl; I was totally selling my body to whoever for whatever. Like that's what I do by trade; it's a living. (Pause) He found out about me and came looking for me to beat the wild out, I guess. Then he pulls me out a there, and I push him in the street, and here comes that big-ass city bus on a run, and … (Pause) No, delete that weak shit from the record. Bring his stay drunk, abusive nasty self back here for seconds, and me as myself, I'll do him up again in a heartbeat. (Pause) DON'T YOU DARE! NO … NO … DON'T!"

Ronnie broke down in tears, sobbing hard, hands covering his face and rocking back and forth. He was inconsolable. Nonetheless, I gave it a shot; it's what I do. I'm the Amazing Hulk of healers. I say jump; you say how high? I may be small, but I am mighty.

"What gives, my man? Share with us. Open the tap," I told him.

"She pulled the plug on me is what gives. She's all like: 'It needed to be you run down, instead.' Then, CLICK … Gone like the Lone Ranger," he said.

The homies supported him with the likes of: "You a baller, Ron Ron." "No doubt, no doubt. It's all good, man!"

"I just shot an air ball, though," he rasped.

I went into helping mode, telling him that he was a survivor, and the world had just better learn to live with that because he was a force of nature, a live wire, and he had the juice.

"Don't write her off," I said. "Your sis will be back on the bandwagon waving like a veritable parade queen to the adoring crowd soon enough, but mine won't, not ever." Score one for Team Ronnie. I'll just sit here alone at the bar and cry into my beer if you don't mind.

Mistakes are how you go pro. Ronnie would realize that, but first he had to deal with a pack of serious consequences, which was waiting to pounce on him and rip him a new one. His time would come soon enough. It was Ronnie vs. Karma. Smart money was running heavy on Queen Karma, who was untied and undefeated and more likely than not to remain so. All bets were off.

"BG, you're up. Lights Camera Action!" "All eyes on you, girl!" "It's showtime!" "Sparkle!"

Our main attraction then told us her plan was to holler at her mother. BG was the impatient sort. "Cue the phone and feed the kitty in advance," she ordered. "Well, man, shit, I don't sign for the deaf! And so, now what?"

"S' up, Mama," she began, "what's the dealio! (Pause) Looky here, my smart Yid lawyer talkin' about I'm a get my walkin' papers up outta this joint today, and I want me some mac 'n' cheese plus a tasty sweet potato pie for dessert, must be chilled down, too. (Pause) And I wanna roll home in a stretch limo in white with top-shelf champagne on ice, feel me? It's proper like that. So, make your girl's day, ah-ight? (Pause) Mama, I had sex with your man just because he was there and just because I could. We got sky high, straight maxed out on some killer shit, know what I'm sayin', and he started to talkin' about you, yeah you and all the things you won't do for him jjust 'cause you, you think they're too dirty, and you, you a practicin' Christian church woman 'n' shit. So, BG stepped up's all. (Pause) … in your bed. (Pause) Well, you always said to share my toys with the boys. I'm 31 flavors of sorry, Mama; I'm just young and foolish and restless and bored, but, hey, shit would not have gone down like that if you were not so damn frigid, though. (Pause) Like get over yourself already, woman, fuck! (Pause) You can do a whole hell of a lot better that his sorry ancient fossil-ass, too. That cocktail-weenie-havin'-come-quick-leprechaun ain't nothin', and he look just like a catfish, too. Why bother with a dude if you gotta ask yourself this question: 'Do I wanna fuck him or do I wanna fry him?'"

The locals were loving it and filled the air with: "BG BG BG!" I joined in, too. That's prime time entertainment in my book! This was worth the price of admission. The phone chat went on. There was a universal hush in the room. It was just that good to them. The ticket price was right, and the seating was dress circle. What's not to like? Maybe, you want egg in your beer, too?

"NO, MAM, I'M NOT JUST A NASTY GIRL; I'M A NASTY GIRL WITH BIG BANK!" BG shouted at her mother. "Mac 'n' cheese, my chilled down sweet potato pie and the white stretch ride with my beverage of choice iced or I'm a kick you to the curb for real this time; I ain't lyn', neither. (Pause) Love you, too, Mama, as long as you stay black. You still my go-to girl no matter what come down the road at us. Pick out a diamond ring you like, ah-ight? (Pause) Cool, and some cut your mouth out diamond earrings, too, that got more carets than Whole Foods. Hit me back! BG is so gone."

I counseled the notorious boyfriend-bandit to play in the sandbox with the guys in her own age bracket and that she'd be way better off because older men would only sing her a pretty love song and leave her blue, seven kinds of alone and standing knee-deep in a puddle of her own tears. Besides, they don't know Tupac from toothpick.

She didn't acknowledge me for that; too busy with her champagne dreams for such droll, I guess. What did I know, anyhow? Healer, heal thyself.

That's when I started to tie a bow on "Happy Hour at Club Juvie Live," hoping to go out with a big bang. I wouldn't be disappointed; just watch this. Where there's life, there's hope:

"My dear dazed and confused play-cousins," I began, "do start forgiving yourselves because nobody can do this for you; you made bad choices because you're human, and this sage wise man, Guru Jerry over here, a healing traumatized burn victim much like you, yourself says: 'All fire walkers go to heaven, and Teen Angels travel there in first class with all of the rights and privileges that go with it, too.'

"You're here because you crayoned outside their coloring book lines, see. Those lines were real blurry, though. I did bad things, too, a whole butt load of those in my fast life and times; it boggles the mind! So, fire walkers, you see: we're all in that same leaky lifeboat together."

The Halleluiah Chorus went: "What you got for us?" "Give your fair share!" "Break it down, yo!" "Tell all the juicy details; we're impressionable youngsters." "I like my shit raw!"

I fed it to them like this with the suggestion that they take it in with small bites and chew slowly: "Cheated on his own kid sister, check. Cheated on his dear sweet auntie by not fighting like a man possessed for her life, check. Cheated on his own wife, too, knowingly and deliberately, check. Didn't take a bullet for his best friend in the whole wide world, check. Go on, just call me Fallen Angel because I answer to that name. I'm just an epic schmuck! I answer to that, as well. I would describe myself as being a very high priority dodgeball target by nature. Don't confront me with my failures; I have not forgotten them."

Panda chirped that, fact: married men do get itchy a lot, and she knows of what she speaks because she is a certified backscratcher, which comes in the Sexual Healing package along with naked ping pong, full-blown no-prisoners-taken mama jokes, erotic choking and scolding with benefits. Of course, there is the V.I.P. package in which she throws in playing the part of 'Deliman' – (ie. She does you with an all-beef hot dog; kosher available upon request.)

I stroked their egos when I mentioned that Misery sure loves herself some company, and I had them for that role. Actually, this was as good as it gets. It's a veritable blues festival in this place, and I was the second coming of Bobby Blue Bland.

The encouragement for me to reach out to my estranged spouse, aka the Queen of Mean, and offer her an olive branch was really touching. They liked me; they really liked me; I grow on people. It was my house again: too little, too late, though. The fickle finger of Fate was pointing my way; I was a marked man.

"Call Wifey and beg for forgiveness." "Sweat that poison out, Portnoy." "How hard can it be, old dude?" "It'll put hair on your chest." "If you fall off your horse, we'll catch you in the act like you caught us; it's our job." "Put your back into it." "Throw her a bone."

Me and my wife as ourselves, we weren't on the best of terms, though, not even close. Why, she has the evil eye; she's the love child of the Dybuk and the Golem. The marriage wasn't meant to be, and I really should've realized that from the get go at the wedding when her mother showed up dressed in black crepe and her father forgot my name, as he handed me an empty envelope.

"Fire walk for us, Mr. P." "Come on down; we're all waiting over here." "Roar, for us man! You're the Lion King." "Oh, dance like Usher!"

And so, I did just that. It blew up in my face. BOOM!

"Hello, Tiffany, Jerry. (Pause) No, I'm Jerry the Sports Illustrated Magazine swimsuit edition trannie cover model. You okay? (Pause) Great just great to hear that, mean it. I never did tell you how oh, so so very sorry I am for what I did to you, all of it, the whole nine yards. So, I'm very sorry for what I did to you; there ya go. You happy now, dream-killer? (Pause) Well, that went well. (Pause) And how is our beautiful little girl? (Pause) You didn't even invite me to her birthday party, Fang, and, gee, that was just so so cruel of you, too! You're cold-blooded. (Pause) Yes, yes, I already know what you think of me; you've made that crystal clear by now. Hey, you even woke me up to say goodbye. Okay then, I so want to explain something to you right quick, okay? Well, all right then, that hot hooker, the one that I got spotted with at the Buggy Whip Club, so it turns out that the guy, he was HIV positive, and I got totally bitten off of that shit. Hey, that right there, that's the worst part. The best part of the story is that my dick worked like a champ. I'm was so proud of it that I sent it a thank you card; it's the Hammer of Thor that bad boy is, a nine inch kosher joy stick with a little body english and a left hook to it. (Pause) Oh, my God! Please let me see her; she's my daughter, too, ya know? Look, I'm begging you over here. (Pause) Yes, fine, you can be at the scene, of course that. (Pause) And your parents, too, just in case? Sure thing. Oh, rush! Hear me out, why not … why not have your sisters and their husbands there, as well; can't just up and leave them out of the picture, and we must must have your Aunt Molly, her and Uncle Irv there, also. Snap! We can make it a black-tie fund raiser for Jews without summer homes. (Pause) Oh, fuck me is it now? Too late. Life's already done that. WELL, THEN FUCK YOU AND YOUR WHOLE MARRIED SWINGER BOYFRIENDS FAN CLUB, TOO! HOPE YOU GET CRABS. AND MY HIV, IT STANDS FOR NOTHINNG BUT 'HIS INCREDIBLE VICTORY!' No one ever looked at me, my whole life, without thinking I'd live forever."

"Okay," I told the kids, "logline for Jerry's life: it's a tragedy in two acts. Act one: a drunken poke with a woman he hardly knew. Act two: a kid that he so regrets, who calls him by another man's name on the better days and calls him "deadbeat scumbag loser" on the not so hot ones."

"Ah, me," I added, "I have no marketable skills whatsoever; I can't fuck, and I can't fight. I'm just a leech, a parasite on humanity. When the revolution comes along, I'll probably be put up against a wall and shot down like the bottom-feeder I picture myself to be. Everyone that's ever been nice to me even a little bit nice I've set on fire."

Hearing that, Jimmy Glitter shouted: "Far out, old dude! You rock!"

Then I screamed like a badly wounded animal, primal stuff that I brought up from my toes, but I quickly regained my composure because there is an honor code that true cowboys, the real deal, they don't lose their cool while they're on the clock. So, I stood there mum, which spoke for me loud and clear.

At first the kids were stunned, then they all stood and wildly cheered for me. My eyes teared up. I felt sorry for them and even sorrier for myself. Poor poor pitiful me. I was dying a death by a thousand cuts, but I wasn't going down alone. Misery sure is a magnet. She never goes home by herself.

Happy Hour officially ended now, as I told them that we should all be happy for a change, at least give it the old college try; might work, might not. RAH! RAH! RAH! FIGHT ON! Leave it all on the field. Win one for the Gipper! Ain't the size of the dog in the fight; it's the size of the fight in the dog that matters.

I'd give the joy thing a shot if they would join me on the journey. It sure beats being down with a bad case of the blues all the time because that gets old fast. People get hooked on sadness and wind up fiends for it like us, down on our hands and knees, the crumb sniffers.

My final words of wisdom were: "Live like you're at Rock 'n' Roll Summer Camp now and always. Get on the love bus, happy campers!"

"BG is camper in charge of star search," I added. "Jimmy does his Elvis on crack impressions; Panda leads old-school karaoke; Ricky models conflict resolution; Ronnie, oh, our Ronnie, he chooses our dinner menu items, and happiness is a choice; Ty, Cool Tee tells dragged-out steamy love stories; and Dee, he teaches us method acting for fun and profit. I judge the hot dog eating contest, which was my college major by the way, I'm just keeping it real."

Then there was the finale: "If there is a God in heaven, after all, he will surely bless you, every single one, and, if there isn't a God, then just who's been playing this chess match with our lives?"

The kids nodded in agreement. Breakthrough! The ice melts! The day is won! And then the rains came. Thunder … Lightening … and Ricky's shouted alert of "Trucha la huda!" ("Watch out! The cop is here.") It was a bust. There was nowhere to run to and nowhere to hide.

The magic bus to Camp Cheerful had been pulled over. All off! There was a toll to pay, and Dr. Crabtree had come to collect it, every last cent. She would do just that, too: the bride of Shylock over there. She wanted her pound of flesh, and she was not to be denied. I'd had my last hurrah. It was good to me, too. Now, I could die happy. Remember my name. They would; I'd bet my life on that, which is exactly what I had done.

CHAPTER FOUR

PAYDAY

"Look it in the eye and don't you even think about busting a move; it smells fear," said Jimmy, #1 in my heart by virtue of his outrageous personality and inmate #36075 on the jail roster by virtue of his incarceration. He liked to be called "Jimmy Glitter" because he had delusions of grandeur and saw himself as the next big thing and It Guy in rock 'n' roll and was offering sage advice to the rest of the young debtors when the bill collector entered the dayroom, a holding pen for

Society's wayward castoff-kids destined for ritual sacrifice on the Altar of Justice by the heavy hand of one Dr. Tamika Sue Ann Johnson Crabtree, known by many aliases including "Crabby" and "Dr. C." Why all those names were necessary I have no clue. She was keeper designate of the flame at this the bleak shrine of truth, justice and the American way called "Juvie," and she did it to death, too. It wasn't a job to her; it was her calling in life. She was not to be denied neither by man nor beast. Legend has it that her shadow killed a dog.

Then I gave Crabby, Juvie's reviled Program Director, the Queen of Mean, here to settle their I.O.U.'s, a proper welcome: "WHOA! There she is. Well, just look at you, Miss Done Up for the Gods. You really do know how to make fabulous entrances and glamorous exits, don't you? And you do work a room. You're like a special effect from a horror movie. What d'ya hear? What d'ya say? Took you forever to get over here. What did you do, Munchies, come by way of the Panama Canal?"

Dr. C. shot back that sarcasm is the purview of teenagers and homosexuals, who just happen to be my preferred social groups. Small world!

"Okay, I take that back because this complex is so huge," I went on. "The average Joe like me needs a Sherpa tribesman guide up in here. I missed you so bad! Did you miss me even a little bit, too? Sure do hope so because, if you didn't, I'd be totally floored beyond words."

"What do you have to say for yourself, sir, and make it good," she told me, "because I've got something for you, and, no, it isn't Hanukkah gelt, either."

"Well, first off, I'd like to thank my manager, my producer, the director and all of the little people that made this possible," I said. "Okay, just put it under the Christmas tree, so that I can stay awake all night trying to guess what it is, and make it snappy, would you please; this is cutting into my nap time, and nothing does that."

"You don't acknowledge Christmas, though, Mister," she said, to which I replied: "So, how about Simchat Torah then?"

"You need to act your age!" she scolded.

I popped back that I didn't have to do anything but stay handsome and die and that she should lighten up on me because I regularly tithe to my conscience.

"Go on," I added, "amuse yourself. Of course, handle me with care; I'm a bomb with a short fuse."

Not one to truck with a jester, she focused on the job at hand. "People, I've just received your case dispositions from the Court. You broke the social contract, and it's payday," she said. "Nobody acts foolish, nobody gets hurt and don't go putting any parts of a Be Kind to Kids sign on my backside because there is a place for kindness, yes. This for sure is not it."

Me, the elephant in the room, waved a red flag in front of her eyes in an effort to disrupt the rotund despot's rant, saying: "Hey, Grim Reaper, doom and gloom, that you know real good. Cue the sunshine!" It bounced like raindrops off a duck's back.

And so, it began and would roll on and on, until I was the last man standing. The heavy hitter swung away. To her, this was just batting practice, and I was playing On-Call Bat Boy. I acted the role well, too, until I didn't. Play ball!

"Panda Ann Logan," Dr. Crabtree, obviously cast as the ruthless villain in this melodramatic dust-up, went on, "report to the Watch Commander. Your charges have been dropped. Process out speedily; we need the bed. There's a waiting line at the door."

Panda jumped for joy and pretended to shoot a basketball, doing her own play-by-play announcing with a shout of: "She shoots; she scores!"

I apparently put my foot in my mouth when I advised Panda to cease gallivanting with psychos.

"You talking to me?" she said.

"No, I'm talking to the Pope," I said. "Sugar baby, you're lucky to be still alive, but Lady Luck is a fickle friend known to run out on you when needed most."

She replied that she didn't have to do anything but "stay cute and party down"; she was so right about that, too. Duly noted.

"After a while, Mr. Magnificent and thanks, thanks for being truly wonderful you; you're all that and a bag of weed, and you really wear those jeans just right," she said as herself, the happy hooker. "WOW! That all you? Why, you dog you, you went commando on us, huh! Guys, all you want is three things in life: grass, gas and ass."

She was wise way beyond her seventeen-year marker; she'd already lived a lifetime; she knew the ways of men so well that she could teach it. I gave her four words of advice, assuming that we had come to the end of the road: "No retreat, no surrender." But she had more to say on the topic of my manly animal-attraction. I liked what I was hearing, too. Keep that on the downlow.

She added that she wanted to be my play date so bad; she worshipped my cock; and she got $2,000 for the "Old Fashioned," which was a basic roll in the hay with a one nut limit; $900 for the "Duet," which she defined as a suck and chuck BJ with her humming to the hits; and market price for the "Bouncing Betty," her two-fisted-four-stroke-shake-and-bake-jerky-boy-pound-off. She swore that she could say "Fuck me" in four romance languages, too. Respect!

She went on that she, the Wonder Panda, would rock my world and that she was totally D.T.F., down to freak, and loved her some strange. She would take me places I'd never been before, and I may never ever come back, so I should pack a lunch and clean socks.

"Oooooooooooo!" the admiring kids went and gave Panda her props for her lofty prices for services rendered. I was impressed, myself. She was a survivor for sure, and she was in the Game to win it. She liked the high life; it was all she knew. She had just one speed, warp.

After Dr. C., the H.W.I.C. (Head Witch in Charge), told our Panda that she was obviously on her game today and asked her if she'd ever heard of STD's. Panda stuck her right back, asking the director if she'd ever heard of Listerine. BOOYA!

Then the happy hooker's focus returned to yours truly. She was much like a siren, luring Odysseus with a beautiful song to the rocks, where his ship would crack up and sink.

"Baby, let me be your very own private party doll," she said, seductively. "I'll make you come like a beagle and gush like a fire hose. Last call, old dude! Come get to this pretty young thing and make my kitty purr. …. MEOW … MEOW … Do me, baby. Come get to this. That's not a request, either. I can play rough. Hey, I know, we can play dress up together. Resistance is futile. You'll owe me."

"PANDA! PANDA! PANDA!" the kids cheered lustfully, as she showed out for them.

All the while, I was thinking: "I'm the best me that I can possibly be. What would Roy Rogers do?"

Panda was feeling emboldened by the court's dropping its hold on her. So, with nothing to lose now, she told me that she knows who I am famous. "Why, you're Peter Pan, leader of the Lost Boys!" she said. Peter Pan never grows up.

Obviously, her ire was evoked by my having turned down the entire Sexual Healing Package; I was on the wagon, see.

I cautioned her to play safe because it's a crazy wild jungle out there, and she'd already been bitten by a poisonous "trouser snake," aka man dick. She told me to save the drama for the civilians because that's what they're there for.

"What's up," she said, "afraid of us young girls? Figures if you are because you're half a faggot, anyhow. No wonder your little wifey so hates your infected ass, swishy male-impersonator! If I had a dick, you'd be singing 'Hava Nagilah!' And your amazing god-like, homoerotic, studly ultimate action hero Lone Ranger was porking Big Chief Tonto and All-Guy first teamer Ramblin' Roy Rogers, too, yes! If you don't know, now you know."

Inmate Dee wasn't about to be denied. He wanted Panda for an exclusive relationship as his very own personal porn star, and he let it be known, too.

"Girl, be my #1 lady, and I'll turn you out proper," he said. "I wanna put my brand on you."

"You do?" she said. "You mean get busy with little bitty me?"

"With that ass; I'll murder that shit!" he said. "Say my name, girl! You know who I am."

"Ooooooooo! You go, Dee!" the captive audience shouted out in unison.

"No money, no honey," Panda said. "The cuddly Miss Panda bear over here doesn't need a broke-ass scrub trying to get some play for a box of Ramen Noodles."

"But you just might eventually fall on your knees to me and beg me hard to be my chew toy by choice before this is all history, though," Dee continued.

Panda told him flat-out that she just might eventually go to Disneyland and blow Goofy, too, but she sincerely doubted it.

The kids roared with laughter, making it hard for me and certainly for the undisputed boss lady with portfolio, Dr. C., to believe that these warriors' futures hung in the balance by a frayed thread, as did their hot tempers.

"Gimme some stink, girl, just the vapors," Dee said, seeking an amicable compromise.

"Say pretty please with a cherry on top, oh, you nasty nasty wannabe boy toy!"

"Pretty please with a cherry on top a that shit. Now cut the cake!"

Panda then slipped her hand into the front of her panties, pulled it out and blew on it in Dee's direction.

"Ooooooooooooo!" The rest of the kids shouted. They were really into it now. Why not? The price was right and so was the seating.

"Now, that's what I'm talkin' 'bout!" Dee said.

"Stay up, my misguided youthful offenders," Panda told the home team. "Keep your head to the stars."

"Well, time to go peddle this tight little hot body off to my Viagra-popping old hippies turned investment banker groupies," she went on, "and pretend I like give a flying fuck about groovy Woodstock, the bitching Beach Boys and Tricky Dick. Tin soldiers and Nixon's coming. We can change the world!"

"Do as you must," I told her, "but don't give up! Don't you ever give up, not ever. You're young, yet. You have ideas. Don't grow old; old people have only fear and diapers going for them. I'm here for you; I'm not going anywhere far. I love you as a person."

"Not as an Aardvark?" she said.

"Wild thing, you move me," I went on. "Look at me as the wagon master. The Indians are out there to scalp you, and they'll be coming for you soon enough. I'm circling the wagons around you; you're safe. I'm giving you the choice to start the first day of your life again or die on the street like roadkill. Go on, become the special person that you were destined to be. Promise me that you will do the right thing. You don't have to be a star to be in my show."

"Do you even hear yourself!" she said. "Okay, okay, okay, me as myself, I am now making you a solemn promise in front of these witnesses: I will hurt and disappoint you bad if you don't get out of my pretty face. Fairy tales are for kids."

"What is that," I said, "the curse of King Tut's tomb?" I joked. Truth be told, she had my laughing on the outside and crying on the inside.

Panda then gave the gallery the V for "victory" sign with both hands. The kids did likewise right back at her and bid her a fond farewell, as she told them to tune in, turn on and drop out, blew me a scented air-kiss using the aromatic panties-hand and bent over to give Dr. C. a full moon shot.

Then she looked me in the eye, pecked me on the cheek and told me: "A cloud of dust and a hearty hi yo, Silver," departing to go hook up with Destiny, her next blind date on the Sugar Daddy Circuit.

She was truly an original, too fast to live and too young to die. I'd think of her fondly and often. She had happened! If anybody could somehow pull it off, that high wire act without a safety net, it was the Panda bear; she would be forever young or die trying.

I like betting on long shots, and I was all in. After all, I was a misfit by nature my own self, another cowboy riding against the wind; it takes one to know one.

Bringing up our inmate BG's disposition directive on her iPad, Dr. C. let it be known that she was truly Fate's messenger of record, the designated shot-caller, no doubt about it, and we had best recognize or suffer her wrath! Snakes bite. So does Reality.

"Countess Electra Crawford, our Earth Angel, better known as 'Baby Girl' or BG, you're next," the Doc announced.

"Got that eye-candy right here!" BG spit out. "The circus is in town, y'all. Gangster royalty BG is a bad micky ficky, and she's fine as cherry wine, too. Recognize, bitches!"

"BG! BG! BG!" the kids roared; it was unconditional love. They had all of her hit CD's and mp3's at home and knew her songs by heart, every last word including and and the. They also had bootlegs of her movies and her posters; it was BG's house in their eyes. She named the tune, and they danced to it.

Our resident big shot, the entertainer known as Baby Girl, sang out: "I'm goin' home! I'm goin' home!"

Then she proceeded to rip Dr. C. a new one in no uncertain terms, telling her that she, Dr. C., and the powers that be took long enough to get around to BG's turn.

"Somebody goin' on Black people's time up in here, Dark Vader!" BG protested to Dr. C., the self-proclaimed standard bearer for all things afrocentric.

Dr. C. wished our ebony star, BG, a fond bon voyage, which was oh, such sweet music to BG's ears. Then the other shoe dropped. BOOM!

The bearer of sad tidings, Dr. C. added that BG's new domicile of record would be the Cybil Brand Institution for Women; she was to stand trial in adult court, no more kid stuff for her. Plus, her bail had been denied, as she had been deemed to be a certified menace to society of the worst kind. The Law had taken its gloves off, and it wasn't to play Patty Cake, either.

The messenger went on to welcome BG to the big leagues and congratulate her on getting just what she'd wanted most all along, which was top billing.

Wobbled but still on her feet, though, BG told Dr. C.: "Don't write checks that your sorry ass can't cash, Color Purple! I can throw down, yo; I may be young, but I'm ready!"

Dr. C. had heard it all many times before; she wasn't impressed by the bravado and told BG in no uncertain terms to move along with a purpose or so wish that she had done so. It was no bluff. Dr. C. was a killer, and she didn't play softball.

BG, not the least bit intimidated by the mismatch, didn't flinch. She countered with: "Oh, hell to the no to the no no no! You only sweatin' me 'cause I'm Black; I know how that go. If I was white, you'd straight be my play-auntie. Tell me I'm wrong, shit!"

Dr. C. broke the news to BG that her alleged victim, the homeless man who had recently sustained such a terrible beat down from BG and her 'pack of wolves,' had passed on. "You know the poor soul in question; I'm quite certain," the administrator added.

BG went into counterattack mode next; she was a real gamer, too, that one, and she was not to be intimidated by a *bougie* lackey in an outlet store sale-rack off-brand business suit. BG swung for north, and she swung from south. It was on!

"Blow it out your ass!" BG said, going on to explain emphatically that she wasn't even at the scene of the alleged crime. That was her story, and she was sticking to it.

"I'm a celebrity: you don't know that by now?" BG told the Doc. "You'd better ask some damn body, shit!"

The slug fest continued. Dr. C. played the trump card now, revealing that two of BG's partners in crime, her very own bodyguards, had taken sweet deals to testify against her at trial, the kill shot. BOOYA!

BG broke down at the news. She was now hysterical and screamed out: "I DIDN'T MEAN IT! I'M SORRY; I'M SO CRAZY SORRY! LORD JESUS, HELP YOUR POOR CHILD; TAKE ME TO THE WATER. I JUST GOT ALL CAUGHT UP IN IT IS ALL. OH, MY GOD, WHAT HAVE I DONE? WHAT HAVE I DONE?"

BG was vulnerable, after all. The kids in the gallery were so stunned by this; speechless. Apparently, BG was merely a toothless recording studio gangster, after all, and her bark was worse than her bite. Oh, my, how the mighty had fallen! Why, she was all show, but no go.

Dr. C. informed her that she would be praying for her so hard, and BG said that she was a praying girl, too. Had Dr. C. heard the news? "He is comin'."

Dr. C. bit hard. "Who's coming, a name?" she asked BG.

"Your daddy," BG fired off, "he's comin' in your mama's face!"

The kids laughed loudly. BG was still on her game. She had her problems, too, yes, for sure that, but, no, a witch with a Ph.D. in divinity truly wasn't one. That girl, BG, she had a lot of heart for her size. I wanted her on my side in a bar fight. Pound for pound, she was still the undefeated champion and undisputed truth, shaken but not stirred.

Told by the administrator to make up her mind to either walk out or be restrained and carried out and to make it up fast because they were burning daylight over here, BG chose discretion over valor and punted, bloodied but still unbowed. She actually strutted out of the playpen and held her chin up high defiantly. I liked it; I liked it a lot. She was still loud and proud. Big props!

The gallery kids wished her well, and so did I. She was sugar and spice and everything nice, until she wasn't, that one. She was now one for the ages.

Fare thee well, our caped crusader, courageous and bold. Thanks for the memories.

"James Anthony Caputo, Jr., alias Jimmy Glitter," Dr. C. called out, telling him that his new address was as of this very day to be a psychiatric state hospital referred to as "Promises of Zuma Beach," really. Some called it Camp Cup Cake.

Jimmy shouted out: "Trippy!" and asked her how long he would be kept on ice for. Until Jesus came back was his answer. The Judge had handed out time like it was lunch.

Staggered by the gut punch, he asked me to spread the word that he, the one and only Jimmy the Freak, had been here for a cup of coffee. To which I told the human firefly to stay positive, which is a lost art much like the elusive double-clutch-jackhammer-hand-job with a twist and a pinch to grow an inch, which was gone but not hardly forgotten. It was the legendary white buffalo.

Life isn't a wish factory, no, but he got his, though: no parents, no problem. Now, it really was Jimmy vs. the world. He was a good actor; he could fool some of the people all of time and all of the people some of the time, but he couldn't fool all of the people all of the time, try as he might.

Ty, who had been riding Jimmy like a racehorse, asked the other kids to give Jimmy some "gay love," and Ronnie yelled: "Hey, Jimmy Rocky Horror, strike a pose and vogue for us now!"

Jimmy laughed long and hard at that; he was the only one doing so.

As Jimmy stood to leave, Dr. C. said: "Pleasing you pleases me. Buh bye, Jimmy Glitter."

And the Best Actor in a Drama Tony goes to you, Jimmy. Applause! "I'll see you when I see you," I told him. It was not to be, though, as you will see.

"Ronald Andrew Chin," the Doc continued, "you're up."

"They got the wrong guy; we all look alike," the Chinese bandit told her.

"You're off to the very plush California Institution for Men at Chino for five to ten years. A post card would be oh, so very nice; put a happy face on it and make us all real proud!"

"It ain't but two days that matter, though, day you go in and the day you come out," Ronnie said.

"When you get up there," I said, "just tell 'em you got cold busted, went to Club Juvie, met a true cowboy's cowboy, saw the error of your ways and all you got was a lousy T- shirt."

Ronnie replied that he'd be a stone-cold original gangster till he got boxed up and dug in; he took it like a champ.

"And until then?" I asked him.

"WHOOP! WHOOP! Picture me rollin'," he answered me back flippantly, pretending that his hands were on a stirring wheel. Then he struck a Kung Fu attack pose for the fans and held it for effect. Time stood still, and then it didn't.

Happy trails, Ron Ron. Don't let anybody get you down. Roll with the punches and take a pass on the canine cuisine. You are what you eat.

The remaining kids started barking like dogs. Exit Ronnie, aka Egg Roll, stage right.

"Tyrone Orlando Otis," Crabby called out.

"What's the big haps, Butter Cup?" he threw at the Director.

"You're sprung due to insufficient evidence. See the Watch Commander," she said.

Ty was pleased to his very core to say the very least. He told the lovely full-figured boss lady that she was so sweet that she made his teeth hurt and that he'd lost his phone number, could he have hers? And then he asked her if it hurt when she fell to earth from heaven. She wasn't at all pleased. Some people!

"You'll be back here soon enough, Romeo," she assured him. "We'll keep a light on for you."

He patted me on the back and said: "You good people, Battlin' Jerry Portnoy; it shows through your disguise. Be yourself 'cause everybody else out there, they already taken last time I checked."

"Dangerous game, running those mean streets, Ty, but ya cannot lose if ya do not play: take that with you. Jail is just a temporary shelter from the storm, not a final destination for your life's journey."

"What is this, 'Scared Straight'?" he snapped. "Ya don't think I can jail, shit! I been caged up like a dangerous jungle animal half of my life already: it ain't no big thing to me. Jail ain't nothin' but a house party, though, feel me? This shit make you strong-minded. Me, I'm untamed and not suitable for a rescue. When I'm in my cell, I free up my mind, and I'm dinin' on filet mignon and lobster tails; I'm drinkin' fine top-shelf French wine; I'm playin' golf with the President; I'm cruisin' the avenues in a chauffeur-driven luxury ride; I'm catchin' touchdown passes in the Super Bowl off of Patrick Mahomes; and I'm knocking out the heavyweight champion of the world with one punch. BOOM! Club Juvie ain't no parts of jail to me; it's Camp Snoopy up in here, I'm just sayin'.

"It gets old fast, though, just like me," I said.

"Say, Portnoy" he asked, "is that your nose or the bus to downtown L.A.?"

We laughed at that. It was good medicine. He needed it; so did I. He smiled at me, winked and left the playing field, totally ignoring Dr. C. She got over the snub fast, though; an occupational hazard. It wasn't her first ride at the rodeo.

"De Andre Alonzo Smith!" she announced loudly.

"Good news only, later on for the rest," Dee told the Doc.

Dr. C. told him that he was free to boot-scoot. The sole eye-witness in his case had come down with a sudden case of amnesia and couldn't even remember her own name; all charges were now dropped. Who knew? Ty needed to see the keeper of the keys; he knew just where. Club Juvie was his home away from home.

Strangest thing, though, he didn't appear to be surprised by this turn of events, not at all. Could it be that the fix was in? Stranger things have happened.

"You did good, Mr. P.," he said. "You're the best social worker around, top dog, and this ain't my first dance with a tourist, neither. Much love, Brother Pale Face!"

I had one bullet left, and I took a shot at him just like this: "Crime doesn't pay enough, young man. No more wrong turns for you. Teen Angels rule; gangsters drool."

Ty laughed and responded that he wasn't even hearing that noise. Then he had a personal message for Dr. C. that she was a "damn good House Negro" and shouldn't let anybody tell her any different. She got a big smile out of him with: "Just wait till you see me as the next Prom Queen."

"You still got a little Africa left in you, though, Sista Soldier," he added. "The man didn't beat it all outta ya before he bought you."

"Hasta la vista, desperado! Don't let the man get you; Johnny Law doesn't fight fair," I warned him. "Give me a pound of your best stuff."

With that we bumped fists, and Ty left me for greener pastures. The Call of the Wild beckoned him. Watch out, streets! Here he comes, and he's ready to rumble!

"Ricardo Nicolas Cruz!" Dr. C. shouted loudly enough to be heard a mile away; they were at best a foot apart. "You're the last of the Mohegans. Take a well-earned stage bow."

He answered up in street Spanish with: "El mas chingon de aqui. Ondelay … Arriba … Come on. Take your best shot! I ain't goin' out like no sucker punk; that's not a option up in here, not today."

"Early Christmas for you," Dr. C. told him, "you are a free bird once again. Take flight and don't even look back. Fly like an eagle before you wake up and find that this is but a dream."

"And stay that way if ya know what's good for ya," I slipped in. "Fly high and soar! Happiness is looking at jail in the rearview mirror."

"Next stop: see the Watch Commander," the Doc added.

Ricky asked her where all the white women were at. I thought that was a hoot. Stoic Dr. C. took a hard pass, though. Women! You can't live with them, and you can't return them for a credit, either. You can't even sell them for used parts.

"Gracias por todos, Maestro Jerry," he told me and added: "A certas luces usted parece uno estraya de sin."

I interpreted that for Dr. C.. It means: "In a certain light, you look like a movie star." Hey, I get that a lot. What can I say? If you've got it, flaunt it. It's a gift, and it's all me.

The eastside street soldier then asked me why I claimed that I was this big bad serial cheater when I didn't cheat on them any and stressed that he knew his cheaters well by their smell; he'd been stung before. Once bitten, twice shy.

"Hang up your gun belt and get a life, Big Scrappy," I told our Ricky. "There's one in the layaway with your name on it, a very cool one, too, yes, indeed; I peeked."

I got a rather sarcastic response that sure, like that'll happen. So, I hedged my bet.

"A part of you is broken, but they didn't get all of you, not yet, though, anyhow," I added. "Wake up! You're slipping into darkness. The world's not a ghetto."

"They ain't never gonna stop the Midnight Rider, though," he bragged. "I'm loco, Mr. P., what's your excuse?"

"I'm no longer age seventeen," I said because it was my truth to share. I was pushing twenty-seven hard, and you can't go back to Sugar Mountain, try as you might.

Before he left, he paid me the nicest complement of my life: "You just a outlaw man like me, Jerry. Por vida, me bueno amigo! Vamos a la cantina. If you pass before I do, be my guardian angel. If I go first, spill the wine and don't you be stingy because I'll know that shit and haunt your ass."

Big Scrappy then raised a hand, with his fingers flashed his gang sign's configuration at us and departed for higher ground. We had struck a deal. I would remember it always, no doubt. It was a win win proposition, the best kind.

And then there was one, namely yours truly. This is the famous final scene where I say that Quick Draw Jerry's work here is done, and I quit this lemonade stand. Don't talk about me when I'm gone because I have big ears.

Now it can be told: my problem is a toxic mixture of fear and self-loathing. You see, I trust absolutely no one, nowhere, no how. I'd been bitten before lots of times, and my mama didn't raise a fool. Kick me in the ass once, shame on you. Twice, shame on me.

It's scary out here flying solo. Isn't life just peachy keen! Well, welcome to mine, and it's never going to change, never ever. I'm just a lonesome L.A. cowboy, riding against the wind, I guess. It's like that sometimes. So, don't confront me with my failures; I quite obviously have not forgotten them. That's not me talking; it's the pain.

Dr. C., much to my astonishment, stood there telling me that I was a real certified card-carrying pain in the butt with a long history of being a square peg in a world of gaping round holes, but I was also a veritable homing beacon for lost souls; I feel their pain and work my magic to stop their internal bleeding somehow, kudos.

I replied that that was just me doing my job, following what was written on the script page for me. This wasn't just my castration complex talking now, either. I'd been flattered before. I didn't fall for the okey doke. She could save the sweets for Valentine's Day. I know the old rope-a-dope move when I see it coming.

Everybody has this unrealistic expectation for me that I will emerge from a cocoon as a beautiful butterfly. Well, I got news for you, this is me in real time. What you see is what you get, and I will die as a basic caterpillar: a day late, a dollar short and a pound light.

Then she opened the flood gate and told me what the Personnel Department thought of me, which was that I am a high achiever, who is totally self-reliant. I have no close friends or loved ones to turn to for support because I don't need anything but myself. While I am desirable to an organization because I am a born leader of men, I am at the same time a threat to stability. I tend to get easily frustrated and act out with impunity in an effort to destroy anyone that frustrates me. There is only one way to control people like me, termination. "The consensus is that you should be shot and thrown to the wolves," she added. "I beg to differ, though. Forget about the wolves."

She admitted to me now at the eleventh-hour mark that, if she had handed me over to the Personnel Department Boys' Firing Squad and had me walked off the grounds, then she wouldn't have been much of a talent scout, after all, but she was the best around, actually, and she was now looking over a legitimate all-star, namely me, the inimical humble hero known as "Special J," Most Valuable Player by acclimation.

I'd done it my way, too. Regrets? Sure, there's a few, but much too few to remember, except for one, the Big Kahuna strangling the life out of me still. I'd been a coward under fire and just couldn't deal with it, try as I might. The yellow stripe down my back just wouldn't come off.

"Shantith. Shantith. Shantith. I want to die," I piped up.

"What's that about?" she asked.

"Why, this is me chanting," I said.

"Sir, you're very weird," she told me. "Alas, diversity matters."

Full disclosure, weird is as weird does. I dream about circus clowns with balloons in their cheeks, floppy shoes, oversized pants and big red noses chasing around naked toddlers. Just kidding about the clowns, though. My favorite vintage '80's groups are "Circle Jerks" and "Alice in Chains." My high school guidance counselor told me that serial killers listen to that music. Not me though, I can't kill time or even guilt. I also fucked a sex doll on a dare. It had a recorded message like a Chatty Kathy doll has; it said: "Sock it to me, big boy!" It was totally consensual. I fucked Touchdown

Tommy Buck, aka Tommy Football, the all-everything high school quarterback, too, also consensual. He bucked like a bronco; he also threw accurate passes; he had a future, but he died of AIDS. I loved him and told him so. He said: "What's love got to do with it?" Some life!

"I'm still so out of here, though! Save your breath for the next sucker up at bat. No stopping me now," I assured the Doc. "Thanks for being you, mean it. You're a way better woman than I'll ever be, mean it, too."

"Just who are you, Stranger?" she asked.

"A visiting prince from the East," I said. "My life is a non-stop round of tennis and golf, and I play a mean game of polo, too. My family crest is centuries old. Oh, yes, I'm a matador, too. Can I interest you in something nice in a bull's ear from my collection? Good news, I've recently found a fair damsel to who I can dedicate my victories. We're getting married. Her name is Gweneth Paltrow. Yes, she's the actress;

I'd see her in anything. She's half Jewish, which is okay because I'm half horse."

"You're crazy!" she said.

"Well, Gweneth has always spoken very highly of you, though," I added. "To sum it all up, inside my head there is a masked ball in progress, and I never know who I'm dancing with. Looks like today's partner by choice is you, and you're more than just a handful."

"Please reconsider, oh, please!" she continued. Then she started throwing her best stuff at me. "Sure, I was hard on you, yes. So, there's that. Just trying to introduce you to my harsh personal friend, Mr. Reality."

"I just can't be the cookie-cutter company man here, swallow my pride and suffer like I'm the Magic Christian. What am I, Rudolf the goddamn reindeer or something!"

"I didn't want yet another hard-headed Calvin's crash and burn on my conscience; I couldn't take the pain, no, not again, no way," she said. "Once in a lifetime is more than enough for this woman. I don't have superpowers; shocking to hear that, huh!"

"Portnoy," oh, you of the shiny nose," she continued, "there are three, count them three juvenile halls in Los Angeles proper, and, so far, you, sir, you have been terminated by the Program Directors at two of them over the span of a single calendar year. Three strikes and you're on the street for good, Mister! Don't even think about returning to this campus for the Homecoming Dance, either. You've pretty much burned this spot, too, for all intents and purposes. You're on my last nerve! The dyke is about to burst."

"I trust that you have a map to buried treasure," she added. "If not, then what's left for you out there? Gigolo is definitely not a viable option; you don't have the goods."

I wanted to know more about this mysterious hard-headed Calvin character, though, and pressed her for a full reveal.

She disclosed that he was her late husband, the love of her life, and he took mess from no man born unto woman in particular, either. We would've been boys for sure, according to her. Birds of a feather flock together and all that good stuff.

"Calvin was my black knight in shining armor," she continued. "You may have heard this: the blacker the berry, the sweeter the juice. Well, my man, Cali, he was sugar on my lips, and it was good to me to the very last drop all the way down. I should've bottled the stuff for a rainy day, but who knew, right?"

"So, we were deep in the heart of Dixie, Atlanta, G.A. to be exact, Chocolate City, Sir Calvin and I, visiting family," she went on with her tale of woe, leading me down the Trail of Tears. "On our way to church, Speedway Calvin runs red lights like he's totally color blind. I'm like: 'Calvin Anthony Crabtree III, those lights are red! That means stop or die in this town.' He just goes: 'Baby, they're just reddish to me. They're going to have to shoot me.'"

"Soon enough, yes, a cop then pulls us over and says in no uncertain terms: 'Remain in the vehicle, sir!' Standing tall, as was his custom, hard-headed Calvin goes: 'I think not!' He jumps out of the car, digging into his pants to retrieve his wallet, and Atlanta's finest puts a round through his heart and, by so doing, he put one through mine, as well. BANG! He took two lives for the price of one with the magic bullet that day. So, welcome to Crabby World that's never going to change and where time stood still. Ah, well, would a, could a, should a. If only. I stopped believing in God that day. Are you one of them, too, a true believer?"

"Well, God is dog spelled backward," I said. "I've kissed his ass regular in temple for years, and where did it get me in the end? I'm dazed and confused on my best of days. God? Woman, please! Me, I now whack off to a picture of Ike Kelly, the two-time Ohio State buckeye all American center/linebacker from the early '60's. On his good looks he wouldn't get far, but he hit like a Mack truck. I have an extra; I'll hook you up."

"Are you okay right now?" she asked me.

"Does the Pope defecate in the woods?" I said. "Tell me something, okay, do you think that I'm crazy or what? Every time I take a breath, I think that I will bust out in tears and stuff."

She told me that she thought I was just lonely and needed to get laid so badly, and I took that personal. Here's my take on that: to score ass by choice these days you need to be either a rock star with your own airplane or a pro football jock like a defensive tackle maybe with a six pack for abs and a bull neck with a SUV with smoked windows and a totally bitchin' sound system.

I was so sorry for her loss and let it be known that I was down for a basic murder-suicide pact if she was, too; it was lady's choice for spot the batting order.

She took a raincheck on the offer and pressed me back for an explanation of my cowboy schtick, both my clothes and my swagger, because she might want to try it one day, herself.

So, I opened a vein and let my psychic blood flow. All of those long tall Texans on the TV screen in reruns on their big white horse in a cool kick-ass white hat, boots and spurs that jingle jangle jingle, they're my virtual besties. I ride alone: it's how the West was won. Go on, you won't be the first; say it: I missed the last ship out of the 20th Century. "I was also trying to dazzle you," I added.

"Well, it worked," she said. "You're good! You could teach how to dazzle and make yourself a fortune. This place is wild enough, but adding you to the mix took it places it had never been before. I couldn't have even hallucinated it would be like this. Know what, Portnoy, neither could that bunch of kids, the usual suspects.

The Doc cut to the chase like a surgeon with a scalpel in each hand. "All that because of your poor kid sister going down in flames," she said. "Well, enough with the grief already! I get it. So, what else is new? Chilly today, hot tomorrow."

What else is new? What else! Was she kidding me with that pull on my chain? I did a terrible and unforgivable thing by letting little Sis die on me and haven't been punished for it, not yet.

Oh, how I loved that sweet little girl! Red hair, blue eyes, dimples and always a smile on her. She looked in my face as her candle went out, as though she was saying to me: "Do something and quick, too, Big Brother Jerry, because I'm dying over here. Something is wrong with this picture." I skated, and that's about it. Blackout. End of play. Curtain!

"You and your guilt! Oh, my God, give me a break. Egomaniac, what makes you think that something you did or didn't do years ago when you still wore Power Rangers PJ's and wanted to be a Jedi knight oh, so bad could be of the least consequence today?"

I added that there was a lot about me that she didn't know and that I carried around like a veritable boulder. A. I have an intimate relationship ongoing with sleeping pills. B. I was impotent for a long time. The shrink said it was the trauma coming back to bite me in the ass. C. I had an affair with a trans man with a panties fetish, who dropped me for a drag queen, who did a killer Barbra Streisand imitation. D. I squeezed my father's hand, the one covering Ruthie's little face, even harder to be sure that she didn't alert the Klansmen to our hiding place. So, there is that.

Crabby then told me that she hoped that I didn't want anything much from her because she had nothing much to give and informed me that she won't be attending my "self-pity party," not really her particular cup of tea, but she had, however, brought along a special gift that she'd picked up for a most unique star in the cosmos, namely me, the mighty Battling Jerry over here, paragon of virtue and defender of the faith. "Try it on for size and we'll talk some afterward," she continued.

That, my friend, is when she reached back and slapped me silly across the face with a blow harder than advanced calculus. CRACK! As my eyes welled up with tears, I screamed out in pain and jumped back. What was this about!

"Oh, the things we do for love," she said.

And, with that, the Doc informed me that Angel Baby Little Sister Ruthie R.I.P. now forgives me; God the All Mighty grants me a do-over; my crying time is all used up; the Fat Lady just sang; and Elvis has left the building.

"Portnoy, in order for you to learn to love yourself, you first off have to accept the truth: she's dead and buried," Dr. C. added. "Let the poor little thing stay dead and buried. She needs her rest. So do you, and, quite frankly, so do I."

"What if I don't want to do that!" I said.

That's when she pulled out her phone and told Siri to give her the number for the closest place that sells shotguns.

"So, just what's that you're saying?" I asked.

"That I will murder your ass before I let you drown yourself in a tub of guilt, sir," she told me. She meant every word of it, too. "This is an intervention," she went on. "It's me, you and the ghost of Christmas past."

I couldn't help it; tears ran down my face like Niagara Falls. I didn't weep because I cared too much. It was because I didn't care enough.

"Was that as good for you as it was for me?" she asked me. "Speak! If the right one didn't get you, then the left one will." That wasn't an idle threat, either. She was not one to be ignored; she was a clear and present danger. You have a witness.

"Good, good, real good!" I said because the Slugger in look-just-like and almost real Prada was no slouch; she was the undisputed truth; and I spoke Slap fluently, having been down this road before more than once. She was flexing the fingers of her left hand, ready to deliver on the promise; this was no bluff. She set 'em and put 'em down with the best.

"No cowboy heads for higher ground on me in this one then, I take it," Doc said.

"Different day, same old horse," I went on. That rerun ending with Good Guy in white and Wonder Horse riding off into the sunset was so played out by now. I had overdosed on it. It was now much too sweet to the taste. It made me sick. YUK! "Nope, I'm not a real cowboy; I made it all up," I said. "Don't you get it, boy wonder," she replied. "We all make it all up."

In the ending salvo, the Doc asks me if I want to hit the saddle and take a test-ride with a sidekick that sure loves her some lonesome L.A. cowboy, and she then opens her arms wide to give me the mother of all bearhugs.

"YIPEE KY YEH!" I shouted.

"Shut up and deal," she said, and I did just that. We embraced each other long and hard like we'd been lost and finally found at long last, kindred spirits were we. She was Dr. Feelgood after all. I'd taken the Cure, and I'd been healed. It was truly my Ah Ha moment, and it was all good.

It felt super comfortable to be with my own kind finally, the family of wounded warriors. I'd be better off now. Life is for the living. I was tired of playing the role of Dead Man Walking and could only hope that I hadn't been type cast by now.

It was a new deal. I was all in. I'd been touched by an angel. Call it a wakeup call by way of a love tap. Life is truly like a box of chocolates. You never know what you'll get.

I stand tall. I pass the taste test. I am a guy's guy. I am godlike. I kick butt in bunny slippers. Lightning bolts shoot from my fingers, and, doggone it, people like me. I am fearless and shameless. I am a conqueror. I still don't believe in God per se, not as this kindly Jewish grandfather with an old world accent that gives us candy and keeps us regular, but I think that, when all is said and done, he might be willing to make an exception in my case that my final ending will not really be so absolutely final after all. I stand by my record, some of which is detailed for you here. So, you be the judge.

Ah, but I digress. Back to the story for I have many promises to keep and bridges yet to cross, at least the ones that I hadn't already burned down along the way.

Okay, a spoiler alert goes right about here and now. See, I die at the end, and it's not particularly at all pretty, still rather operatic, though, when push came to shove. You do, too, nothing to write home about, either. So, we have that going for us.

Ride on, Listener! We have many miles to go yet before we sleep. Everybody up for the kickoff!

CHAPTER FIVE

HARDLY STRICTLY LOVE

Two years back, Tiffany and I found ourselves in the office of the good doctor, Dorothy Cole, a couple's counselor par excellence, known to do more good than harm. Actually, she wasn't the first of her kind that we'd aired our dirty laundry out for; I've lost count by now.

We merely wanted her professional opinion on whether this turbulent union between a bi-curious wannabe movie cowboy/erstwhile social worker and this pampered Queen Bee with a wandering eye for potential new bedfellows, preferably well-endowed tops with salami-girth schlongs, could be saved, if it was worth saving at all that is or not.

We had been on this herky jerky rollercoaster ride called marriage for three years now. Every day of it had seemed like an eternity plus a year. Do I sound happy to you, yet?

One of my problems, according to wife Tiffany, was my financial irresponsibility. I only wanted the very best of cars, clothes, restaurants and jewelry. Get the picture? "You just go around once," I figure, "so go for the gusto or don't go at all."

"Yeah, right," Tiffany mocked me, "and that would be why we're teetering on the brink of bankruptcy: the Great Gusto Quest."

Compulsive gambling was yet another of my major bugaboos, and we'd come here to the good Dr. Cole to resolve that, as well. Hopefully she had a magic wand handy or some love potion at the very least.

You see, I had a few bucks in pocket. I'd lucked out with an admittedly scandalous crotch book, a pulp memoir about a torrid affair between a college professor and a carnal coed, blow by blow. I'd scored a $100,000 advance from the publisher, which was a dollar and a quarter more than I intended to spend.

With that in mind, I'd been known to lose as much as $10K on a single race at the track. The horse's name was "Eventually." She'd finished last. Who knew?

"I could have ran faster than that my own self," Tiffany complained to me.

"Oh, so now you're telling me," I said.

"Oh, yeah?" she snapped. "You'd better watch your mouth because I know women who would snatch your package for a double-scoop of chocolate chip."

When I was single, I'd dabbled in online dating, a total disaster at best. As I told the Doc, every woman I'd met on the Net, they all wanted the same things from a guy: money, money and more money. Did I mention money, yet?

Today's metropolitan man about town always has to justify his love. What's up with that! Me, I prefer to just kick it old school: guy as shot caller, feel me? Make Jerry's game jersey of choice a vintage model, if yo please.

Simply put, these JDate/E-Harmony.com female contenders wanted the best dinner out that money could buy, which was universal on their Wish List. In woman-speak: "It's good grub, it's good love." And, of course, there is always: "Pie doesn't lie." As if a large pizza with everything just for her was only a snack, right?

You'd think that I was offering them Alpo if I merely hinted at KFC, the way they went on. Gold-diggers! Well, Jerry ain't the one to fall for the okey doke, ladies: start spreading the news.

Know what they call a woman with PMS and ESP? ... A bitch that knows everything. Can I get a witness, brothers out there? When I married Tiffany, she put the ring through my nose, not on my finger. Now, the story can be told.

So, Tiffany, the very poster girl for penis envy, herself, hears that barb and spits at me with: "Okay, where do you want it? You're about to suffer the wrath of Tiffany, and it won't be pretty, either. I'm calling for backup now. That does it. My girls are as good as on the way! You, you're a marked man now. It won't be pretty."

Well, you see, Listener, this was to be my absolutely final try to keep this thing of ours, this masquerade, afloat in a churning sea of trouble. All indications were that it was "ballgame over." See, I'm not your everyday naïve Nancy, so to speak, although I have dabbled in the occasional Estee Lauder product for that certain *je ne sai qua.*

As I explained to the Doc in no uncertain terms, I wouldn't wager on "Success Story" to win, place or show in this race. I'm a textbook realist; I call a skunk a skunk; and I told Tiffany that if the shoe fits she should wear it.

"Are you a realist about your having maxed out all of our credit cards, too, all of them," my pet wolf in sheep's clothing, Tiffany, said, "or about your being overdue on the mortgage and the car note for the third, count them the third month in a row or, especially, about me being in my fifth week and starting to show now? And that's not blowback from the cheeseburgers and onion rings, either, baby. Go on, wave your hand in the air like you just don't care!"

She was on a roll now and went on to tell the Doc that there was also the issue of my erectile dysfunction to dissect here today. This was shocking news to me because I had come in for counseling, not a circumcision.

"My dreamboat, Doggie Daddy over there, the ultimate cocksman, he has big big trouble getting Mr. Mojo rising, and, when he can get back in the game, by the good grace of a merciful God in heaven, he's up and running for like two minutes tops if he eats his Wheaties and the planets are aligned just so. Then pop goes the weasel, and all bets are off. It's like beating a dead horse."

So said the lovely demure Tiffany, my blushing bride, as we were standing there going toe-to-toe and throwing haymakers from out of left field.

My turn … I said: "Maybe, if you were a better lay, then it wouldn't be an issue, feel me? So, right back at you in your face then. BOOYA!" She took it like a champ, not even so much as a flinch.

Her turn … She threw: "Maybe, if you stopped comparing real life with all of that skank pornography you lust over, you could change your name back to Big Game Jerry from Droopy!"

We had the issues of the pregnancy, keep it or sweep it, and financial mismanagement plus habitual gambling plus pornography addiction and, last but not least, how to put more lead in my pencil to deal with. All aboard the Love Train!

Let's go way back to the Big Apple when the ball first started rolling. Tiff and I met at a Halloween party in Brooklyn. I was 21; so was she. We were both of us seniors at NYU.

Tiff came as herself, a wicked witch, and she cast a spell on me. I was drunk as Ned the Wino that night and look what it got me, the bride of Frankenstein. What's more, she farts in the bed. Alert Homeland Security, somebody! Okay, here's something else: when she comes, she screams like the chick getting stabbed up in the shower scene in the movie, "Psycho."

"Well," Tiff told the Doc, "when he comes, he pats me on the head and says with a straight face mind you: 'Good pussy. Good pussy. Good pussy.' The hell!"

Cupid shot his arrow, and zing went the strings of my heart. Then I dragged her home by her hair, caveman style. It's all about that Jungle Love, though, right, Listener? So, call me Jungle Jerry.

Actually, my girl, Tiff, was pretty good looking, though, albeit majorly weight-challenged. Yeah, I said it. We're talking fat girl and not pleasingly plump or big-boned, either. Slick her hair back and put her in a diaper, she easily could have wrestled pro Sumo on the circuit and made a nice piece of change for herself. Never say never.

She was built for comfort, not for speed; big butt, big heart. She had a caboose on her like a frigging Winnebago. I swear to you that the thing snapped at me more than once. I still don't know what she fed it, big old pumpkin patch dimpled show-pony butt.

Tiff didn't take that lying own. "Listen to the last of the red-hot lovers," she said, "my hero, Sir Pack-a-Lunch; Casanova in a Kia!"

"Sliding into you is like rubbing down with sandpaper, and I mean you are parched, as in the frigging Mojave Desert," I said.

To which she let loose with a veiled threat that I had to sleep sometime, and she knew where I lived, and get a hold of this, she blamed the sexual dysfunction all on me, saying any problems were due to the fact that I didn't turn her on.

What was that about? Most of the women I've known would eat a mile of my shit just to get close to my asshole.

I belted her right back with: "Hey, a prairie dog runs by your bed every night, and you have sage brush and tumbleweed in your bathtub." She wasn't a good sport about it, though, Listener, telling me that my days were numbered, no joke.

Marriage is a give-and-take proposition, isn't it? I gifted her with a huge diamond ring, and, in return, she gave me a bracelet engraved with the words: "Jerry is the devil." Is it any wonder that her side of the waterbed is frozen solid? I wake up with frostbite.

Tiff then wanted me to tell her why I never shout out her name when we're making love, and I told her that it's all very simple: I just don't want to wake her up.

She went on to tell the Doc that at first there was a lot of steamy sex in the mix, which fit right into my meager entertainment budget.

Tiff argued back at me that she could have done a whole lot better for herself than me and married up, though, because she had the opportunities by times of ten.

"I was very popular," she added. "The hospitals were full of guys with twisted necks from turning to look as I walked by."

"What's that, the Vagina Monologue?" I said.

Listener, it wasn't all bad all the time, though. Tiff gave me oral pleasure on the first night we met. She had mad skills, too, I must say. But she needs some work in the attitude department. She licks my cannoli once, maybe twice if it's my birthday. Then she looks up at me and grins like the cat that just ate the canary, and, all the while, she's sucking wind, as if she had just finished running a marathon.

Hey, Listener, just between us, the secret to real man-bliss is, in a word, "whores," anyhow, and I'm a witness. So, call me Mr. Cash for Coochie if you must. With a hooker, you know that you're going to score on your very own terms every time out. So, I have that going for me.

I have this favorite escort that I see to get my business straight: Tasty Touché, she multitasks: gives me a BJ and hums the hits. She never misses a beat, that one, just like a bobbing chicken head. That woman can sure eat her some jelly roll, though. She knows things.

"Sure sure, tell Dr. Cole everything, why don't you, boy on a budget?" Tiffany said, not one to go heavy on the ego stroking lest it should go to my head.

"You're not ready to run with this pretty young alfa dog here," she added, "so stay in your own league, rookie! In your face! BOOM … How does it feel to be posterized?"

Tiffany was definitely feeling her oats now, Listener. She had no shame and went on to tell the Doc that we were in her car on our very first night together, and I whipped out my pink "thingie" totally without any parts of her permission. Then she went down on me because that's her best move, and I cheered her on with stuff like: "Suck it! Kiss it! Slap it! We'll do pizza sometime. You look like a pepperoni person. I'll call you, promise, mean it."

"Gee whiz! What a guy's guy this one is. He really brought his A game to the ballpark," she went on.

We had our fun, too. It wasn't all doom and gloom all of the time for sure. Okay, so, for example we'd go to my place, drink off-brand sodas, eat knock-off potato chips and watch highlights of my porn stash, epics all of them, such as "Dykes on Bikes vs. Roller Derby Dolls," and then, of course, there was "The 50 Ft. Woman vs. Thong Thing," but my all-time favorite by far was "Spring Break Confidential," starring the hot tamale, Miss Junk in the Trunk herself, Senorita Beanie

Wild Thing Sanchez, who is billed as '300 lbs. of spicy mamacita.' She had made quite a splash in her debut film, "Fat Chick, Hot Pants."

Listener, let it also be known that Tiff really got into "Nookie Stop," starring the horseman, Rex Thoroughbred, and introducing the tag team of Rowdy Randy Sprout and the stuck-up redneck, Bobby Joe Header, aka "Blue Balls and Dixie."

Tiff had something to add to that: "Doc, I kissed a whole lot of frogs along the way to being sacrificed at the sacred Altar of Love.

"Not what it says on the men's john stall, though," I popped off, garnering a scowl. Score one for me.

Listener, you've heard the expression "one and done" before. Well, this particular dark comedy, "The Jerry and Tiffany Show," could be summed up in three little words, namely: two and through. This was hardly strictly love.

You see, we had been down this same rocky road to ruin once before, potholes and all. This was our second go-around; we had been married to each other once before. Misery is as misery does, huh!

The first cruise on the "Love Boat" lasted all of ten months before it sank to the bottom of the sea. The headline read: "TOTAL DISASTER!" I wish that I didn't know now what I didn't know then; I'm still running against the wind.

But we both answered the bell for another shot at it, though. Why bother? Just chalk it up to being young and new. I guess that there was some amour left in the tank, yet. At this point, however, we are riding on fumes.

"Okay," Tiff said, "sometimes, he wasn't all that bad between the sheets when push came to shove; I'll give him that much; credit where credit is due."

Listener, I don't like to brag much, but I've got the fire down below; I'm definitely packing; I'm hung like a Christmas stocking; and that bulge in my sock isn't my ankle, either.

Tiff chipped in with: "He likes to play Horse and Rider. He's rider; quick rider. Two more words: premature ejaculator."

"Well," I said, "it's a real fast world out there! Deal with it."

"When I complain about it," she added, "Speedo over here, he comes right back at me with the ever-so-clever: 'I got mine, get yours.' Hey, maybe I should have chosen someone else instead of Zippy here, ya know what I mean, somebody not so frigging eager."

Listener, I told her that, next time, she should try a real jockey then. BAM!

Well, fight fan, as I explained to Dr. Cole, Tiff and me, we were there with her that day to decide whether to stick or split, and, if we couldn't agree on it either way, then the good doctor, she would cast the deciding vote, something non-binding, just a mere nudge in the right direction as she saw it to be is all we wanted.

The counselor asked us to start with the first break up and go from there.

"Okay, cool," I agreed, "but it's way complicated, though."

"Yes, it's some complex and very malignant shit for sure," Tiff said.

You see, Listener, my friend till the final out, when we were just newlyweds, I was a part-time community college instructor, trying to bring home the bacon and make ends meet. It was a battle to keep my hands off the co-eds, though, a heavy cross to bear for sure. It's so hard to be a saint in the city! There I was, the professor of desire, raking in a whopping $16K a year.

"Give it up for Bill Gates II," Tiff said, "my big baller shot caller. WHOOP WHOOP! Hail hail to the conquering hero, the champion of the West!"

Well, that didn't stop me from taking her out to the finest five-star eateries in town, best seats in the house for concerts and even the occasional Las Vegas getaway, too, feel me? Nothing was too good for my baby.

"Man is God's gift to women. So, live with it," I told my blushing bride. "Guys rule; chicks drool."

"All of that on an enormous $16K, incredible!" Tiff slapped me back with. "You were Pauly Plastic on a tear, the Credit Card Kid, even charged my engagement ring to the tune of $50K, didn't you?"

"I thought I could cover it all with a small bump from the Tooth Fairy, though," I said, "or perhaps my Fairy Godmother would kick in."

Tiff went on to tell Dr. Cole that the bill collectors were calling our house non-stop those guys, and she was so freaking out that she'd wind up homeless, and the prospect of living in a tent didn't exactly make her love come down in the least. "No! A woman like me, Dr. Cole, sister please," she added.

You see, Listener, this high roller, Winner's Circle Jerry boy over here, I went belly up and landed upside down, and my lovely bride and I, we were rudely evicted. All the furniture was repossessed, as was our new car and her fifty grand bling bling ring of love, too. Now you see 'em, now you don't. I was on my ass now.

You can't make this stuff up! So, Listener, this has no doubt led you to just one conclusion; I was an accident waiting to happen. BOOM!

That brings us to the current pregnancy now. I should go first merely because I have the one and only penis in the room; I'm assuming.

"He didn't use protection," Tiff told the Doc. "So, I got bitten by a poisonous snake. Wow! Talk about a frigging angry inch."

Well, that just may be so, friend, but she swore to me on a stack of bibles that it was "safe," that she couldn't possibly get pregnant at that time of the month, no way. Rhythm Method Calendar Mama over there.

So, I'm thinking to myself: "What the hey, Slugo? Batter up! It's your deal now, and everything is wild."

Her famous last words to me were: "Drive it home, Big Papa! Pedal to the metal. Ram it! Man handle me!"

"Selfish deadbeat!" Tiff called me.

"Sleazy slut!" I snapped.

"Numb nuts!"

"Blowfish!"

"Limp biscuit!"

"Thunder thighs!"

And so, it went, this lovers' duet in two-part harmony a little off key.

Then she called me the lost boy who refused to put his big boy pants on.

Who, me?

"On that happy note, Dr. Cole," Tiff continued, "I had an abortion that first time knocked up by him, our guy, Mr. Warmth. He was pressuring me; he really didn't want a baby, no frigging way.

"This is me," she added: "'Jerry, I'm pregnant.' This is him: 'Oh, yeah? Sweet! Like I'm supposed to know you from somewhere? Give me a hint.'"

Get this, noble Listener: she was on the phone to the hospital to schedule the procedure the very same day she got the positive test result; she didn't as much as even mention it to me, not word one. So much for love between a boy and girl can be oh, so wonderful, right? I would've offered her a ride both ways and paid for the gas, too.

Tiff didn't take that shot lying down, either. She told the Doc that she was scared and that I wouldn't understand, adding that, if I'm so frigging manly, why do I cry when I come?

"Fix him, Doc; I can't," she went on, "maybe try an exorcism or a blood-letting. Erotic asphyxiation is getting so very big these days."

Truthfully, I was torn to the max over this. That's me right there; I'm just too good to be true; ask around. I mourn over roadkill.

Guys have feelings, too. My kid might have grown up to be the next Supersize Johnny Wad or even the Booty Bandit, Long John Silver, that one. I would've been some kind of a dad, too. I could've taught him the four F's of dealing with women: "Find 'em, feel 'em, fuck 'em, forget 'em."

I'll keep it real for you. Sure, I was a little relieved, too, yeah. There's that truth and mix in a healthy helping of anguish, as well. Bottom line: young man about town Joltin' Jerry is seven kinds of sensitive. I'm tuned into my feminine self, and do I ever look good working a miniskirt and heels!

"But only women bleed," Wifey scolded me. She was breaking my heart, Bloody Mary over there, the lady in red.

And then, of course, there is the matter of the current pregnancy to deal with. If not now, then when, right? That Dutch oven is on a timer. She has the boogie in her, and it's got to come out. Basically, she seduced me, plain and simple; she mates, then she kills.

"Hey, Dr. Cole," Tiff said, "all work and no play makes Tiff a dull girl, though! So, I climbed right back on that painted pony, rode it hard and put it away wet. But even cowgirls get the blues, though, and I'm the Sweetheart of the Rodeo."

"So, do I tell the Doc about the Prince episode now or just bite my tongue," I asked our all-around cowgirl.

"Okay, sure," she agreed, "tell it, Eager Beaver, before you explode then. It is kind of unique, actually. So, speak your truth, boy, and I might let you stick your little clammy little hand in the cookie jar just for old times' sake."

Green light!

"Tiff, she knows all of the jams on Prince's "Greatest Hits" album," I revealed. "So, this one time, we're going at it hot and heavy just like a couple of bunnies in heat, and you know how they do. Your boy, Jerry with the juice, laid much pipe.

I really was getting my swag on, and my mojo was working overtime, too, high gear. I was the King of Bareback Mountain. You know, they don't let you join the Players Club for nothing; you've got to come correct!

In the heat of passion, Tiff, she screams out: "Do me, baby! Pluck me like I'm your guitar, Prince!"

That was the moment I knew for sure that she was totally howling-at-the-moon whacko, and she was truly the shorty of my wet dreams, my one and only, my ride or die.

More than anything else in the whole wide world, I wanted that we would remain the very best of boos forever and a day. I'm like that, you see: I like my music funky; I like my food spicy; and I like my women freaky.

So, Freak of the Week Tiffany over here, she winds up barefoot and pregnant once again. Can you say "rerun?"

"Oh, you he-man oozing testosterone," Tiffany said, "you club-swinging caveman, why don't you just lather up and shave for us now? It's such a turn on!"

She cheated on me. Yes, Listener, you heard me. Terrific Tiff slept with her boss, no less, kid you not, and I'm telling everything. This is a real page turner now. You wanted it; I had it; you've got it. This is the featured attraction.

Yep, she opened Pandora's box. Well, okay, full disclosure: I cheated on her first. Yeah, I said it. Monkey see, monkey do.

"His name was Ron for the record," Tiffany said, "and me, I was just blowing my pipes out. See, if you don't use it, your good thing sure as hell turns to shit on you. Use your tools. A rolling stone gathers no moss. I was the cheater. Ron was the cheatee.

"As for Jerry, he just wasn't getting his homework assignments in on time, and my allure has a short shelf-life. So, I went out shopping for a stand in for love. It's just the Gypsy in my soul, I guess."

Ron, good old Ronnie boy, let's put him in play, while we're doing our Spring cleaning over here.

"Bring it on, party-girl," I told Tiff. "Put your game face on for us and let your freak flag fly high. That's how you do."

Sure, Listener, I admit it: I played a mean game of "Hide the Salami" with that little vixen hot to trot on the cusp of jailbait groupie of mine: I'll cop to it, yep. Enough said. And we're off!

My tramp-stamped and tongue-studded teen tramp in a halter top's name was Passion, and, yes, she was my own personal passion fruit, ripe, juicy and all mine for the plucking. I was the plucker. She was the pluckee.

I can't stand here and, in good conscience, point the Finger of Guilt at Tiffany because I follow my dick around like it's a GPS, and I'm Chief of the Fuckahwee Tribe, as in "Where the fuck are we?" Maybe so, but I do have my standards, though, namely a pussy and a pulse.

"Well, Doc, Ron was my boss at the firm," Tiffany began. "I'm a lawyer, see. At first, it was innocent enough, all of that attention I was getting at the office, okay? That's all it takes to heat my little engine up, a tad bit of attention, and, next thing you know, my legs are in the air like football goal posts, and I'm calling out my train time."

I told Tiff that I want attention, too. So, where is mine: somebody who'll miss me and welcome me home at the door?"

"I look like a cocker spaniel to you?" she barked at me.

"A dog is man's best friend, though," I said.

"A wife is your best friend, wrong!" she snapped.

"Okay, if I put you and my dog in the trunk of the car, come back in two days and open it up," I said, "who is happier to see me?"

"One for you," she said.

"It's always a disappointment for me coming home," I told her.

"Why, because no one's throwing you a parade?" she said. "No buxom cheerleaders. Not even a covered dish."

"I think I'd better leave before I commit a crime," I said. "I'm tired of being with a woman that's afraid of making a commitment. From now on, it's just married women for me."

"But you're already married," she said.

"Shit!" I said. "It's always something."

"Then, Doc, there was this big case," she went on, "and Ron asked me to go to D.C. with him to appear before the Supreme Court, the big tuna. I put my happy face on fast. It looked good on me, too.

"So, we won, and Ron and me, we went out on the town that night to get our party on. Well, yours truly threw down; I mean I totally balled out!

"That night, he told me that I had just made partner at the firm, and I'm not going to lie to you, I was revved up. VROOM VROOM! I burned much rubber doing wheelies that night."

"Those power players turn me on," she added, "and the mighty Ron was my Superman. So, I took a shot; I'm a rebel;

I was doing it and doing it well. I was hot to trot and chomping at the bit.

"Okay, I slept with the Man of Steel, my very own caped crusader able to leap tall buildings in a single bound, faster than a speeding bullet, more powerful than a locomotive, my big hero, Ronnie, that night and every other chance that I had after that, and it was so good to me, too," she continued. "He was the true King of the Jungle, much unlike someone else, a purring little pussycat that I kept at home as a pet, who shall remain nameless, unless, of course, he should piss me off, in which case all bets are off."

"Ronnie could really do the Hokey Pokey," Tiff went on. "He nailed me like a union carpenter. Is it hot in here or is it just me?"

"Where did it all get you in the end, though," I pressed her. "Tell us that, okay? Go on, Fling Thing, pour your cheating little black heart out, two-timer."

She explained that the affair got her fired, that's where, kicked to the curb, out on her cute derriere. BAM! That just happened.

The perky office intern tickled the wonderful Super Ron's fancy more than Tiff did now, and, like they say: "Two is company, but a threesome gets overcrowded." She was Asian, and her name was, get this: My Pie or, as the guys at the firm called her: Kung Pao Pussy.

So, Listener, it was goodbye, Ronnie Rock Star; goodbye, company car; goodbye, 401K; and hello, unemployment and cheese burgers every frigging night of the week.

She told Ron that, if he fired her, she would go straight to his little wifey's door, look the hunchbacked cyclops in the eye and dish about everything, one blow at a time and no humpty hump left behind.

Okay, Listener, he did, and she sure did. Tiff was on a mission, search and destroy. Ron's frumpy house frau simply said: "Girlfriend, what else is new? Tell me something that I don't know." End of soap opera, right?

Not even close because Ron gave Tiff a raging dose of Herpes, just a little souvenir to remember him by. Thank you for the party favor, Superman!

"I'm all manners of sorry, baby," she told me.

"You're a sorry-ass lowdown cheater," I popped.

"And if I had a makeover, then what?"

"You're a made-over sorry-ass lowdown cheater."

"Thank you for sharing, baby," she went on. "You're an honest and decent man sometimes, and you're most definitely a keeper in my book. What's up, you don't have a nice compliment for me?"

"You look pretty in pink, about it," I said. "Oh, yeah, you give a good hand job, too. You can really pop that thing." Now what?

"It's all in the wrist," she said. "Upsie Downsie … Upsie Downsie … BOOM! … We have launch! I shoot an arrow into the air, and it lands I know not where."

"Jerry," she went on, "that interlude with Ron, it just happened's all; had myself an itch, scratched it off. For every hot dog, a bun.

"I was panicking, you know, the age thing: Father Time creeping me out and the Evil Twins, Sagging Booty and Susie Cellulite, about to visit me soon, and they come over to stay, the tramps. Mary, don't even ask!"

Listener, would you like to hear about my Passion now? Get it while I'm feeling it. Stories don't tell themselves, now do they? This really happened; true one; I kid you not. If you think that fiction is wild, try reality.

Passion was a stone-cold psycho killer; it's what she did. Here in sequence are the foreplay, the good stuff and the aftermath. Be advised: don't, do not try this at home. This is not the stuff with which dreams are made.

As mentioned, I am an author of some renown with a bestselling novel under his belt, namely: "Hollywood Raw." Can I get a WHOOP WHOOP! More than likely, you've heard of it and, consequently, of me, as well. Hot stuff in there, a real sizzler. Guaranteed that those pages will get sticky and fast.

Humble me, I'm America's Most Wanted. Everybody and their sister craved a piece of me to this very day for what I wrote. Thanks, Oprah, mean it! All things will soon be revealed.

Actually, that cunning scheming bimbo character in the novel is, yep, based on a very much alive and kicking predator from here on to be known as "Passion." She was my creative inspiration, oh, for sure, although I'd never put that out there for popular consumption. So, Listener, it will be our little secret.

Believe me, that particular party girl, she likes to get her knees real dirty; she's seen more dicks than the old school phone book.

Okay, that said, Missy Passion was a freshman at City College, where I was teaching and barely making my nut. It wasn't easy paying the cost to be the boss and the Poor House was only a hop skip and a jump away.

Anyhow, she was enrolled in my Intro class, and there she was on the very first day, sitting in the very front row in a very hiked-up miniskirt. She was totally going warrior without even a hint of drawers on her, just sitting there, airing her good thing out and flashing me like a neon sign: "Eat here!" "Eat here!"

She was a foxy young thing, too. It was just like the hand of God had come down and tapped me on the shoulder. It was my turn, and I took it; I made a deal with the devil: big wealth and global fame and the occasional elusive snapping pussy for my hot buttered soul. Play now, pay later.

Passion was a perk, and I was ready to walk the dog; I was totally smitten by her; I'm living proof that a hard on has absolutely no trace of a conscience. Passion may not have been Miss Right, but she was Miss Right Now. In short, I couldn't do the one I loved, so I did the one I was with, and I popped that thing like a champagne bottle cork.

I'll put it to you like this: Passion was about to surrender the pink and become my secret Santa. What wasn't to like? I was married, sure, there is that, the X factor in this equation, yes, but I wasn't dead, not yet. Carpe diem. Showtime!

She came to my office right after class on Day One, and then she baited her trap, as big game hunters do. I was prey in season now, and her love gun was locked and loaded.

The cunning vixen told me that she would be my "wildest fantasy come true," and that she was totally down to make me rise to the occasion and do me on the spot. That girl could make a blind man see and a dead man come; she knew it, too. It doesn't take a weatherman to tell which way the wind blows.

Alas, nobody rides for free, not even us at the cool kids' table. What she wanted in return for recharging my batteries and making me glow in the dark was a guaranteed A grade in my class, which she bluntly explained she had no intention of ever showing up for again in this lifetime. It was a textbook case of Pop and Hop. Forbidden fruit is always the sweetest, until it isn't. You couldn't tell me nothin'!

Who was yours truly, Sir Cheatalot here, to turn down a fair damsel in need? I was now totally caught up in her web. The more I struggled to get free, the direr were my circumstances. This Passion, Listener, oh, but she was a man-eating shark on the hunt, a natural born killer.

That was her agenda. Myself, I had a simple action plan of my own design: I was going to tap that ass and write about it, therefore making myself the literary new star in the galaxy and an author's author, a totally and ingenuously fool proof game plan, right? I was camera ready for my close-up now. F.Y.I. I dressed from the left.

Cha-ching! It was time to get paid, and I stepped up to the plate. Bring the heat! Beware of what you wish for, though, because you just might get it. The fucking that I got wasn't worth the fucking that I was going to get. Who knew? Go figure. Life is stranger than shit; quote me.

As if I actually cared, I asked Passion to tell me all about herself. It was the teen schemer's favorite subject by far. She was the poster girl for the #Me First Generation, the second coming of Lolita to my Humbert Humbert. I was in over my head now, about to be eaten alive. Help!

Here is what I got back, word for word: "I'm a weekend exotic dancer, a true frisky Scorpio and an on-call motivational speaker. I so like chocolate milk; I was in a porn flick called 'Chain Gang Chicks vs. Swamp Thing'; I put out big time and surrender the pink at the drop of a hat; I take what I want, and, baby, I want Y.O.U. and that spells you."

She added that she was hosting a party the following Saturday night, and I was invited to be the guest of honor. Fancy that! Rank has its privileges, and the hits kept right on coming.

"Run through my crib," she told me. "I'm throwing a set, and it'll be totally like so off the chain with: champagne and reefer and jungle love. Dress to impress. Be fly or be gone."

I was all in. She was a certified canine catcher, and she had just thrown Jerry dog here a juicy bone. RUFF RUFF! My tail was wagging like an angry mother's finger.

Meanwhile, I'm keeping a journal about this tornado that I was now totally swept up in because sex sells, and it was her currency. Man does not live by bread alone. Occasionally, he needs some strange. Isn't a pity? It's so hard to be a saint in the city.

The set mouse trap was about to be sprung, too. I'd learn the hard way that there is no such thing as free cheese, and there is always a catch; it never fails. That's the way it is. I wanted her peaches, so I shook her tree, that simple. Then, I bit off more than I could chew.

Okay, Saturday night comes around. I show up at her swanky Beverly Hills proper address, and wouldn't you just know it: I'm the only party guest there. Surprise! Surprise! "My my my," said the spider to the fly.

Sidepiece Passion greeted me at the door totally in the buff, yep, butt-naked with: "You know what you have to do now, Cowboy." And I'm thinking just two words: "Ride 'em!"

That Saturday night lasted until Monday morning. We played non-stop one-on-one, hot and sweaty, too, some totally drastic stuff went down. Wild Thing and me, we were twerkin'! It was a hot game of Booties Up. She gave as good as she got, and I'm no slouch, either, with a fungo bat in hand. Passion turned me every way but loose. She chewed me up and spit me out. And that, dear Listener, is as good as it gets.

At the end of it all, hot tramp put on a fashion show for me. Check this out: she was now dressed to kill with diamond earrings, diamond bracelets and an eye-popping diamond tiara.

You see, my femme fatal, this delicate hothouse flower, sidepiece Passion, she was an accomplished shoplifter, as well; high-end merchandise exclusively, and far far be it from loyal Scout Jerry here to blow the whistle on Miss Teenage America Hot Lips, aka "Sticky Fingers."

Talent recognizes talent, feel me? I was good to go. My book was virtually writing itself; I was just a conduit; I was going to ride that sleek filly as far as she would take me; I wasn't even breathing hard, yet. Soon enough, I would be gasping for air, though; watch me unravel.

All the while, she was videoing the bedroom fandango, under the pretense of editing it into the ultimate sex tape, supposedly for our eyes exclusively, hers and mine. She called us the fabulous saddle buddies.

It's still being sold on eBay; it's entitled "French Tickler," starring Passion as Nymphet, the French maid, whose best line is: "Eat it like your mama made it!"

Well, the semester ends, and Passion gets her A grade, of course, because a deal is a deal for sure where I come from, and I was deeply into writing my get-your-rocks-off-and-feel-oh-so-good-cookbook about our torrid affair with visions of riches dirty dancing up a storm in my swelled head.

But it isn't over, not yet. Passion now desperately needed big money for a criminal defense lawyer, you see, as in she'd been busted for extortion. Our girl had been servicing a Saudi prince, a movie mogul of note, plus the Dodgers' ace pitcher and a billionaire captain of industry and blackmailing them all with compromising pictures of them dressed up in drag as Dorothy from The Wizard of Oz, cartoon character Daisy Mae, Ann Frank in striped pajamas and Little Bo Peep, respectively. My girl played hardball, and she was ready for prime time.

I told her that this sounds like a personal problem and hung up pronto. BAM! There it is, Listener, the story's plot point of no return.

Passion threatened to burn my house to the ground if I didn't pay up big time and fast track it, too. She tacked on that she would turn my butt in to the college's chancellor and trash me on social media and, all and all, torch this new cushy life that I was enjoying to the fullest thanks to the huge advance on the book from my publisher, hallowed be their name.

What, me worry? Hardly! I laughed her threats off and kept on writing. She's only Little Red Riding Hood, but, me, I'm the Big Bad Wolf with a big mouth to eat her with, and it was time to put my bib on and chow down.

Well, I soon concluded the writing, and the world was having a feeding frenzy over this, the ultimate guidebook to enjoying the pleasures of extra-marital trysting, a celebration of lust Americana. Sales were off the chart, making me a certified mega-bucks lotto winner. Drinks on the house! Party on! When I say hey, you say ho!

My "Hollywood Raw" was the best-selling novel, setting new records with every passing day. Say TA DAH, somebody! Who's the man now? I was doing the Moon Walk and feasting exclusively on Swiss bon bons and chocolate eclairs. Life was grand, an ongoing sugar high, and it couldn't be happening to a nicer guy in all modesty. It's not bragging if it's real, right? I was the man hands down! Recognize, bitches. In the end, talent will out, never fails. To the victor go the spoils.

Then I went on tour to promote my blockbuster masterpiece, lots of media appearances from coast to coast, which included no less than being the featured guest on ... Hold your breath! ... Drum roll if you please. ... Can you saw Oprah, the patron saint, mother confessor and personal savior by choice of those with totally lost causes, herself? The be all end all awaited me. Hail to the victor valiant, brave and bold!

Yep, I was the new Golden Boy, the People's Choice. The world was my oyster, and me, I was as happy as a clam. Bow down! Make it twice.

It was now all Jerry all the time. Soon the bill would arrive, though, and I'd have to pay up in full for the sin of Gluttony in the First Degree. My eyes were so much bigger than my stomach: I know, right? Hindsight is always twenty twenty, and I was now the designated Monday morning quarterback by acclamation.

So, I'm Oprah bound, few are chosen. I was this year's boy, and nobody stood up to challenge me for the crown, not a single solitary soul, until there was one, and I would take a knife in the back.

You will never in a gazillion years guess who was on the show with me that day, though. Give up? It was none other than the oh, so very delightfully demure, pure as the newly driven snow Passion, herself. True story!

Yep, Listener, the stunningly beautiful kleptomaniac-extortionist-seductress had learned that I was going to be there that day; it was no heavily guarded government secret. TV Guide was her date book.

She'd contacted the show's executive producer and tantalized her with a tempting promise that she would blow my ship totally out of the water, and, Listener, she delivered the goods like Chinese takeout.

Passion stone told our saintly host, her Royal Majesty, queen of all she surveyed, Oprah, may her big heart only be blessed now and forevermore, plus the studio audience and millions of viewers, too, that I was a bold-faced-full-blown-thief, something right up Passion's alley.

She added that I had maliciously stolen her book idea, hers, and cashed in on her misery, she being a poor, trusting, vulnerable waif. So, there's that! She played the crying game like it was Guitar Hero. She was in it to win it. I was burnt toast now, and I knew it. Pride goeth before the fall. Rome was burning.

It was textbook revenge of the slighted femme fatal, and hell has no fury like a woman's scorn. I was still the Chosen One, but the script had flipped on me drastically. It's a fast fall from the penthouse to the doghouse.

Spoiler alert: The worst was yet to come. Passion said that I had even dared to fat-shame the sacred cow, Oprah, who ate up every word of Passion's testimony with relish. It was a classic juicy "Oprah burger" with everything on it, and America was famished for it. Her fans ate that shit up, too. Yep, Oprah and Passion were joined at the hip. Sisters united will never be defeated. Men are just good for one thing, and they aren't even any good at that.

There she was, the Goddess Oprah, sister-hugging Passion tightly like she was the second-coming of Mother Teresa. My mind was now officially and completely blown to smithereens. BOOM! Pick up the pieces, somebody please.

The incensed studio audience then started hurling vile insults about me and my ancestry and horrid threats at me and booed me off the set. Can you now start to feel my deep pain at long last, Listener? But I hadn't seen anything, yet. The overture to this tragic grand opera kept right on playing with every single note of it a new gut punch. Rock bottom awaited me.

Post the Oprah-palooza debacle, I went straight from zero to total-loss-crack-up in virtually nothing flat. The college kicked me to the curb on the spot; my new pride and joy BMW was torched; and my hate mail included threats of great bodily harm without mercy in the name of Jesus about who I'd only said good things so far.

Then, cue the proverbial last straw, a nervous breakdown hit me like a ton of bricks. I was now hallucinating that I was being chased by an angry foaming-at-the-mouth lynch mob, and the accompaniment for all of this madness was a chorus of screamed threats from invisible haters, ghosts and goblins out to do me in and pull no punches. Your now downward facing dog, the celebrity known as Jerry boy from the Bronx, formerly Man of the Hour, was up for grabs, and he was running for his very life, wanted dead or alive.

The most prominent imagined voice of them all, though, the Alpha was telling me to take the quick fix out of this swallowing quicksand and off myself without any further ado. Not one prone to argue with Fate, I slit my wrists and bid this cruel cruel world and Passion, that ruthless vindictive spawn of Satan, farewell.

Right on cue, my dog started howling like a banshee with hemorrhoids, which alerted my very nosey neighbor lady, one Tilly the Gossip, an *uber yenta* among *uber yentas,* that something on the day's menu wasn't board-certified kosher.

In a flash, the ultimate wag, who was prone to wear her full-length mink coat all summer and complain non-stop about her ungrateful children, called in the police, who got to me just as I was about to enter the Land of Light where there is free gas, food and lodging for eternity.

Not to be denied, loose lips Tilly had also taken photos of me doing the backstroke in a pool of my blood, see; splish splash. And she sold both her photos and story to the tabloids, claiming that this formerly famous but now sullied man on the run over here had revealed his choicest dark secrets exclusively to her, and she would only share them with our vaunted Oprah dearest, herself, and none other.

"Hey, Mr. Entertainment," Tiff shouted at me, "do tell the good Dr. Cole all about your psych ward timeout, while you're on a roll, why don't you? Let it all hang out."

"Yep," I told her, "season my nervous breakdown with a death wish and a pinch of a bad attitude. That led the attending shrink at the hospital to decide that I so needed an extended vacation at the cuckoo's nest, aka the funny farm. I filled my time there with Play Dough, coloring books and masturbating by the numbers like a man possessed, really jerking myself to Jesus. It was all good, too. I had game: I was a Play Dough master/coloring book Picasso/jackoff champion to be recognized and proud of it, too, a triple threat for sure.

Finally, I got to go home to my dearly beloved shorty, my loving wife, who hadn't once written or visited me, her boo-for-life, her young love first love filled with true devotion, not even a post card with something like: "Get better soon or else. P.S. Your dog is dead."

Well, I get home, and it came as no big jolt to me that my lovey dovey dream girl and goddess wife had vacated the premises, skipping out with everything that wasn't nailed down; divorced me at my lowest: frigging Sneaky Pete over there.

She had left a note for me, though: "This is all on you! How ya like me now?"

And that, my faithful Listener, officially signaled the end of round one. DING DING DING!

"That wasn't his first visit to the psych ward, though," Tiff told the Doc.

"Yeah," I said, "there was the chapter in my book about my nightmare in Cleveland. Every page of it was stained by my salty tears."

"You see," I continued, "once mom and dad were out of play, I went north to live with my Auntie Carol in Cleveland. My uncle, Sgt. Mike, U.S.M.C., was deployed in Afghanistan, so Auntie Carol had room for me. Pretty soon, I met my main man, Billy, and we became blood brothers. It was all good there on shores of Lake Erie, almost heaven, until it wasn't anymore."

"Tell, Dr. Cole, the story," Tiff added. "Do me a solid. You know it as good as I do; it's too painful for me to open that door again. I'll owe ya one. What d'ya say? You can do it; you're good for something."

And so, my disgruntled two-timing bride, a theater major no less, channeled her inner Meryl Streep and raconted the "Ballad of the Ambush" like this for the rapt audience of two:

"How could they possibly foresee that the events of this day would irrevocably redirect the rest of their lives? The naiveté of youth and the great anticipation of cinema bliss negated even the slightest chance of any premonition of the doom waiting in the wings.

The tandem strolling along Cleveland's lower eastside Kinsman Avenue that Saturday afternoon in the fall of the Year 2004 appeared to be the happiest ten-year-olds in their entire working-class neighborhood: Jerry, yes, our very own Jerry Portnoy, and sidekick numero uno and water-carrier first class, Billy Andrews.

Jerry, by far the shorter and more frail of the pair, had mastered the nuances of four dialects of his native tongue: the Yiddish-English of the Old World Jewish immigrants who inhabited the Kinsman Avenue enclave; the southern rural black patois gleaned from his best pal, Billy; movie cowboy slang absorbed from a multitude of sagebrush-cinema classics and, by edict, the grammatically precise textbook-English insisted upon with an iron fist and relentlessly monitored by his third grade teacher, Mrs. Goldfarb, known to certain of her students, Billy, in particular, as "Old Fleabag the junkyard dog."

Billy focused on an imaginary baseball, hit by an invisible member of a nondescript opposing team. He positioned himself and lunged at just the right moment, making yet another miraculous, game-saving catch. He was the tallest, fastest, toughest and loneliest boy in Mrs. Goldfarb's class; feared by virtue of his fists, unaccepted by virtue of his skin color. The calendar may have read 2004, but in that hardscrabble neighborhood, it was still 1950. Jerry was his only friend other than his blue-nosed pit bull, Pete, who tended to be rather moody, much like his master. Since Jerry trended to be decidedly more upbeat, he won the popularity contest that day. Plus he was low-maintenance; he didn't have to be walked or petted.

Jerry had various nicknames. He was sometimes called Tex by classmates teasing him about his obsession with movie cowboys. He was frequently called "Kleiner" (a Yiddish pejorative, the equivalent of Shorty) by other Kinsman Cowboys (as the Kinsman Avenue Jews were, themselves, branded by their upscale co-religionists in bordering Shaker Heights.) He was occasionally addressed as Jew boy by the Italian and Irish kids who shared Jerry's turf. Kinsman Avenue wasn't for sissies, not by a longshot. Its history was one of storm and stress to that very day. Only the strong survived. For the dynamic duo, so far, so good: they were still there.

Jerry liked to call his pal Bronco Billy. Others taunted him with Little Black Sambo, Sunshine and Chocolate Chip.

Billy's friendship had been proven in numerous schoolyard dust ups; Billy stepping in to protect Jerry from bullies, lunch money extortionists and kids who had unquestioningly accepted their parents' hatred for all people and all things Jewish. Few kids confronted Jerry when Billy was on the scene. Billy's quick fists were respected. Racial taunts were hurled at him from far beyond striking distance.

To Jerry, loyalty, above all else, was an essential. Anyone he chose to be his partner had to be trustworthy. He had chosen Billy Andrews, and Billy had never let him down, not even close, not yet. The Lone Ranger had Tonto; Gene Autry had Smiley Burnett; Roy Rogers had Pat Butrum; and Tex Portnoy had Bronco Billy.

The boys had been going to the movies together on Saturday afternoons for a while now. All told, they had seen all of twelve low budget, filmed in black and white westerns, every one of them starring the same '50's movie cowboy, Randy Bob Laredo.

The Imperial Palace Theater, you see, was an art house owned and operated by a former neighborhood kid of the vintage '50's era, who had become a software entrepreneur of considerable note. The now multi-millionaire had a soft spot in his heart for the young, believing that what they needed most in life to ward off Evil and keep them on the straight and narrow shining path to do a Christian God's work was a weekly dose of the movie cowboy mystique.

Just for the sake of agitating his easily-provoked thin-skinned pal, Billy began to belittle in no uncertain terms what both boys already knew for certain would soon unfold on the theater's silver screen.

"It's always the same boring-ass stuff!" Billy complained.

Then he quickly blew a bubble with his bubble gum and popped it for emphasis.

"But it's always fun, though!" Jerry shot back, popping his own bubble.

"Randy Bob Laredo...," Jerry sang.

"The good guy...," Billy added, with mild disdain.

"And Smoky Joe Jones...," Jerry continued, undaunted by Billy's interruption and lack of enthusiasm for the celluloid action-hero, an icon in Jerry's life.

"The sidekick...," Billy chirped in, lackadaisically attempting to disrupt the rhythm of Jerry's flow.

"Show up in Dodge City...," Jerry went on, oblivious to Billy's efforts.

"They'll save a lot of nice people, all of them white ...," Billy guaranteed, sarcastically.

"From Montana Jack the *farcockda shtunk* outlaw...," Jerry laughed.

"A man with no conscience...," Billy said, contributing to the movie villain's character analysis.

"And Montana Jack's gang of *nogoodnick* cutthroat thieves...," giggling Jerry continued.

"Men with no soap!" Billy shouted, biting his lip to keep himself from laughing, too.

"Well, hey, I call that fantastic!" Jerry shouted back, smiling victoriously.

"Well, hey, I call her fantastic!" Billy counter punched.

Billy's her referred to the pretty little girl who was walking toward the boys. Blond hair in a ponytail, big blue eyes, white patent leather shoes with red bows and a nifty new skirt replete with ruffled hem line; ten-year-old Carly Sue Lipkowitz was the real deal. She put the C in cute and the S in spoiled.

In the heart of every boy in Mrs. Goldfarb's class, even the most fervent girl-haters, Carly Sue was their very own dream girl from the neighborhood.

"Hi, fellas!" perky Carly Sue greeted.

"Hi, Carly Sue!" the boys shouted at the same time.

Billy elbowed his frail companion to the side and stepped up to Carly Sue.

"Who you like better, Little Bit, drop-dead handsome me or skin-and-bones little munchkin Jerry over there?" he pressed.

If there was one thing that Carly Sue enjoyed more than instigating a boy-fight, it was being the reason for the confrontation.

Consequently, this mid-afternoon's jousting between two local knights, Sir Jerry and Sir Billy, for the affections of a fair damsel, Lady Carly Sue, was favored entertainment.

"Well, Jerry, you're nicer than Billy, but all you ever talk about is cowboy movies, and that makes me sick to my stomach!" Carly Sue explained matter-of-factly to the diminutive little guy dressed in chaps, blue jeans, holsters for his two fully-loaded vintage cap guns and his signature white cowboy hat. "Texele," as his beloved Auntie Carol liked to call him, was temporarily crestfallen.

Opportunistic Billy wagged a finger in Jerry's face and taunted him.

"Billy, you're funnier than Jerry, that's very good! Big yeh!" Carly Sue continued. "But you tell lies, that's very bad! Big boo!"

Jerry now wagged a finger in Billy's face. Smack for smack, taunt for taunt; those were the rules. If you can't stand the heat, get out of the kitchen.

"That means I like you both the same, sometimes; tie score," she concluded, leaving the issue open for interpretation for yet another week.

Jerry and Billy stared at Carly Sue. Then the two amigos locked eyes. Dissatisfied and confused, they shrugged their shoulders, indicating acceptance of their lot. For the moment, it was to be a most disappointing draw with an option for a rematch.

"I've got to leave now," Carly Sue proclaimed. "I'm going shopping with my mommy. After all, a girl never has enough pretty clothes. Bye-bye, boys! I'll play with you at recess if you're very lucky! So, pray hard on it."

She waved to her admirers and skipped off. Her beaus drew deep breaths, exhaled simultaneously and, in turn, bid Carly Sue so long and happy trails.

Jerry and Billy walked on toward the Imperial Palace, the neighborhood theater, where they had a scheduled interlude with fantasy heroes. Soon enough, though, they would encounter Fate. Kids plan, and Fate, Fate just laughs its butt off.

A bit further down the Kinsman Road trail, a sign painted on a window announced to the travelers that they had arrived at:

The World Famous

Tushman & Son Market

Fresh Produce & Kosher Poultry

Moishy Tushman, also aged ten, was arranging fruit and vegetables in bins in front of The World Famous... He was known to the Jewish kids as Moishy the Nosher.

"Hi, Moishy!" Jerry greeted him.

"Hi, Portnoy! Still peeing the bed?" shouted the squat scion to the Tushman family's emporium of great renown. He was overjoyed to have been addressed with civility, a rarity in Moishy's young life. He was snack food from heaven for the hungry bullies.

"Billy once again seized the moment. He stuck his thumbs in his ear holes and wiggled his fingers, a ploy to get Moishy's goat. It had proven effective every Saturday afternoon for as long as Billy could remember.

Billy sang an original ditty: "Tushy-man! Tushy-man! Moishy is a Tushy-man! Nah! Nah! Nee! Nah! Nah!"

"Meshuggener!" Moishy shot back, flushed-faced, eyes welling with tears.

"Don't be calling me crazy in Jewish, you gefilte fish eating mama's boy! I'll kick your fat ass from here to Woodbury School and back again!" Billy threatened, lunging at the very frightened Moishy, who beat a hasty retreat into the sanctuary of his father's store.

"Calm down, Big Fella!" Jerry told Billy, who had worked himself into a fine tizzy.

"Okay, Jerry! Moishy started it, though!" Billy replied.

"Are we going to the movies or not?" Jerry insisted.

"There's nothing else to do; sure we are," Billy said. "My electricity is off because Mama is a little tardy again. She put it under my name, and my credit is shot."

"You shouldn't pick on Moishy," Jerry scolded.

The requisite dance routine, Jerry's and Billy's posturing with petite Carly, who was also known around Kinsman Road as "Goldie Lox and Bagels," was now old business. So, too, the recreational harassment of Moishy Tushman had been played out with its usual cliff-hanger ending.

Jerry expected that the remaining two blocks' walk to the Imperial Palace would be the usual, uneventful and dull.

Since boredom is the universal bane of ten-year-olds, Jerry chose that moment to share his big news.

"My Uncle Mike's coming home from Afghanistan next week; the fighting is slowing down; my Auntie Carol got herself a email!" he blurted excitedly.

"Wow! That's great!" Billy concurred.

"I'm so happy for me! I don't have the words for it," Jerry shouted.

"I don't know when my old man's coming home; I don't even know where he went," Billy lamented.

That was for effect. Billy was too well aware of when his father was due for release, in fifteen to twenty-five years. He was also cognizant of his father's whereabouts, The Ohio State Penitentiary.

Billy's mini-melodrama was effective; never failed to evoke Jerry's sympathy.

"I'll share my popcorn with you today, old trusty pal of mine," Jerry promised.

"Will you buy my ticket, too?" Billy cajoled. "My mama was a little tight with the movie money, and I was thinking, since we're ace buds and all, you might help a needy brother out in honor of Dr. King's birthday in a month."

"This happens every doggone time we go to the movies!" Jerry chastened. "I'd like to know why! Well? Well!"

"Because you always give it up, that's why, and, if you don't like it, you can sit through those dumb-ass cowboy movies by your own self!" Billy said.

"This is the very last time, and you gotta pay me back because I'm saving up for something special," Jerry explained, "such as a Power Rangers costume for Mrs. Goldfarb's Halloween Party."

"Oh, that's special all right, yeah, boy!" Billy mocked. "I'll be going as childish Michael Jordan; he's my biological father, and I have papers on him, too."

The boys walked on in silence; only one more block until they would arrive at the oasis, the Imperial Palace, at which time Jerry would hand over yet another ticket, in addition to the lion's share of his popcorn.

Assured of gratis entry to the theater and free snack-food to boot, Billy felt obliged to make at least a token show of conviviality.

"What you gonna be when you grow up?" he inquired, although he was already aware of what the answer would be.

"A movie cowboy like Randy Bob Laredo!" Jerry responded, as expected.

"Be a landlord or a banker like the other Yids of note, but not a movie cowboy, not you, uh-unh! I just can't see it," Billy argued. "You ain't got no parts of the goods for that particular line of work. Besides, it's a calling, not for Jews, my Black brothers or Orientals. You've been told that a million times already by me. I thought you people were smart."

"Like I said, a movie cowboy just like you know who, then I'm gonna marry Carly Sue!" Jerry continued.

"Oh, I get it," Billy said with disdain. "What I'm hearing is that Carly Sue will be your cowgirl."

"Exacto!" Jerry shouted, naively assuming that Billy had seen the light at long last.

"Exacto nothing! Carly Sue is mine! We're ebony and ivory. I found her first!" Billy snapped. "Finders keepers, losers weepers. Girls fall out at my sight. Besides, I'm finna put my brand on Carly Sue's tush. I take what I want."

The boys faced off, both of them were bluffing hard.

"Oh, yeah?" Jerry challenged.

"Yeah!" Billy responded. "Ya little bedwetter you."

"Let's race for it!" Jerry challenged. "First one to the box office gets to marry Carly Sue, and, if you beat me, you don't have to pay me back for all the movie tickets I've ever bought for you, a tidy sum with interest and service charges included."

"I wasn't gonna pay you no way, chump!" Billy shouted. "Kiss my pretty young, gifted and black ass, Texele!"

With that, Jerry darted off. A fair start would guarantee his certain defeat, and he knew it, too.

Jerry ran fastest when the heat was on, and it was on full-blast when he was being chased by Joey Leonetti, aka Joey Farts, and Johnny Pantone, aka Johnny Pants, the alfa bullies in Mrs. Goldfarb's class.

"It seemed that there were only three options for a Kinsman kid trying to escape the ravages of boredom: shopping with Mommy, which was Carly Sue's routine outing; trekking to the Imperial Palace for a cornball western, which was Jerry's particular nirvana and Billy's lot by desperation, as he had but a single friend, Jerry, those and harassing smaller children for the fun of it, while stealing their candy: Joey Leonetti and Johnny Pantone had a particular penchant for that, too. Billy blamed their anti-social behavior on their watching too much TV. He said that they needed to "stay in their bible."

While Jerry had the courage of a lion and the endurance of a marathon runner, he also had the foot speed of a sleepy sea turtle. Nevertheless, Billy had not surged ahead of him; he had not even begun running.

Lingering at the contest's embarkation point, Billy reached into his pocket and withdrew a ripe tomato, purloined from Tushman's vegetable bin. He held the juicy sphere in his palm and addressed it with stern insistence:

"Be there, baby!" the Ebony Prankster demanded, thus defining the tomato's mission and his own sinister intent.

Meanwhile, Jerry chugged closer to the finish line.

Unaccustomed to being in the forefront in any test of physical prowess, particularly if it involved running or jumping, Jerry turned his head to ascertain fleet-of-foot Billy's proximity.

At that very instance, Billy launched the projectile: BAM … a perfect strike! Jerry's white cowboy hat, his most prized possession, was splattered. It was as of that moment indelibly blotched with sticky, dripping tomato juice.

"Ambush! Ambush!" Billy screamed with delight. "I got you, fool! Ha! Ha! Now what, Tommy Talmud the Yeshiva boy!"

Jerry yanked off his Randy Laredo look-alike chapeau and assessed the damage.

"It's ruined!" he yelled, tears streaming down his cheeks. "You owe me a new cowboy hat!"

In a flash, Billy was by his side.

"I'll buy you a new cowboy hat for Christmas, you big crybaby," he teased. "Good enough for your ass?"

"I don't celebrate Christmas!" Jerry sniffled. "It's not for us; we don't even celebrate snow."

"There goes your new cowboy hat, chump," Billy laughed. "Win some. Lose some. Sometimes, you just get rained out."

"My Auntie Carol gave it to me for my birthday. Just look at it now!" Jerry complained, crying harder.

"Yup, the chapeau has reached the end of the trail. Looks like this is your last roundup," Billy agreed. "Okay, Jerry, I'm sorry. There, I said it, satisfied?"

"That's not good enough!" Jerry objected. "Do better."

"I'm sorry with frosting on top!" Billy added.

"I won the race, didn't I?" Jerry continued.

"You cheated, but you still won," Billy conceded. "Luck of the Irish."

"I get to marry Carly Sue!" Jerry gloated. "I'll call her by my name."

"Yeah, you get the heifer, and you'll have lots of little pink-cheeked bowlegged babies, too," Billy conceded. "I don't even like Carly Sue no more. She smells like gamey sweat socks to me. So, hold your big nose when you go in for a kiss, boy!"

"And I'll make a good movie cowboy, too, won't I?" Jerry prodded. "Say it loud!"

"Jerry-man, you'll be better than Straight Shootin' Rootin' Tootin' Randy Bob Laredo," Billy guaranteed. "And, partner, I'll always be your most faithful sidekick through the thick and the thin times; I dare Joey Leonetti and Johnny Pantone and their dago Mafia henchmen to try stealing your shit or try kicking your slow of foot ass for sport again because they'll be fighting me first, and they don't want none of me; this we well know. I'm badder than young Mike Tyson on crack! I'm dangerous, fool! What's my name!"

Billy demonstrated his pugilistic prowess by doing a shadowboxing routine. He tripped over his own feet and flopped onto the sidewalk in front of the Imperial Palace. Jerry and Billy burst out laughing.

Jerry had won the rights of first refusal to Carly Sue, validation of his potential for stardom as a cinema caballero and a pledge of fealty then and forevermore from Billy.

Billy had enjoyed the singular thrill of the ambush. Albeit perverse pleasure, he would do it again in a heartbeat; it's just what he did. He rolled like that; the boy had skills and he was battle tested, too.

All worry, fear, woe, apprehension, regret, vendettas, deadlines, responsibilities and obligations in these lads' lives were, as of that moment and for the next three hours, put on hold. It was movie time!

Jerry paid for the tickets, and the guys entered the theater, where they would be tickled pink by the back-in-the-day cartoons (Mighty Mouse, Bugs Bunny, Donald Duck, Porky Pig, Wily Coyote, Casper the Friendly Ghost and Krazy Kat) and by the played-out serials (Batman, Buck Rogers, Flash Gordon, the Green Hornet, Rocket Man and the Masked Rider). The generous software mogul went all out on the nostalgia.

Jerry would be emotionally consumed by the piece de resistance, "Trail Pals," a Randy Bob Laredo epic.

Billy would feign nonchalance and make raids on Jerry's popcorn. Jerry didn't care because this interlude at the oasis was heaven on earth to him.

In a Randy Bob Laredo western, plot-points were consistent to a fault. There was poetic justice; there was affirmation of the American Dream; there was validation of the family unit; there was total abstinence from alcohol, tobacco and physical affection. Kissing horses on the nose, though, was extolled as virtuous. There was responsible ranching, crop rotation and humane cattle-drives; there was a celebration of country music, square dancing and all things rodeo tossed in for good measure, as well, no leaf left unturned there. In a word, it was a pure sugar rush, and Jerry was sky high on it.

All problems would be resolved in favor of the hero and those he designated as being worthy, who were more often than not were: sheepherders, the clergy, liberal newspaper editors, widows, orphans, cripples, the blind and the good natured dim-witted among them all, who provided comic relief dancing through life with their two left feet.

All evildoers would be brought to bar of justice. They would then realize the error of their ways and, contingent upon the depth of their contrition, they would be forgiven for their misdeeds and granted another chance to see the light and lead a righteous life with a passion for a home on the range for all, *pax Americana* and the white man's manifest destiny.

No minorities would ever appear in speaking parts of consequence. They would be depicted as irresponsible, lazy, stupid and conniving underlings, clowns and outsiders. They need not even apply.

Women would be relegated to the singular parts of Wife, Mother, School Marm or Saloon Floozy. Their universal jobs were: cooking, cleaning and kids. They always stood by their man, too, and would go through fire and water for even the worst of them.

There would be singing, gunfights, a showdown on Main Street at high noon, a sucker-punch, a saloon brawl, an ambush at Box Canyon, fatherly advice for children and a glorious "black and white" sunset. The plot was simply a symphony in three movements: Kick Butts, Take Names, Repeat.

These movies were unabashedly a collective testimonial to the primacy of the straight white Christian American he man, long may he run.

Billy Andrews obviously lacked the whiteness prerequisite for inclusion in the dream world of: immaculate white cowboy hats, lariats, leather chaps, perfectly-tuned acoustical guitars, cowboy boots, spurs that jingle-jangle-jingle, pearl-handled six-shooters, hand-tooled holsters, rhinestone-studded shirts with a rose on front, bandanas, silver-adorned saddles, operantly-conditioned horses, obedient sidekicks and subservient womenfolk.

Billy claimed that he couldn't care less about playing the Cowboy Game. The truth was: he couldn't have cared more.

The Christian criterion had eluded Jerry Portnoy, who lived his life by the cowboy gospel according to Randy Bob Laredo and his kind. He dressed like the movie cowboys; he walked like them; he talked like they talked; and he even sang an original cowboy ditty in Woodbury School's Talent Show.

I'm just a lonesome Kinsman cowboy,

Riding an invisible horse.

I'm just a lonesome Kinsman cowboy,

Yup, it's Tex Portnoy, of course.

Yipee, Ky Yo; Yipee, Ky Yeh!

He told his teacher about the kids who were naughty when her back was turned, and he named names and pointed out birthmarks, too. He carried salami and cheese, peanut butter and jelly and egg salad on rye sandwiches to school in an official Randy Bob Laredo lunch box that his dearly beloved aunt had found on eBay. He wore cowboy pajamas to bed, and he slept on sheets with likenesses of cowboys on them.

Down deep, however, he knew that, for a Jewish boy, becoming a movie cowboy like Randy Bob Laredo would be unlikely at the very best and nearly impossible, at the very least.

There simply were no Jewish cowboys riding from one end of the movie screen to the other; there was not a single Quick Draw Cohen, a Gold Dust Goldberg or an Alibi Axelbaum. Nevertheless, Jerry dreaded the thought of settling for anything other than Hollywood horseman. Besides, Hollywood had stopped churning out westerns all together in favor of "Star Wars" and its clones, and what a hard pill to swallow that sure was.

Billy had resolved that, having been denied access to the Good White Cowboys' Club, he would cast his lot with the unloved outcasts, the bad guys. After all, it was they who toiled so arduously to grab their share of life's bounty; to smack the gloating smiles off the good guys' smug white faces. Billy wanted to do likewise in the worst way.

All the while, Fate awaited the boys outside their sanctuary, the no-worry zone known as the Imperial Palace. Soon enough, it would strike them down with a particular vengeance. This was but the lull before the storm.

The theater was filled to capacity.

"Every kid from school must be here today!" Jerry observed.

"Yeah, including the two Italiano meatballs, Billy warned, pointing out their mutual nemesis, the badass tag team of Joey Leonetti and Johnny Pantone, who were sitting in the center section.

"Stay close, Billy," Jerry requested. "Once the lights go down, I might not be able to see you."

"Just what's that supposed to mean?" Billy snapped, assuming malice of forethought.

"Those are some highly treacherous hombres over yonder. I can't whip 'em both, not by my lonesome, catch my drift?" Jerry explained, slipping into cowboy vernacular befitting the occasion.

"As long as you don't be playing stingy bastard with the popcorn, I'll be right next to you, my dear ol' battle buddy," Billy promised. "I got you, little man."

The house lights began to dim. The fellas, now certain that they wouldn't be spotted by the feared Joey and Johnny, dashed for the only two vacant seats in the front row.

Seven cartoons. Three shorts. Five serials. A second large box of hot buttered popcorn. The featured presentation, at long last. Anticipation and longing made it even sweeter.

Fade in: Resplendent in white cowboy attire, embellished by a red rose in full bloom embroidered on his shirt front, directly over his heart, and sitting tall in the saddle astride his noble steed, Thunder the Wonder Horse, an impressive white stallion or proven valor under fire, Randy Bob Laredo, guitar in hand, is singing a country song to his sidekick, Smoky Joe Jones, Randy's educable special needs comrade in arms of proven good humor, loyalty and valor under fire.

Without warning, Montana Jack, the notorious outlaw, races by, hell-bent for leather. Not only is Montana Jack in violation of the *prima facie* speed law, but he is abusing his mount, spurring on his poor black horse mercilessly. OUCH!

Montana Jack is a mangy, sleazy, unkempt, unshaven villain. He is dressed in black; the total bad guy package that one.

Randy Bob Laredo initiates hot pursuit, leaving Smoky Joe in the rear, assumedly to tend to his guitar and rustle up some grub, beans, beans and more beans.

Montana Jack swivels in his saddle and fires his pistol at Randy Bob. Randy Bob draws both of his guns and, while holding Thunder the Wonder Horse's reins in his teeth, returns fire. Randy Bob hits the outlaw in his shooting hand, causing Montana Jack's weapon to fly off. Montana Jack examines his wound, mouths a curse and spurs his horse.

Randy Bob cringes at the sight of this inexcusable mistreatment of the pathetic animal and shouts at Montana Jack.

"I'll get you, Montana Jack!" he promises. "Horses have feelings, too."

Montana Jack responds with a sneer. Body language and facial expression say it all: "You'll never get me, sucker!" He's studied the Method.

Randy Bob pulls his lariat from the saddle horn and twirls the rope in circles, high overhead. He lets go, and the rope sails through the air, settling around Montana Jack's torso. BAM!

Randy Bob pulls the jail-breaking, bank-robbing, claim-jumping, land-grabbing, card-sharking miscreant from his horse and hog-ties him, rodeo style. That is reason enough for our heroic Randy Bob to raise his arms to the sky, celebrating victory, which he does. He knows he's cool. He is sure comfortable in his skin and as confident in his sexuality as he is spry in his unscuffed shiny cowboy boots.

Nature's delight is short-lived, however. Montana Jack's gang arrives on the scene. They get the drop on Randy Bob, who "reaches for the sky," once again. This time, it is to surrender. Forget the ode to joy for now.

Suddenly, Smoky Joe, the ultimate sidekick, springs from the bushes, six-shooters drawn. The bad guys give up. Game over? Not hardly.

Oh, no! Montana Jack has struggled free from his bonds. He pulls yet another gun. (It was hidden in his boot.) He shoots Smoky Joe in the shoulder. Our Smoky Joe is badly hurt, which doesn't faze Randy Bob, who has his own problems. The bad guys have the upper hand now. Mother Nature is unhappy with this turn of events, and so are Jesus and Santa Claus; you can take that to the bank.

Randy Bob speed draws both of his Colt .45 pistols and blazes away at Montana Jack and the outlaws. He hits every one of his targets, their shooting hands, of course.

All of the bad guys' weapons fly out of their grasps. The entire motley crew, all dressed in black, examine their wounds: no blood is visible, miraculously. What a movie!

Randy Bob nods to Smoky Joe, somehow indicating exactly what the Smoker is expected to do next, tie all of the bad guys' hands behind their backs. Smoky Joe does his job well. It takes him five seconds to complete the whole task. His shoulder wound has healed by now. No blood is visible on him, either. A miracle has happened here!

Randy Bob's white clothes have remained unsoiled and unwrinkled all the while, and his hair is picture perfect. He turns to the camera, smiles, removes a bandanna from his neck, dabs his brow dry and smiles.

The kids in the theater on cue cheer lustily as a "black and white sunset" appears on screen and Randy Bob, accompanied by faithful companion Smoky Joe, rides off. The movie has ended, as all good things must. It was a long time till the next Saturday; it felt like a century.

Randy Bob and Smoky Joe are surely headed for more adventures and feats of even greater glory, trust me. As for Montana Jack and his band of desperadoes, well, they can stay out there, tied up on the Great Plains, snack food for the buzzards and coyotes. No one, except for Billy Andrews, really cared about them at all. He had been in their boots for a long while now, himself, running from the devil.

The bulk of the kids exited the Imperial Palace en mass. Jerry and Billy were the last to leave, lest Joey Leonetti and Johnny Pantone, the real-time bad guys, would get ahold of them and let the dogs out.

The walk back to Jerry's aunt's house was comparatively uneventful. Jerry blew enormous bubbles, loudly popping every one of them. He jabbered excitedly about the montage of marksmanship, horsemanship, gallantry under fire and sartorial splendor he had witnessed on the Imperial Palace's big screen that afternoon. In the afterglow, life couldn't have been better. To Jerry, this was truly the rapture. It didn't get any better than that.

Billy seemed oblivious to Jerry's very presence. He was preoccupied with making theatrical, game-winning buzzer-beating jump shots with an imaginary basketball, thusly winning the NBA title for the Cleveland Cavaliers.

"Randy Bob Laredo's is surreal. Two words: incredible!" Jerry announced.

"Damn, you've said that a hundred times in the last minute. Boy, give me a break already!" Billy objected. "Can't you see I'm finna block Lebron James' shot? Have you no shame! Respect the artist within, shit!"

"Randy Bob zinged every outlaw in the shootin' hand!" Jerry continued. "He got Montana Jack twice! Double bingo. BLAM BLAM!"

"Of course, he did, genius; it was a damn movie," Billy retorted. "The fix was in."

The fellas were now standing in front of Jerry's house, where Billy would bid him a fond adios and walk on for three more blocks along Kinsman Road, until he, himself, reached his own home in the housing projects that he called the "roach motel," where you could check in but never check out.

"Looks like your TV broke again," Billy said, pointing to the truck parked in Jerry's driveway. A sign on the back of the truck read:

Lucky Louie De Fazio

Television Repair

Every customer a happy customer!

"It always breaks down on Saturdays, while we're at the movies; go figure," Jerry observed.

"Your Auntie Carol must've got the TV set wholesale," Billy deduced.

As the boys stood in front of Jerry's house, pondering the puzzling regularity of Louie De Fazio's visits, a cab pulled to the curb, just a few feet away.

A tall, brawny soldier paid the driver, swung a door open and alighted. He was carrying an Army duffel bag and a bouquet of flowers. Medals and commendation pins attested to his bravery. The stripes on his uniform jacket identified him as a Sergeant Major. A badge bore the surname, "PORTNOY."

Jerry's eyes opened wide with the sight of his uncle.

"Uncle Mike! Uncle Mike!" he shouted, running toward the man, arms outstretched.

Sgt. Portnoy didn't lift Jerry high into the air and hold him tightly, as he had hoped for. Then again, he never had done so before, so why start now?

"You didn't expect me today, did you, young fella?" he said to the jubilant little guy.

"Auntie Carol told me next week!" Jerry shouted.

Billy stood nearby, watching the reunion. His emotions were mixed. He was happy for Jerry. Yet, he was also green with envy, now as always. He could count the number of tender moments he had shared with his own father on one hand.

"You've gotten taller, Billy," the Sergeant said.

"Yup, that's sure what happens," Billy responded, hesitantly.

It wasn't that Billy had singled out Sgt. Portnoy as particularly undeserving of his trust. All adults were devious and potentially dangerous predators to little boys, as Billy saw things. Like they say in the westerns: "I don't like this; it's too quiet out there."

Biblical admonitions, full-blown lectures, public ridicule, corporal punishment, innumerable punitive writing exercises ("I will learn self-control." "I will not talk out of turn." "I will follow directions." "I will not cheat on spelling tests." "I will not cheat on math tests." "I will respect Mrs. Goldfarb."): five hundred repetitions, on many occasions; these had left their brand on Billy's psyche, not to mention scars on his arms, legs, back and buttocks from his mother's swats with an extension cord. Worse yet, they had left him leery of even the most well-intentioned grownups.

Billy kept a space of ten feet between himself and Jerry's uncle. He had detected no signs of danger, not even a hint. On the contrary, not a thing seemed amiss. That was what frightened him; it was too good to be true, a possible setup. The devil was a devious one; this he knew.

"And you've gotten very handsome, Billy. The little girls must really like you," the Sergeant continued.

"They sure do," Billy bragged. "It's a gift. I'm blessed and highly favored by a touchdown."

"Stay with the Black ones, young man; it'll go better for you in the long run," the sergeant told him.

"I'm real glad you didn't get none of your legs or arms blew off in the war, Sgt. Portnoy," Billy said, saluting the soldier. "You kept your head on straight."

"Me, too, Billy," Jerry's uncle chuckled, as he returned his attention to his nephew.

"He extended the bouquet toward Jerry, suggesting: "Let's give these flowers to your auntie."

"She's gonna be awful surprised!" Jerry guaranteed.

"Adios, Redskin, my faithful half-an-Indian by nature companion!" Jerry bade his pal.

"Adios, Pale Face," Billy responded. "Don't get caught in no more ambushes, I'm just sayiin', you heard?"

"Welcome home, Sgt. Portnoy," he added, once again acknowledging the decorated combat veteran with a crisp salute. "Much thanks for your indentured servitude. You made us Kinsman cowboys proud; you ran a good program, too. You're a regular guy in my book."

The war hero didn't return Billy's gesture, though, yet again.

"Home sweet home, right, Uncle Mike?" Jerry blurted, laughing all the while.

"What's this thing doing here?" his uncle asked, as they sidestepped Louie De Fazio's vehicle.

"Oh, that, well, it's like this: Auntie Carol, she got us a TV set wholesale, cheap and good," Jerry explained. "It always has technical difficulties on Saturdays, while I'm at the movies; it's quite a coincidence that we have on our hands over here, huh! It's beyond my pay grade."

The smiling nephew used his house key to unlock the front door, allowing them to enter and make Aunt Carol's day really special.

She was not in the kitchen, not in the living room, not in the dining room, not in the den. Jerry and the highly decorated warrior searched for her in vain.

"Where the hell is she?" Sgt. Mike grumbled.

"I think she's taking a snooze," Jerry whispered. "Let's not disturb her. She needs her rest."

"Oh, let's!" the uncle countered, as the faint sounds of a lovers' duet emanated from the master bedroom.

Jerry had to run to keep up with his uncle, who strode through the house, as though he were stalking prey, toward his bedroom and paused at the entrance.

In a flash, Uncle and Nephew stood in place, next to each other. Only a closed door separated them from the source of blissful serenade of moaning on the other side.

"Uncle Mike, you dropped the flowers," Jerry said cautiously, as his uncle was grinding petals into the carpeting.

Jerry stared with wide-eyed disbelief. This was hardly the cheerful man who had, only a few minutes earlier, been greeting him, almost but not quite like a long-lost son. On the contrary, Jerry was in the presence of a veritable snarling beast, hunched for an attack. Killers kill.

Jerry's instincts screamed for him to flee, yet nonetheless he lingered on. While he feared the worst (that his aunt and he were in harm's way), he would have been out of character were he not expecting the best, that somehow there would still be a joyous family reunion coming up and soon.

Literally every movie Jerry had ever seen had been a western, and every one of those had had a happy ending, no exceptions. That the good guys would win was as certain as day following night in those sappy flicks. Righteous wranglers, they never got bloody; they never got bruised; they never got mussy; and they never ever ran away: Jerry stood his ground. He was one of the good ones, too. He talked the talk and walked the walk.

Sgt. Portnoy burst into the bedroom. Jerry and he were now the audience for a passionate performance of a between the sheets ballet. The role of Ballerina was being played by Auntie Carol; Dance Partner was being played by loverboy Lucky Louie De Fazio.

"Daddy's home!" the Sergeant bellowed, as he exploded into the room.

While his wife provided an accompaniment of entreaties, begging for her very life, the trooper pounced on the interloper.

Jerry stood in the doorway, bewildered by a stranger's presence in his aunt's marital bed and transfixed by the savagery of his uncle's attack.

Previously, the most pressing issue in Jerry's life had been ascertaining how it was that Randy Laredo, having fired two rounds from his pistol, could consistently zing four outlaws, all of them in their shooting hands without fail; magic bullets.

The sage companion, Billy, had provided his canned explanation: "It was a movie!"

This was the Portnoy' house, however, not the Imperial Palace. Randy Bob Laredo would not be riding Thunder the Wonder Horse into the bedroom to set things straight, and Billy was not at Jerry's side to provide enlightened commentary.

Meanwhile, Louie De Fazio, the lonely ladies' lothario, was on the horns of his own dilemma. His head was being beaten like a drum. Sgt. Portnoy's fists had turned Lucky Louie's face into steak tartar.

For an encore, Uncle Mike kneed Louie in the groin. Then he grabbed the gigolo by the scruff of his neck and slammed him, face first, into a dressing mirror.

"You aren't good looking anymore!" the soldier shouted, punctuating his maledictions with a wad of spit directed at the what had previously been a singularly appealing visage.

Louie De Fazio, nose smashed, lips lacerated, face oozing fluid, was now lying on the floor. He groaned, as though he were acknowledging the accuracy of Sgt. Portnoy's observation. He truly was not good looking anymore.

Sgt. Portnoy exhibited an altered countenance, himself. He was flushed with furry and was perspiring profusely. His uniform jacket, shirt and trousers had been splattered by the gush of De Fazio's blood.

Jerry's thoughts drifted to Billy, who had always been one to extol the merits of horror movies over cowboy movies.

"'The Mummy's Curse' is way better than 'Randy Rides Again' or 'Randy to the Rescue' or 'Pecos Partners' or any of those other stupid cowboy movies!" he had often told Jerry. "The Mummy can't be stopped, not by man nor machine. It's ruthless, and it shows no mercy for mere mortals! It's all consuming, too."

"Jerry, still frozen stiff, a virtual ice-carving, theorized that his uncle and the Mummy must have been one and the same; unstoppable, merciless!

The Sergeant turned his back on the writhing home-electronics technician and focused a laser-like stare on Aunt Carol, who was huddled in a corner. She had wrapped a sheet around herself, a scant shield from the icy terror closing in on her next.

It was that moment that Louie chose for a last-gasp attempt to escape the bestial furry that had so unexpectedly descended upon him.

Groggy from taking wicked shots to the head and a face-off with the mirror, Louie reconnoitered the bedroom; a dash for the window was his only hope.

While the Sergeant's glazed eyes were glued to his cornered wife, Louie De Fazio, clad in his birthday suit, staggered to his feet, grabbed his pants and shirt and charged the window.

He was yanked back to reality by Sgt. Portnoy's outstretched hand, which had closed around his neck. Louie's legs wriggled in the air, like a fish struggling for survival, after having been hooked and reeled in.

"Must you be leaving us so soon?" Uncle Mike asked.

Louie's face had, by now, turned purple, the Sergeant was strangling him. He could not speak, even if he had wanted to; he could barely breathe.

"Answer me!" the Sergeant ordered, slightly loosening his grip.

"Whatever you say," Louie rasped.

Sgt. Portnoy responded by tweaking Louie's broken nose, eliciting a piercing scream.

"Allow me to show you out," he continued.

Then he tightened his grip on Louie's neck and smashed him through the window, face first. Blood-splattered chips of glass exploded through the room, like shrapnel permeating a battlefield.

The savagery escalated. Sgt. Portnoy, recipient of a Silver Star for bravery under fire and a Purple Heart for getting wounded, had saved his hottest lava. He would now spew it on his wife and Jerry.

He had pinned Auntie Carol to the floor, face down. By pressing his foot and all of his body weight on the back of her neck, he kept her immobilized.

"Slut! Tramp!" he bellowed.

Jerry could bear no more of this.

"Leave her alone, you big bully!" the little boy commanded. "Some hero you are, beating up on a woman!"

His enraged uncle lunged for him, momentarily freeing his wife.

"Run, Auntie Carol! Make for the hills!" Jerry yelled, an instant before his uncle's slap scorched his cheek.

"I hate you! I wish you got killed in the war! I wish you never came home!" he added, trying to hold the Sergeant's attention while his aunt made a break for it.

"You knew, you little bastard!" the man shouted at Jerry, as he drew back an open hand for another slap.

"Knew what?" the boy whimpered. "Use your words."

"You knew what was going on in this bedroom, and you didn't let me know about it, not word one!" Uncle Mike continued. "You had my email address. Are you retarded?"

"No!" Jerry shouted. "I swear I thought he was just coming here to fix the TV set, honest! I don't tell lies; it's not becoming for a gentleman."

The second slap let him know that his denial was unacceptable. The blow sent him reeling against a wall, where he slumped into a sitting position.

"What the hell could I expect from you, anyhow?" Sgt. Portnoy hurled at the traumatized child. "You're not my nephew! You were born illegitimate; your mother had you from a one-night stand with a African American spear-chucker. Tell that to your little charcoal buddy boy, Billy, out there that he has a new cousin."

"Better yet, watch this," he continued, as he forced Jerry's aunt to her feet. She had stayed there to protect her beloved Jerry. A lot of good that did her because her husband turned her head toward her nephew, put one hand under her chin and his other hand on top of her head and snapped her neck with a twist, instantly killing her.

With that, he turned his back on the boy, righted himself into a proper military posture, tossed his head back and marched from the room.

Standing in the Portnoy driveway all the while, Billy overheard the commotion. He also witnessed the battered Louie De Fazio's crashing through the bedroom window and scampering for his truck.

Billy tried to fathom the living hell that Jerry was surely facing within his formerly tranquil abode. He was certain that Sgt. Portnoy's homecoming had been the harbinger of doom, just as he had suspected all the while; all of the screaming and crying guaranteed a worst-case scenario. The hell hounds were loose and barking.

He concluded that Louie De Fazio, he of gored face and smashed nose, was Frankenstein reincarnate, and, if Frankenstein had gotten his butt kicked so convincingly, then there was sure one frightening demon rampaging through Jerry's house.

Billy was at as much a loss as his friend, Jerry, for the right moves at this moment of major peril. While he had the courage of a lion for pulling off a Randy Bob Laredo-type rescue, he lacked the expertise.

Sure, he had often saved Jerry from the clutches of miscellaneous local tough-kids, but fending off adult assailants left Billy in a quandary. Consequently, a frontal assault was quickly ruled out a mismatch.

He could forget the whole thing and haul ass, Billy figured, but Jerry was his one and only friend. If Jerry sustained debilitating injuries, necessitating a lengthy absence from Woodbury School, who would share a lunch table with him? Who would go to the movies with him on Saturdays? Who would Billy throw tomatoes at? Nobody! Thus, desertion was not a viable option, either. What to do now!

Strutting out the front door of his house, Sgt. Portnoy had a psychotic look on his face. Truly, no one could confuse him for the Grand Marshall of the Happy Ending Parade.

Billy hid behind a tree, in front of Jerry's house. In his haste, he had dropped his baseball hat. His heart pounded, as the monster that was his best friend's highly-touted uncle, approached the tree. Sgt. Portnoy noticed the hat, scooped it up and hurled it into the street.

"Where are you, you deep purple gape-mouthed sonofabitch!" he cursed, scanning the vicinity for Billy.

Billy held his breath, fearing that even the sound of respiration might reveal his whereabouts. He risked a peak at the man turned monster, who was now reenacting a battlefield encounter with invisible Taliban enemies.

The Sergeant bellowed commands to troops under his command, seen only to himself; imploring them to fight on, conserve their ammunition and, if need be, die for the Stars and Stripes and Uncle Sam.

In the war hero's mind's eye, the skirmish had run its course, it was a victory. He grinned and shouted, "Well done, men! Your country is proud of you today!" With that, he marched down Kinsman Road.

Once the decorated war veteran was out of sight, Billy emerged from hiding.

"Now, what I'm gonna do, go inside that haunted house or not?" Billy pondered.

As though the Lord, himself, was answering Billy's question, a resounding thunderclap rippled through the darkening pre-storm sky.

"Yup, I'm goin' in," Billy thought to himself.

He looked toward the heavens and spoke, "You mostly done me real good so far, Buddy Jesus; I owe you a solid; I'm good for it, too. You know me. Us, we go way back. We have history. Amen. Over and out."

Billy quickened his step in route to Jerry's front door, just as the rains came. He entered the house and walked cautiously through the rooms.

Arriving at the chamber of horrors, he tiptoed in. Jerry's aunt was lying in a heap. Her face was bloodied; her lifeless body was covered by a sheet. Billy walked to another corner of the room, where Jerry sat, crying uncontrollably. He placed a hand on Jerry's shoulder, and Jerry looked up at him.

Tears ran down Jerry's bruised cheeks where his assailant had tattooed a farewell message with his fists. Jerry tried to verbalize his pain but was incapable of speech, so heavy was his grief and so deeply wounded was his soul.

Billy sat on the floor, next to Jerry and hugged his wailing friend.

"It's gonna be okay now, Jerry-boy," he promised. "The darkest hour comes just before the dawn or something like that. You white folks are sure a trip, boy! This sure ain't 'Leave it to Beaver'."

It was to no avail, Jerry wailed even harder. The candlelight of hope seemed to have been extinguished for this boy, who had always believed in a turn for the better, a silver lining, an eleventh-hour rescue and the cowboy code of honor: do no harm.

"Aw, Jerry, you know cowboys aren't supposed to cry no crocodile tears into drop buckets like that," Billy reminded his pal, as he embraced him.

Billy could barely get the words out of his mouth. He was crying too, sharing Jerry's pain. Big boys do too cry.

Jerry, accepting Billy's support, pulled Billy close to him and returned his hug. And that's that. So, it ends.

"I'm afraid that we are out of time for today's visit to Shangri-La, and Lovers Lane is shutting down for further repair work," Dr. Cole told us at that point. "Shall we continue with this romantic rhapsody say next week or move on to greener pastures?" she continued.

"All depends on the vote, of course," Tiff said. "Two yes's and we see you again as a married couple. Two no's and it's "Hasta la vista, baby!"

"Time to vote then, valiant gladiators," Dr. Cole said, as she gave each of us a piece of paper and a pen, adding: "If it's a tie, I'll do my very best Judge Judy impression. I also do a mean Barbra Streisand."

Well, Listener, we voted. It was a tie, much like kissing your sister.

"Hey," I told Tiff, "let's vote again, one more once, all right? You just never know."

"Cool by me," she agreed.

Dr. Cole was puzzled, though. She asked us why on earth we wanted a revote anyhow when one of us clearly chose to opt out. "And don't tell it to me, either; tell each other; I'm just the piano player in this combo," she went on: Molly Metaphor over there.

That's when Tiff poured her heart out. "Jerry," she said, "you're the Romeo to my Juliette, which is code for I love you even more than a hog loves slop, and I hereby always and forevermore forgive you for all the pain and suffering, too, every last drop of it, and we're talking about a sea of trouble here."

"Okay," she continued, "after carefully considering all of the compelling hard evidence against you, and there is for sure plenty of that, I've decided not to turn your philandering ass over to the Women's Retaliation Hit Team for the time being at least or even pop you upside the head because I can go from zero to screaming banshee in like nothing flat."

"We're in this together, sink or swim, for better or for worse," she add. "So, let's turn the page, okay, and together we'll write the next chapter of our hot romance novel before I have to neuter you as a public service and really make a name for myself in the sisterhood."

"Yes, you're an unreliable cheating jackass, but you're my unreliable cheating jackass," she wound up with. "Here, take it, Big Papa; I'm giving you my still-beating heart. Handle it with the utmost care because I know where you stay, and you have to sleep sometime."

"That's all I got," she tacked on to the end. "Don't leave me hanging. Come with you're A game or don't come at all! Be so good or be so gone."

"Baby," I began, "I love you even more than I love Miss Bunny Buns, the star of the epic, "Beaver Hunting," and trust me: Miss Bunny Buns is the truth! Even love you more than I love playing the ponies, too, and, from this day on, I promise you that I'm strictly a one-horse cowboy. Me, I'm gonna do so much better if you'll still have me; you'll see, just watch my smoke. So, what d'ya say, Sugar Booger, let's go over those scary red-hot coals together, hand-in-hand like storybook children? I'm game if you are."

"That is that," Dr. Cole said.

"That is that?" I popped back. "We ring our hearts out and that's all we get, three words? I didn't realize we were being counseled by a Freudian." "Who is this person?" I asked Tiffany.

"Oh, her, she's the third Musketeer," the love of my life said. "We are, the three of us, joined at the hip now. It's a threesome. Kinda kinky to me."

At that point, Dr. Cole distributed new pieces of paper for the revote. Then she announced the result with: "Congratulations! You are both still in play. I'll start doing the Wave now."

So, this love story for the ages would go on, and the train kept rolling, until it wouldn't anymore.

"And you will call the new baby just what?" the Doc asked us.

"Speaking for myself," I replied, "I'm totally down with Michael for the King of Pop or Aretha for the Queen of Soul."

"Or Goofy for yourself!" Tiff said.

CHAPTER SIX

CUE THE SUNSET

When Panda, the reigning Teen Queen of Steam, asked me why I became a social worker in the first place and I went into the stock cover story, "The Mama Lion and her Gooey

Cubs," it was just a quick fix, though, a dodge; I didn't know the notorious Gang of Seven well enough at the time to go into the real litany of woe and reveal where the bodies were buried at. The timing wasn't right back then, but it sure is now. Here is the whole enchilada. Listener, get out your handkerchief. Allow me this moment to put ashes on my forehead and tear my garments.

Shortly after Sister Ruthie's tragic death, my stepmother took her own life. The pain of tragically losing the baby was too much for her to handle, I guess. She was pretty good to me while it lasted, though, but, hey, you just don't leave people you care about that way; it's like you're stealing their life, too. A month following that, Papa got mouthy with the wrong red neck at The Silver Dollar Cafe and was gunned down, leaving me alone, an orphan without a clue as to which way was up.

Well, after the brief but devastating nightmare in Cleveland with Uncle Mike, Auntie Carol R.I.P. and my dear soul brother, Billy, God bless him, I wound up living with my grandma in the South Bronx, New York, which was real good for all intents and purposes.

The locals called it "Southie." To me, at first, it was heaven on earth, featuring killer egg-creams, tasty Nathan's hot dogs and a delicious New York's finest Dr. Brown's soda for a wash. As they say in Southie: "Forget about it!"

The locals were all so friendly, too. They never met a stranger that they didn't welcome to the neighborhood with open arms and the three stock questions. #1 – "Who the fuck are you?" #2 – "Do you know who the fuck I am?" #3 – "What's your fucking problem?"

Then, in a New York minute, BOOM ... it wasn't my little piece of heaven anymore; it was the fiery furnace of hades. Why me? Why the perpetual black cloud over my head? Well, Listener, you ain't heard nothin', yet. You just can't make this stuff up, try as you might.

Grandma died when I was just 13, leaving me a ward of the borough. Soon enough, though, I wound up in a series of foster homes, which was pretty frigging miserable to put it mildly. Mrs. White's was the worst of the worst of them all for sure, no doubt about it, and the competition for the title was sure strong. All she was missing were horns and a tail because her house was a real hell on earth. She needed to post a sign on the door: "Abandon hope, you who enter here."

She put on a good enough dog and pony show for the inspecting social services workers to get a pass with, but she let it all hang out when they were gone. She hated Jews with a vengeance, and let it be known. Portnoy wasn't exactly your generic Smith or Jones. When she learned that I had black blood coursing through my veins, too, well, I was marked for death, literally. It wasn't a question of if it would happen to me, only a question of when. My life was no walk in the park on a sunny day.

Mrs. White was kind of stingy with the food, too. On a good day, I got a bowl of off-brand stale cereal with powdered milk. On a bad day, I went so hungry that I thought my stomach was going to eat me. There were more of the bad days than good ones in her house, though. I was all skin and bones.

Well, I had one and count them only one friend, Miguel, better known as Micky, a street-smart Puerto Rican kid of my age, who knew how to survive in spite of his abusive old man, who had more than a passing fancy for the young boys on the block.

If it wasn't for Micky, I wouldn't have made it through the darkest period of my life, and, if it wasn't for Micky, I wouldn't have become a social worker with a soft spot in his heart for suffering kids, especially the unwanted defective throwaways landing in my lap at Club Juvie for a total rewiring job and the mother of all tune-ups. I really gave a damn, too, you see.

That made me unique. For the most part, I got them. We were all on the same page.

The last time I saw Micky was Halloween, 2007, thirteen years ago. It was my fourteenth birthday; I was depressed and hungry, that day more than usual. Being scared out of my young fragile mind hadn't set in, yet, but it was still early in the day. Total Paralysis was just around the corner and headed my way. I still had most of my wits about me, but, before the sunset was cued that memorable calendar day, my world would be turned upside down. Some birthday that was! The pits.

When I complained to Mrs. White, she merely showed me a magazine picture of a birthday cake and told me to blow the candles out. Then she laughed. I'm a funny guy, I guess.

As usual, Micky waited for me on the stoop for our ritual morning walk to school. He knew all of the neighborhood gang kids well enough, as his old man was more likely than not their own father's go to guy for ganja, betting the daily number and kinky porn, especially animal acts and niche dramas like "Lollipop Shop" and "Tongue Bath."

He could always make me laugh the blues away with stuff like: "Hey, man, my mother is a trip. She told me that I'm her best friend. I said to her: 'Then why did you fuck my dad?'"

The local thug chapter, they liked my man, Micky, and the wolf pack out there let him pass through the panic zone unscathed. They didn't like me at all, though, but I got a pass, as well, because I was Micky's plus one amigo, and we were on the Buddy Plan. I was a lucky fella, albeit with a sad face and a fiercely growling empty belly; Double Trouble was tag-teaming my hungry broke butt something fierce, and I was going down slow.

In honor of the Halloween holiday, Micky was in costume with a red cape and a blue Superman T-shirt with a red-letter S on front. He didn't see me approach him because his nose was deeply imbedded in a Superman comic book. He had a backpack slung over his shoulder; I thought nothing of it then, but I sure should have, though. It was much more than a prop in this tragic grand opera about to unfold. The stage was set; the curtain went up; the scene was a broken heart.

I got close, and he looked up by instinct. He was a survivor that one, and he wasn't about to be bum rushed by a stranger up to no good. Recognizing my familiar mug, he said: "Yo! Halloween Harry, trick or treat on this!" Then he gave me the finger and laughed like crazy; I was silent. "Why you ain't smilin', my kinky-haired Hebrew brother by another mother?" he asked me.

"What are you, writing a book?" I snapped.

"Old lady Mrs. White got stingy with the food ration again, I take it," he said. "The evil bitch won't even give you a wish sandwich: that's two pieces of bread and wish you had some meat. She needs to get herself laid in the worst way. That's why she's so satanic. Maybe, Mike Tyson's available; he'd poke a stray dog with fleas. That's what she needs most, a stiff man dick and a good enema with a fire hose."

"Boy, you don't know pussy from pepperoni," I said.

"Do too!" Micky objected.

"You wouldn't recognize a pussy if it walked up to you, tapped you on the shoulder and asked you for the train directions to Midtown," I said.

"Jerry my man, I'm a certified pussy hound, and I sure know how to carry the bone," he said. I laughed so hard that my eyes watered up. He was that good! The boy had real potential to be the second-coming of Freddie Prinze. He added that he was so horny that he felt sorry for the crack of dawn, which made me laugh so hard that I sounded like I'd been bribed. Then the dark cloud returned, and I was blue again. That right there, though, was no laughing matter in the least.

Micky knew that I was troubled; we were tight like that. He felt my pain and vice versa; I bled, he bled, too. That's the way it was. "Go on, Birthday Boy, Mr. Fourteen Candles, express yourself to me. Take it to shul. You keep that shit all bottled up deep inside of you, you'll blow for sure, and it won't be nothin' nice for you to write home about, neither. Come on, Jew boy, talk to me. Speak! What we playin' over here, charades?

I opened the tap and the pain gushed out. "I'm hungry, fool! Good enough for your nosey ass?" I told him. "I haven't seen food per se as we know it to be in this neck of the woods since twelve o'clock high noon last Tuesday, two whole days without even a single slice; I'm living on vapors over here, shoot! Kill me now! I'm on my last leg. I'm about to sell off my body parts. Who needs a good working warmed up kidney around here? Keep your eyes open and your ear to the ground for me, ah-ight?"

Micky was duly impressed by that news. "WHOA!" he shouted, and that said it all, too. "You for sure won't get much for your stunted-growth little dick," he taunted. "I'll ask around the neighborhood, though. But, be advised, they got two-fisted dildoes on the market of late for nine-ninety-five, batteries included. The brand name is 'Mister Buzzy.'" The extra-large model is called the Whopper because it takes two hands to handle that sucker. That calls for a woman among women, huh!

Then I asked him if he could help a friend in need out because I was so broke that the ducks were throwing bread at me, mean it, every word.

That was Micky's cue to unveil his fool-proof solution to the problem. "You still lookin' out for me because I'm still lookin' out for you, Young Kipper," he told me, much like the proverbial spider to the proverbial fly. I was to fall for it like a ton of bricks, too, though. I took it all: hook, line and sinker.

"Boy, what's your scheme this time?" I asked him. Micky, who wasn't a stranger to the fine performance arts of shoplifting and pick pocketing, tried his very best to look innocent, but I saw right through the smoke screen. This wasn't my first dance at the party.

"I got a future!" I said. "I'm not down with any of your Jesse James shit today. Be advised! I have your number. You're a devious one, everybody in Southie knows that."

"Is it because I'm brown?" he said. He now played wounded warrior, but, finding that to be an ineffectual move, he laid his cards on the table for me with: "Choose, boy! Either we steal us up some kind a grub for you or you starve to death because you look like you're already knockin' on heaven's front door."

I gave in. What! Listener, you wouldn't have? Man, please!

"Steal some grub, it's gotta be done!" I said. "But this, this is my last time; I play Good Guy." I officially signed on with the program, as Micky told me the stone-cold lock foolproof master plan for us to get over on the Man and score our fair share of life's bounty.

Step #1: We would saunter over to the market on 187th Street at Belmont Avenue. Step #2: I would cool as a cucumber slow drag up to the cash register and start chatting up the Asian American cashier, something like ask the dude which canine was tastier, an Irish setter or a border collie, just to hold his attention on common ground, so he wouldn't throw a monkey wrench into Micky's works.

"That's all I gotta do in this, which is to namely play second fiddle for a hot second?" I asked my co-conspirator. He wasn't good at very much, but he was sure the guy to see for solving world hunger. Giving credit where credit is due, he also flashed olympic speed in hopping subway station turnstiles and harassing the local nuns just because he could, and, according to him, that's what they were there for.

It's a tough job playing the part of slick Micky in this saga, but somebody's got to do it. In polite society's eyes, he was flat out a loser, hands down. Maybe so, but he was my flat out loser. When he liked you, he went all the way. I'd made the cut.

Micky insisted that he would be doing all of the heavy lifting, every little bit of it, too. My job was simply to occupy the head Asian in charge of the till and poke my nose out of doors in a timely manner to see if the local beat cops were in the vicinity and headed our way, in which case we would beat a hasty retreat and head for the hills like runaway convicts from Rikers Island.

"Heavy lifting meaning just what?" I insisted. "Talk business because I'm dying fast over here; I'm seeing visions and hearing voices."

"Meaning I'm a clear slimy boogers out my nose with my left hand and tug on my nuts with the other one," he replied.

"Stop acting like Bobo the clown, silly rabbit!" I said. "We got us a damn life-or-death situation on our hands over here, and you're all twisted up over some slimy boogers and a bag of mixed nuts!"

"You need to chill better, shit!" he ordered me. "I'm a get busy in there, stuffin' up my trusty backpack here with foodstuffs, yo. What's your pleasure? Ain't nothin' too good for my main man, Jerry the Jews' Jew, trust me. You came to the right street guy. Micky is the name. Boosting grub is the game."

Enough with the meet and greet, I told him to get me a chilled Dr. Brown's celery soda from the cooler, some Oreo cookies, a bag of Doritos, beef jerky and a couple of large Snickers, which would cover all of the basic food groups and provide me with the breakfast of champions.

"And then we make the dash," Micky said. "Boy, go till I say stop and not one second sooner! You heard me?"

I had a bad feeling about this whole caper from the get go, though, and I let it be known in no uncertain terms. Let that be noted, too, whenever and wherever the Bronx tale is told down the line.

Micky blamed my reluctance on the fact that I didn't read enough Superman comic books for my age. Oh, really?

"Can't nobody stop us, the Supreme Team from the Justice League, nobody, try as they might!" he said. "Plus, I got prime time homeboy Roscoe on my person, just in case it should be some technical difficulties with the authorities along the way to Fat City and push comes to shove. Jerry, allow me to introduce my little friend Roscoe; he don't like no stinkin' badges, neither. Small world!"

Micky then pulled a gun from his pocket and waved it in the air, shouting that, with Mr. Roscoe in his hand, he stood ten feet tall and change. "I'm a Ninja warrior, motherfucker!" he shouted. I was convinced, too. Micky had more than enough swagger for the both of us.

In an effort to change the subject and tune my instrument, I told Micky that, hey, I want to be Superman for Halloween, too, and that he should give me a share on wearing his cape just for old times' sake. We were tight like that: he was my ghetto pass in knockoff Nike Air Jordan's, and I was his conscience in a yarmulke, tsitsis and ear-locks. He had lots of trouble playing any parts of good basketball, though, and I had lots of trouble playing any parts of good Jew. So, there's that. We were strange low-hanging fruit on the Tree of Life, and we were both of us about to get plucked up.

Mrs. White called me the anti-Christ. Well, everybody's got to be something, I guess. Sure, Jesus caught a raw deal and took the fall, but enough about him. I had troubles of my own. That was then, and this is now.

"Yo, you're shit outta luck, partner, because I die in this cape," he said.

My friend told me that should Death come calling on him first, I should just say: "Decansa en pas" and lay him down easy.

I told him to do me a solid and speak English to me because he wasn't in sunny San Juan, P.R. anymore.

"Look over there on the street, fool!" I went on. "Those are what we call street legal motorcars in the South Bronx, not your dirt road porta-donkeys, yo. Get with the program! Shape up or ship off."

"It means rest in peace, White Chocolate! Okay then, move out," he instructed, barely audible over the angry grumbling of my empty stomach, which had run completely out of patience with me and was announcing that it was now a case of do or die. Some birthday this was! How blue could I get? I was now down and about to be counted out.

So, soon enough, we entered the market, and I chatted up Asian Man at the register, while my accomplice of record wandered through the place, deftly shoplifting food.

"Say, Mister Asian Man," I said, "you speaky the King's English or just your native yang shit?"

"What do you want!" he snapped back.

"I'm collecting for African Americans without leather jackets."

"If you're not buying anything, then leave the store and take that sneaky boy with you! The police come in here for coffee all the time; takes one word from me, just a word and off to jail he'll go. Tell him to try the baloney sandwich special down there. It will take the edge off."

"Everybody's a comedian," I said, which was when quick hands Micky from the East knocked a bottle off the shelf, and it shattered, as though he was adding ending punctuation to Asian Man's warning.

"Hey, I see you!" the cashier shouted at Micky, who shot back at him with: "I see you, too, Buddha-headed bitch!"

"Your mother must be so disappointed in you," the cashier scolded.

"Gimme all ya got in the cash drawer … chop-chop, bloodsucker! Your money or your life, makes me no difference," Micky went on. "I'm a southside gangsta till the casket drop; I'm recyclin' brown people's dollars up in here. Fork it over, fool!"

Like they say, "Fate is no joke," you see, because at that very moment, two cops entered the market. Pointing at Micky, Asian Man shouted out that my boy was robbing him.

Micky could take a hint. He broke for the door, but Officer Beer Gut was quicker. He snagged Micky by the arm. Just as Beer Gut started to pat him down, Micky jumped back.

"You don't need to be feelin' on me, shit! This ain't Touch Up on a PR's Butt Day in Southie," Micky said. "This is racial profilin'. You'll hear from my Jewish attorney, and he's from Manhattan. I don't play that doormat shit. Bet your bottom dollar on that, donut hound! I bet Asian Man over here got a little somethin' somethin' glazed for your pudgy ass, too, Jelly Belly."

I tried my best to finesse our way out of this predicament and told the Bronx' finest that Micky and me are just a couple of innocent neighborhood schoolboys, trying our very best against all odds to grow up and be somebody special and then to give back by times of ten.

"My friend over there, he intends to be a man of the cloth. Jesus called on him personally," I said. "Jesus says jump, you just say how high, right, Micky? Okay, now, tell these fine gentlemen in blue over here how cool God's been to you, my dear born again brother in the Lord, go on. Won't he do it?"

"Fuck the police!" he said, setting the table. "They be blazin' away at us like we in open season 'n' shit, just talkin' about some weak stuff like: 'I thought the kid was pulling a gun on me; I feared for my very life,' when all the young suspect in question was actually doin' was, he was just reachin' down his pants to take inventory."

I laughed at that. Micky was good in a pinch, real good. Pound for pound, the kid was really courageous for his half-pint size, too. He could hold his own with the best and gave as good as he got. But he led with his chin, though, which was his fatal flaw.

"Just look who we dealin' with here, Jerry boy," he continued. "We got French poodle-eatin' Asian Alvin and the two overweight gay for the stay chipmunks."

Micky and I roared with laughter, but this was truly no laughing matter, though. Oh, what to do! What did I know; I'm just a kid on the rise over here with a whole lot to learn, yet.

Officer Beer Gut then told the aspiring blue comic: "Okay, Superman, cuff up. Hands behind your back. Do it now! Don't make me get ugly."

Micky then whipped out his gun and aimed it at the rotund cop, as Beer Gut's partner looked on helplessly.

"Do you believe in Jesus?" Micky asked the cop.

"Yes, I do," the big guy replied.

"Good! You're about to meet him," Micky went on. "Eat lead, pig!"

"Stop! Don't do it!" Asian Man shouted at Micky, who turned to glare at him and redirect the gun barrel, which was when Officer Beer Gut pulled out his own piece from a holster and shot Micky in the chest. BOOM!

For a hot second, Micky just stood there, as if he really believed he was truly Superman in the flesh and the bullet had bounced off of him, but, of course, he wasn't; of course, it hadn't; and, of course, he collapsed on the spot, oozing life.

Somehow, I found the strength to plead: "Micky, don't die. Don't you dare die on me; I need you. Don't give up! Boy, you're too strong for that. Fight! Superman doesn't die; he's indestructible. Ask the Riddler and Lex Luthor about that. Come on, Micky, talk to me. Something. Anything. You're a talker; speak!"

"Jerry, I'm so cold," he said. Those were to be his last spoken words ever, and the rest, as they say, is history.

The hefty officer felt Micky's neck for a pulse, administered CPR for a minute, checked for a pulse again and announced that he was now a checkout. Then he examined Micky's pistol and said: "A toy! It's a damn replica. The hell!"

The cashier observed that Micky was so young and so angry; a terrible terrible thing. Too fast to live. Too young to die.

"I'm just crazy hungry's all," I explained to the men. Hunger bad, food good. "He was boosting me up some last-minute survival-rations. I didn't know anything about a stickup, though, honest. That's on the Father, the Son and the third joker, whose name I forget, and he's the Big Tuna, too. Might be Moe for all I know. Gotta believe me, guys, just gotta. Oh, please! I have a future. Open up your hearts to me; I'm begging you over here. Gentlemen, think about it: I might have been you or yours. Let the sunshine in; you can do this. That's about it. I rest my case and throw myself on the mercy of the court. Have your way with me; go on. I'm but putty in your hands now."

Asian Man told me that, had I just asked him, he would've given me food, though, and gratis, too. It was a little too late for that now.

Slender Cop told me to I.D. Micky. So, I did as told: "His name was Miguel Angel Garcia Santa Cruz Gomez better known in the area as Micky. Don't even ask me why all of those names were at all necessary. Lived with his mom at the River Projects, 1202B. He sucked in school, never kissed a girl and couldn't hang on the basketball court to save his life, but he was still my road dog, though, and that's through the thick and thin of it. He stretched the truth, yes. Sometimes just a little bit, sometimes a whole lot like today for instance. He could've been a contender. He was a true-blue friend to the end; he had a lot to learn; but now school is out forever."

Officer Beer Gut then asked the cashier if I was in on the robbery, as well. The kindly man replied that he couldn't say for sure because his eyes were so bad.

The second cop said to his hefty partner: "Tell me that you're not entertaining the notion that I know you to be entertaining right now, namely letting this little Hasidic Harry perp bounce and dance down Belmont Avenue."

"Bingo!" the Bronx' finest replied. Big belly, big heart, I guess. "You owe me a solid for not making the collar on your no-good coke-dealing nephew, Frosty the Snowman," he added.

"Go before I change my mind," the fatherly fat man told me, and I did just that, but not before I eulogized my friend, saying: "Decansa en pas, rest in peace or whatever, my dear dear best and only local pal of my age group. I'll never forget you, partner, even in my golden years, mean it. You were the coolest guy on the block! Thanks for letting me be down with ya; you were my rock when the stuff hit the fan, and those are real hard to find in today's dog eat dog world, trust me. I'll dedicate my life and times to you I promise; that's all I got to send up over here. You'll be forever in my heart. If I have a son, I'll either call him Micky after you or Clark Kent after Superman; it's a game time decision. Some life! Go figure. Ya know, homie, the times that you impressed me most were the times you didn't even try. I guess your number was just up. Till we meet again. See ya around, Micky. Stay gold, my beloved brother. Planet Earth to Capt. Micky … Planet to Capt. Micky … I'm losing you! Over and out."

I proceeded to take the just now out issue of Superman comics from the rack and laid it on top of my friend's chest, kissed my hand and placed it on his forehead. Then I covered his face with the cape and beat a hasty retreat because miracles, well, they just don't happen every day, especially in Southie, and that is the rest of the story.

The Black kids didn't like me; they thought that I wasn't down. The Jewish kids didn't like me; to them I wasn't down, either. Micky liked me, though. To him, I was down enough, and that was sure a big frigging relief. I was lost, and I was found. Found was better.

In closing, my dear Listener, I sure do hope that you will remember your resilient narrator for this above all else: I tried my very best with what I had been given to be a real superhero; real superheroes in my eyes aren't people that run off to play out a comic book fantasy, no; they are the ones that stay to be good people.

CHAPTER SEVEN

THEY'RE BACK!

So, the one and only alias Snaggle Tooth and me, we hugged up on it, buried the hatchet and I stayed on at Club Juvie for another tour of duty, the last hurrah. Happy Hour was a total success because: A. No one got carried out in a body bag. B. The stampeding elephant in knockoff Jimmy Choo pumps that the kids were running from got winded, threw up its hands and gave up the chase, at least temporarily. C. I could finally exhale and D. I had earned Dr. C.'s undying trust and respect, no easy feat. A miracle happened here!

As a peace offering, she gifted me with these creative scribblings, unique works of literary art from the pens of the Wild Bunch that the esteemed Doc had wrung out of them as their personal penance for infractions ranging from public masturbation and spectacle flatulence to "keistering" (i.e. butt-cheeking) cookies and then, of course, the oh, so highly dreaded by the authorities, yet a cathartic natural high for the desperate sensory-deprived inmate, the tribal ritual known to this very day as, okay, all together now, WHO BANGING, and here's what that looks like: the back story uncensored. Proceed with caution. A pretty collage it isn't. Two words go here: reality bites!

RICKY

It's just me, Big Scrappy, writin' to you from a jail cell the size of a fucked up broom closet. I'm not doin' this to try to scare you out of gangbangin', shit! Do whatever you wanna do with your fuckin' life, ese. You're your own shot-caller in this life. Chinga! So, run your own program. I'm just the messenger, and this kite is for you alone.

So, I just wanna tell you a little bit about thug life. It's fun, and I mean it's fuckin' fun: cruisin' the streets, always fuckin' that loose shit, always gettin' fucked up. They often used to call me "Ese Stay High." We take what we want, and we don't ever look back. Hit and split, rip and run: that is how we do it if you want to be down with us.

I used to wake up at one o'clock in the afternoon every day. "Fuck school!" was the first thing on my mind. So, the day began for me like this: shower, eat, get fucked up and repeat.

It never changes, always the same old shit: your mom worrying about you to death, wondering if today is the big day that she's gonna get that feared visit, the famous one from the cop, Officer Donut, tellin' her that I'm layin' in the street deader than fuck. I made my poor mom old and gray before her time. That's the price you gotta pay to get into the coolie club house; the name of the place is "I like it like that."

Well, bein' a gangster has its ups and its downs, too. You kick it with your homeboys, just fuckin' around; they're like your second family, real close 'n' shit. But, once you get your ass locked up, most of the time you don't hear nothin' from them till you get released.

Meanwhile, they're out there fuckin' your girlfriend 'n' lots of other drastic shit of that nature since you're on your vacation. Yet, when you get out, there they are for you once more, still your homies, still your brothers, still the posse.

I'm only age seventeen; I been locked up most of my teen life. But, hey, I really don't give a fuck because I love my gang to death. When I get out, I'm still gonna be a dope-headed gangbanger till I fuckin' die and go to hell, ese. Just watch my smoke!

So, shit, if you still wanna fuckin' gang bang, then chinga, firme for you. Like they say: "Smile now, astronaut, when you're out there gettin' sky high on that rocket fuel and havin' your fun and cry later when you're locked up, beatin' your meat raw and missin' the ones that you love so bad it hurts. Don't quote me; I ain't said shit.

RONNIE

As they say: "What goes around comes around," and for me it sure did just that. Check this out and feed your head, bitches!

One night, I came home and found my enemy gang's name sprayed up all over my house. It meant: "Hey, we know where you stay! We'll be back." It was their business card. I thought nothing of it; saying it sure ain't doing it, though. Only time would tell.

Another night soon after that, me and my homeboy, Eddie Boy, we were out there partying like a motherfucker on crack with some real hot females. Eddie said he was tired and was going to go home, but it was too late for that now. So, we both of us went to my cousin's pad to crash out for the night. We were all buzzed and laughing like crazy. Life was good, shit! No end in sight. We would be forever young! It was no stopping us now. Together, brothers!

Little did I know that, while I was out there running the streets and having my fun times, my mom was at home scared and crying her eyes out and my twin baby brothers, the age of two, were screaming their heads off because that night my enemies decided to pay me another little visit. They shot up my house because that's what they do. So, it was now game on for reals. I play that shit for keeps, and no prisoners would be took.

Well, of course, me and my homeboys, we paid them back for that real hard. We took that shit to the limit. I won't say what happened next or who did it, but put it this way, okay, somebody else's family suffered, too, but their pain is eternal. That was our own business card. Right back at ya, bitches! In your damn face, shit!

What I'm trying to tell you is that you ain't the only that hurts. Your family don't got nothing to do with your gang, but they will still get shot at because of your dumb ass actions.

Also, when you go to jail, who takes the blame? Your parents are the ones that are feeling down. It's as if they did the crime themself because they feel they didn't do their job, which is bringing you up proper.

I'll tell you about the first time I killed somebody now. This shit rocks like Jagger, too! It was a Wednesday, the day before Thanksgiving. Me, my homeboy, Lil Devil, and my home girl, Smiley, we were driving around the city of El Monte, and we found some girls sleeping in their cars. So, we hit 'em up, and they claimed their gang, and then Smiley told me to shoot, which is exactly what I did, too. Why the fuck not? I'm in it to win it, just ask anybody.

Next thing I knew, one of those now dead bitches, she flew back from the shotgun blast. BOOM! Then Lil Devil, he up and jumped out of our car and started blasting on them other bitches with his Uzi. Three girls died. I get props and a teardrop tattoo for one of them. She took a head shot. It was a beautiful thing. She was eighteen with a bullet. L.O.L.

I still have nightmares because of that dead skunk, but that's not what I'm busted for this time. That shit went down almost two years ago, but they still haven't caught me for it, yet! I'm Casper the Friendly Ghost. Catch me if you can, bitches!

I got to close you out about now. I'll see any kid that reads this soon in jail; I'm from Westside Assassins. Don't let nobody put us down or else they'll get their bad ass cut down!

I'll leave you with this; it shows you just how your so-called homeboys are not always what they claim to be. Yeah, getting fucked up and partying with them is maxed out fun 'n' shit, but, when it comes down to it, they just are not there for you.

You see, I was at a party with some of the homies, and the shit was hard banging, too. We had hot bitches and drugas for days. What's not to like, right? It was really the shit, until some night riders from 18th Street drove by and let off a clip on us.

As I tried to duck, I saw bullets hit my best homeboy, Happy. It blew his head clean off, and, when I looked up, I saw his blood all over me. It was a fucked up horror movie, and I was dead in it, too.

But what happened next really tripped me out, though. Check this out: I was the only one of our click to turn up for goodbyes 'n' shit at his funeral. He was supposed to be the #1 homeboy, but, when it was showtime, nobody came out for him.

TYRONE

I ain't about to tell you no fake ass shit about how cool being in a gang is. Sure, there are some good times, but, homie, don't get your ass all happy 'n' shit when something good happens 'cause it will soon get worse, a fuckin' whole hell of a lot worse.

When I was younger, all I had was fun like twenty-four-seven, yo. At least I thought it was fun, but that was then and this is now. I used to run around saggin' and actin' like I was the shit. I would rob people, and I thought that I'd never get caught for it, either. Life was good, and I sure hoped to die before I got old; I'm as serious as a major heart attack.

If I would catch you slippin' with somethin' on the Christmas list that I wanted bad enough, I would just tell you to give your shit up, and, if you didn't give me service with a smile, most of the time I would like work you over with a aluminum baseball bat; I would bust your face all up and not think nothin' of it, feel me? It was my autograph, feel me?

I thought I was so cool, too, but, homie, I had not even scratched off the lotto ticket, yet. Compared to the older dudes that I used to kick it with, I was just a raw rookie. So, to get my props, I went out one big night when I was the age of sixteen and climbing.

Somehow, I knew ahead of time that I was in for some crazy shit that night. Also, my mama had feelings that something God awful was gonna happen to me. She said: "Son, listen to me good! Stay in the house tonight." I felt bad 'cause the homies came first to me, not her. That was sure fucked up, huh! So, I left the crib ready for anything to go down. At least, I thought that I was ready. Are you with me?

To get to the bottom of all this, I wound up in a dope house way out in East L.A., which is enemy territory of the worst kind; I was kind a scared, but all of that fear disappeared after I smoked some of that "Sherm." Then I felt ready to kill, but I was so out of touch, though.

An older guy came in and wanted some angel dust. I never fuck around with that shit. Dude, all these guys in that house was tore up.

Another guy jumped up and started to spill a lot of his blood 'cause he had been shooting up that big bad King Heroin like a motherfucker with his hair on fire.

I got scared and so did the guy I rode in with; I barely knew him; I did not know what to do. The bleeding guy needed help, but the last thing we needed at the pad was the fuckin' Crash Cops Unit on a mission to serve and protect.

Then this bleeding guy pulled out a knife and came after me. Damn! I ran for it, as my older homie blew him away with a gauge. Blood was covering me now from head to toe, and the guy's meat was all over the place.

But he was not dead, not quite yet, far from it. He got up, and my homie let the bleeding-ass motherfucker have it again. BLAM! This time, his leg flew off!

I prayed to God to send down a angel of mercy to help me, and I ran outside, not knowing where to head. Some guy called me over to his car about then, and I got in. Dude, the crash cops were coming from everywhere by now.

Then the dead guy's friend ran out into the street and let off with a big-ass clip, and he hit six guys. One of them was my homie, who we called "Baby Kong," and he fell, while I sat in the car watching. I was so high that it did not even look real, not at all, but it was, though; sad but true.

I ran out to help him. He was begging me to call his mother. Then my big homie got out of his car and ran over to give me a helping hand. He got shot two times in the neck, just as the crash cops arrived. I ran away, so that I would not get snagged and pulled in 'cause this was some serious shit right here, and I was up to my neck in it. There was a big price to pay and the bill was coming due for full payment.

That night had started off pretty cool with me and the homies drinking "Old English" and doing a fine ass hooker.

I said to myself that me and my big homie, we were gonna be tight forever, but he got snuffed, chalked up on the street and carried off to the refrigerator that night.

I got into the gang the very next week, but things did not get any better for me, though. The shit was not as advertised.

I have done all kinds of bad things, dude, but the thing that I hate more than anything else is that I ran over a little boy, as I was D.F.U. or driving while fucked up. He did not die, but he is in a wheelchair for life, though, just because of me. I have to live with that memory. It's hard to be me sometimes, true story. Society don't want to give a player no parts of a even break. That is why we run wild in the streets, people. Now you know.

I would tell you more, but I do not really trust nobody that might read it. They might two-face me and throw rat; never can tell these days because it ain't nothin' but a big-ass talk show now days. I hold my friends close, but I hold my enemies even closer. Your best homeboy, he is the one that will snitch you out in the end. Sometimes, it be just like that. It's all in the Game. Nice motherfuckers finish last.

If you come to jail for some shit and, if you fuck with me, I am gonna kill you with my shank, and that is a promise from this gang member. Watch your back, soldier. You've been told. Ah-ight then, you are dismissed.

BABY GIRL

When I was just comin' up from ages eleven to fourteen, I sure admired the way gangsters dressed and the cars they had and their clothes, too; I thought that these dudes and bitches were oh, so cool, and I wanted to be down with them badder 'n' a motherfucker.

So, by the time I lit up fourteen candles on the birthday cake, I was kickin' it with my cousin in his hood on Compton Avenue in the wild wild West.

One day, some of his homies, they asked me if I wanted to be from their set, and I said: "Oh, hell yes, I do!" Then they called some of their little homies to jump me in, and I was thinking to myself: "OMG! I'm gonna be a real live gangsta female now! I'll have backup for life. Bring it on, shit! I can handle mine."

After the very long initiation fisticuffs, I sat on the curb, very exhausted from the punch out. Then one of my now Gee homies came up to me and said that I sure know how to box, and he gave me some PCP to smoke. I got so high that I didn't even know what I was doing. It was like I was living in a cartoon, feel me? I was all like fuckin' Dora the Explorer 'n' shit.

That same night, my homie from the Rollin' 40's gang was standing across the street from his house talking to some girls when a car posted up and two guys named Benzo and C-Bone got out. They asked my Rollin' 40's homie where he was from, and he said it real loud and proud; he had much heart that boy had. Respect! Now what?

Then they started shootin' at him with a twelve gauge and hit him right in the face twice. BLAM BLAM! But he was still alive, though, and he ran toward the porch where his mother was at all freakin' out 'n' shit.

The dude with the shotgun chased after him, though, and blasted him two more times in the head. That finished him off, and he died there and then, while he was lying in his mother's arms with half of his skull missing.

Later that night, my other homies were planning on going on a payback run. So, they gathered some guns, and they looked me in the eye and wanted to know was I gonna go my own self; I told them: "Oh, fuck yeah!" I was all in now; I was a lifer. That said, one of them tossed me a loaded .38, and we began to walk through our enemy's hood, just as bad as we want to be.

We got halfway through their hood, and we then saw them out there shootin' dice and talkin' to some females. They were drinkin' forty-ouncers, too, just boastin' and toastin' and shootin' the shit with their war stories. All of 'em auditioning for the part of Billy Bad Ass, Young Stud Warrior Prince in this movie.

We were gonna start to shootin', but we saw some little kids out there. A few of them moved out the way, not all of them, though, but such is life. You gotta take the good with the bad, feel me, and count your chickens.

So, we said that on the count of three we're gonna blast, which is just what we did, too. Then we ran back to our hood.

Well, about a week later at school, a girl I knew said that two guys had got killed in the shootout, and a little boy got shot in his mouth with a .38. Then I thought to myself: "Oops!

I shot him." I'm real glad he didn't die, though, but he does have brain damage, and that ain't no joke right there. Ain't a damn thing funny!

Two weeks later, one of my homies got caught and was later on convicted of the two homicides and a attempted murder on the little damaged boy. I feel sorry for my homie, who got a bid of thirty years to life out of it all. He took it like a champ, though.

On Christmas, I be steady sendin' the brain-injured defective youngster a pretty card and a little spending cash; I'm his imaginary friend. Everybody knows that that girl, BG, she got much love in her heart for the young children of the ghetto.

PANDA

This is my story untold about my early years BBH: "Before Beverly Hills."

In the past, my mom had me and, when I was age six, she left me with drug dealers as a deposit on take-out drugs.

After three weeks, they called my grandma, and she came, paid them off and picked me up, snotty nose and all. Things were definitely looking up for me now.

A year later, my mom wanted me back, so I went to live with her. She was still doing her drugs and coming home drunk with strangers at all hours, though, which totally sucked if you ask me. She was no parts of a TV mama at all.

When school came around, I stayed home to watch after my little sister, Barbara. I didn't pass that year, but I did teach myself how to read and do some pluses and takeaways, though. I watched so much "Sesame Street" that I thought I was Big Bird.

One day, Grandma came over for a surprise visit and found my mom passed out on the floor and me and Barbara crying like there was no Santa Claus after all. She took us and all of our clothes back to her house with her, no if's and's or but's about it.

I never met my real dad. Actually, I didn't even know his name or whereabouts. Much to my surprise, Grandma told me that I was going to have a visitor. When we came back home from the park, there was a strange guy on the porch. I told Grandma that I didn't know him, and she said: "He's your daddy, girl!" I didn't know what to say, so I walked up to him, and he gave me this great big bearhug. I cried happy tears this time for a change.

He swore to me on the spot that he would always and forevermore be there for me and never ever leave me again no matter what goes down. Two weeks later, he was gone without a trace. I'm the Goodbye Girl, I guess.

Pretty soon, my mom told Grandma that she would like drag her to court kicking and screaming if she didn't send me back to live with her. I really didn't want to live with her again, but I didn't want to hurt her feelings, either. Grandma said that she was real fragile like that and had such a thin skin covering.

One day, everything was building up inside of me, and I tried to commit suicide by pills; I failed at first, so two days later I tried it once again. This time it was by slicing and dicing up my wrists real bad with a razor blade. There's more than one way to skin a cat I guess.

Grandma got me to the hospital just in time to save my life and get myself all stitched up. They wanted to stick me away in a psych hospital some place, but Grandma pulled strings and got me off.

My grandma's boyfriend moved in with us, and he was such a sweetheart to me. He said I could tell him anything, and I could trust him with personal stuff. Yeah, right! That's what I thought. Don't do not trust anybody over age thirty; they're all old and nasty and smell like mothballs.

He started giving me things to drink and, before I knew it, he molested me all up. So, I ran away by bus travel this time around because I didn't want to tell anybody about him.

After a week on the street, I returned just in time for the boyfriend's, his name is Bob, birthday party.

I wouldn't come out of my room to join in the celebration, and that's when Grandma told me: "Panda, pack your trash! I'm sending you and your sister to Kansas to live with your mother." Grandma said that my mom was a "kept woman" these days out there and had a man of means paying all of her bills for her, which meant that I had a ticket to ride on the Good Ship Lollipop, too, I guess.

I ran away again. Kansas was out of the question and living with good ol' trusty lecherous Bob wasn't even a possibility for me anymore, either. I wasn't nobody's play toy. Fuck the world!

I needed my clothes and money, so a week later, I broke into Grandma's house and took my stuff and her TV, jewelry and purse, too.

Well, the cops caught me while I was on the lamb. I wound up living as a ward of the county until I turned ten, which is when my mom married into big Beverly Hills old movie studio money, and I went from stray mutt to Best in Show, so to speak. I went from soiled Raggedy Ann doll to this pretty Cheerleader Barbie doll, but they couldn't put me together again, not on the inside.

My life stinks to high heaven so far, but I think that it sure beats the alternative, which is death, an endless sleep. We shall see, though. Never say never.

I haven't gone wanting for food in a long time. As for love, though, that is a story for another time; to be continued. Hug a kid today.

DE ANDRE

I really didn't care about getting arrested by the cops because like I knew that I would always be back on the streets like so fast. Witnesses do change up their minds right quick when asked to, ya know what I'm sayin'? Sometimes, you gotta make them a offer that they just cannot refuse, I'm just sayin'. Connect the dots, bitches! Then do the math.

So, I would drink a lot and do drugs like a fiend. It seemed like I was always gettin' away with shit. I was straight thinkin' that I really didn't have nothin' to lose by gettin' my bad self arrested because I was always so sure that my mama would be there for me to bail me out in a hot second 'n' shit. You can't keep a good man down.

But now, though, it seems like I lost the whole wide world because now I ain't arrested for just a little thing, though. What they got me down by law for this round is two counts of first-degree murder, and I could be spendin' the rest of my precious life behind these bars up in here. They call this place the "Hotel California." There's always room. Welcome to the terror dome, brothers!

The worst thing is that now my family don't want nothin' to do with me; they haven't come to visit me for a very long time, and, to top it off, my girlfriend, Vanessa, she says she's havin' my baby, and I can't be there for her.

One thing, though, I been locked up fightin' my case for over a year. How can Vanessa's baby by mine, too? It don't add up, right?

I cry so much here in my cell. My tears are running low. Keep that on the downlow, ah-ight? Only the strong survive. I'm down, but I'm not out.

JIMMY (2017)

I was born January 1, 2003, and at age four, I was adopted by my father and my first mom. She died when I was only six, though. Me and my big brother, Richie, adopted a year after me, lived with my dad.

I had a real hard and messed up childhood; I was so upset and angry that my mom had up and died out on me. So, I would get real mad dog pissed off at the drop of a hat and do bad in school by choice. My dad thought that I was crazy, and he kept shipping me out to special help schools and child psychologists. Doing that only made me feel more bad, though, and really really crazy angry. I one time found this stray dog, poured lighter fluid all on it and lit it up. Pooch screamed in pain, just like I do. It didn't help any. I also pulled wings off of birds. You might ask me why. It's because a dog doesn't have any wings.

My dad remarried, and my new stepmom was so mean to me and Richie. I also had a new stepsister. She was way cool and the only one in my whole family, other than brother Richie, that I was even friends with.

I was growing up, getting in trouble with stuff like smoking dope and ditching school. Because of these little things, which were just my way of crying out for help, I guess, my dad sent me to a boarding school for troubled kids much like me in upstate New York.

They had real crazy strict rules up in there, and they went and shaved all of my long hair off, too, which was the worst part of it. I got out after two long years without a single visit and went back to L.A. to live with my dad and wicked stepmom from hell. It was like the "Rocky Horror Picture Show" for me now.

She was always on my case, and that made me hate her even more than before. So, her and my father hated me even worse, too. And so, that's the way it was.

I started missing school again and staying out real late. My parents were always putting me down and talking bad about me, and that's about when I started getting more and more into drugs and grew my hair back real long. I wasn't sick; I was just damaged.

I listen to death metal music and go to concerts, too. My dad said it wasn't right, and I was the spawn of the devil because of the music I listen to.

I hated school because I was the only long-haired white boy there; I got jumped on a lot and had to pay out big money for protection. I got raped twice, but never told anyone about it because they would have thought it was just another druggie's fantasy.

I would still do drugs with my friends and brother, like buds, acid and other messed up stuff; I was also getting into satanic worship a lot about that time, and I cut upside down crosses on my chest with a razor blade.

I was doing minor crimes for money because my dad never bought me any clothes or food, and he never ever not even once took me to see the doctor, either.

One hot night last summer, me and my friends got drunk and drove over to the Sunset Strip to pick up some chicks in our stolen bomb-ass car that we had found with the keys still in the door.

We got busted by the cops for having beer, and the cops found out that the car was stolen. So, they booked us all up.

All my friends got to go home because their parents got them out. But, no, not my dad, though, uh uh. He just said: "No! Keep him in Juvenile Hall; he needs some seasoning."

I hate my parents so much. I want to hurt them really so so bad when I get out. Just watch me do it. You're going to hear about me one day, wait. I have a little somethin' somethin' for them. It will be the end game. Keep me in your heart for a while.

Dad, trust is a thing that few people are ready to receive, and you betrayed mine so many many times. I hate to just disappear and hold all my pain in, so I won't do that now.

The sad truth is that I'm just a copy of you, a clone. You came back from fighting in the war with a Purple Heart on your chest and a poisoned heart inside of it. Will you be there at the finish line, cheering for me, win or lose?

Everybody is allowed to have one addiction in life. Mine is loving you. It's harder than you think, though. That is my emotional truth.

Now, tell me your truth. Why have you been out there shredding my soul? I'm just so tired of wishing a happy Father's Day to a ghost. I'm having a bigtime cry now. Tears happen.

Not everything that you face is changeable, no, but, until you do face it, though, nothing can be changed at all, not even a little bit.

Love, Jimmy (aka Glitter), age 14.

EPILOGUE

MORE GLITTER (2021)

YEH YEH! There he is! 'S up, Cool Breeze? What it do? What it be about? I bid you a warm warm welcome to my cherried-out movie lot dressing room. The producer sure hooked a featured player up righteous, as he should; as he sure should; I'm monster money in the bank: this we know, guaranteed.

They call me "Jimmy Glitter" 'cause I show out. You came for a star, and I got your Golden Boy right here! Hey, just check me out, sportin' these smokin' designer jeans low and the kick-ass hoodie to die for and rockin' these more-bounce-to-the-ounce Jordan's like they was meant to be rocked, yo. I'm Star Child, King of the Universe; I'm just sayin'. I rep the few, the proud and the chosen; I'm the people's choice, and they have spoken; I've been called up for active duty.

Yo, my publicist, he told me this little chitchat, it's for print in "Rolling Stone" no less. WHOOP WHOOP! That's my shit right there; huge huge fan. It's young America's magazine, and I'm Johnny B. Good, thee all-American boy. My brand is fierce, and it's global, too. Bow down, motherfucker! Bow down two times.

Cool with me, too, yo: I know the Q & A drill cold; it ain't my first ride at the Rodeo Show, neither. Ya know what I'm sayin'? You get paid; I get famouser 'n' a motherfucker, feel me? Win ... win. God is good, and, hey, if you don't believe in God, then next time you need him, just call Santa Claus, shit!

I'm a keep it real from the jump for ya, Mr. Journalist Man; my stuff is totally certified Boy Scout honest. My aim is true, ask around: one shot and one kill.

Ah-ight, am I ready? I stay ready; I'm a rock the mic like it ain't never been rocked before; I'm a levitate this shit before we're through here today, too; just you watch me do it from a front row seat. I'm a action hero. What can I say? I'm a throw down, yo. Let's do this. Ready. Steady. Go!

And so, it begins. Now, I'm a spit at ya strictly off the cuff and impromptu; this right here and now is the world famous

"After Party," ya know what I'm sayin'? What time is it? It's time to get real down and dirty. That's how I roll, in the dirt and nasty.

I'm in free-fall talkin' mode at this point, and word on the street, it's you know how to keep your head on straight when it comes down to writin' negative shit about celebrities, the truly blessed and highly favored among us, feel me? Big props! "Silence is golden," thus sayeth the Lord somewhere. Unpretty shit said in here stays in here or you'll sure wish it had. Take heed: let the poker chips fall where they may.

So, homeboy, like I said: "I'm a spout some shockin' toxic stuff." It's time for me to get down to the nitty gritty, and you, you sure better show serious wisdom 'cause, should you be so inclined as to write anything unflatterin' about me and my drama on the way up the ladder, especially that I did time at Club Juvie, fightin' my case, and kicked back in a psych hospital for a hot second, too, I will not show favor in the least. You ain't too hard to find, feel me? And I got my ear to the ground, too.

The charge was murder in the first, two counts; I beat the case with the greatest of ease, though. Every cop is a criminal, and every sinner is a saint. They had nothin'.

"That was then, and this is now," which is what a real cool Club Juvie social worker told us in group therapy; Jerry Portnoy, my partner in crime for life. It's good like that. Big shout out to my main man, Jerry P., reppin' heaven now, rest n peace, a social workin' motherfucker and the real deal. They'll fool ya sometimes; they're slick like that, posers, straight sheep in wolf's drag.

He got took out in a riot at the Clubhouse, protectin' the director, a hefty nasty bitch with a very hostile attitude that one. The Clubbies cut her down to size, too. They tell you to only say good about the dead. She's dead, so good!

Mr. Jerry Portnoy of blessed memory, well, he got in the way of a blade with her name on it. All the Club coolies weren't down with Cowboy Jerry like me, I guess. The good die young. We all meet again, though. I spilt a droplet or two of the tasty purple grape on his grave when I got out; that's how we do. He didn't love the part too much; he just loved the part too well. Rest up in peace, Cowboy Jerry. You made it home. Thanks for the memories.

Scoop, should you not let that sleepin' dog lie still and talk shit about me, I know people that'll cut you short and punch out your time card for thee Big Bad Three: a dime bag, a forty ounce and a Big Mac. So, be advised or be gone; just keeping it real for you. If you don't know, now you know.

Hey, bottom line, if I don't conversate about my life and times like right now, feel me, I'm a explode and go seven kinds a white boy crazy. BOOM! Now, pick up the pieces. I could go off the rail all mad dog style and flat blast on a loaded school bus, feel me; I'd off my own self, too, in the twinklin' of a eye.

The hand writin' is on the wall, but I got shit to do yet, you heard me, like make all that mad Bill Gates cheddar, just sayin'. Then I'll do nothin' but walk down the street all damn day long smokin' weed, while sippin' on gin and juice, yo. Bottom line: if you wanna be a player, make yourself a player. This is America, motherfucker! The last shall be first. It's a warrior's world, yo! I got mine, go ahead on and get yours, too, shit!

I bet the Tinseltown trifecta and cashed a winner's ticket on that puppy, too: "Money for Nothin'," "Forever Young" and "Young Girls for Free." Lucky is as lucky does.

Yep, I wanna get crazy rich and bone all hot-to-trot at the drop of a hat eager-beaver star-struck females of all colors of the rainbow, and, hey, that shit be with my eyes wide open, too; I mean I'm so down to bone my balls are neon blue; I'm lookin' for it with a flashlight in the daytime. "As goeth the dick, so goeth the man"; that's the gospel according to your brother witness for Jesus over here, the bold knight of the round table known as Sir Hollywood: the true fresh prince.

And those knights knew how to party down, too. Nothin' but wall-to-wall loose bed wenches, killer weed for days and the very choicest fruit of the vine. They had a steady diet of big-legged whores, tall cool Coors and succulent s'mores. What's not to like? Hollywood, Cali, USA, yo! Almost heaven.

I'm a paint you a word picture: I'm pantin' like a dog in heat in anticipation of takin' that carnival ride that's located dead center between their legs. One thing, though, and this is not negotiable, neither: they gotta have a head on their shoulders; they gotta be able to bone and chew gum at the same time. Too much to ask for? I think not.

Women! Hell, take a good close look at a full-grown woman under the panties, yo. It looks like a damn bowling ball up in there. Plus, you can't no way trust a bitch at all, nope. There, I said it. Take me for instance; I just can't believe in somethin' that bleeds for a week straight and still doesn't die. So, go on, say it: I'm a credit to my gender. My favorite toy is PlayStation. All my other toys all have tits.

My biggest worry, it's being a solo act, alone on the big stage forever, and my second biggest worry, it's bein' tied down with somebody in a relationship from hell, such as marital bondage. I'm always afraid that wherever I go, the person I'm a like the least when I get there will be nobody else but yours truly. Ya know what I'm sayin'? I have met my enemy, and he looks just like me, too; my fucked up evil twin that's finna pounce on me, chew me up and spit me out. Brother. Brother. Brother.

My prison, hey, my prison, it's walkin' through this world all alone. I'd better like let somebody, anybody at all love me. Pretty soon, yo, it'll be too late.

So, go ahead on with it. State the obvious: "That dude, Jimmy Glitter, the boy is one deep motherfucker!" Yep, I'm the darin' young man on the flyin' trapeze, and, if ya don't believe me, just watch. And I work with no safety net, neither. I like the drama; it makes my nature rise.

Till I got my fame workin' for me and dropped outta the playpen they call public school, they had me in the special ed hopper. Last Chance High School Principal Dougie Do Right. sportin' a jheri curl with a serious activator juice drip, told my stepmother, and I quote him word-for-word. He goes: "Your boy never speaks up in class; he just sits apart from the group in that provocative hoodie wear of his and his indecently sagging trousers, freaking everybody else out, and the homework that he so rarely turns in, well, full disclosure coming up over here now because I'm a straight shooter: it's full of sadism, sexual violence and fury."

Legend has it that Mr. Do Right's shadow killed a dog. Like forget that senile, cantankerous, musty old rotten eggs-smellin' fool and all them teachers too and the horses they rode in on if they couldn't take a damn joke, feel me? Ah, homie! It ain't my mind playin' tricks on me, neither.

Hey, marchin' to a different beat box ain't no crime in America the beautiful, not yet, no how. I guess that don't make me a loser. Wanna compare paychecks with me; big bank take little bank? Oh, no? I didn't think so. I'm blessed and highly favored. What can I say?

Like I said, I only have a basic early bird high school dropout education under my belt, but I do have my Ph.D. in pocket with highest honors possible in payback, though, and that shit is best served while it's still cold to the touch, too: that's in the soldier's cookbook. I don't know karate, but I mos' def' do know me some crazy, and I ain't hard to find, neither. Don't start none, won't be none: let it be known.

So, be advised and start spreading the news: don't mess with the mighty Sir Hollywood or you're goin' down hard and that shit is for the full ten count. BOOM! Step up. Try me out. Take the Hollywood challenge, yo.

What's it like bein' Jimmy Glitter and joy ridin' about town in my pimped out bat mobile? Hey, Gee, it's amazinger 'n' a motherfucker; it's like every day is your perfect Christmas, snowy and white, and you are the moment; I can swagger in anywhere, ya see, anywhere at any time of the day or night, player's choice, yo, and have whatever or whoever tickles my fancy and whets my appetite on the house; nobody ever says any parts of no to me, like never, ya heard? Not even close, feel me? I pity the fool that tries to flip the switch and shine the stop light on me: that's a death wish, you know what I'm sayin'? I'm Bruce Lee, motherfucker, shit! I smoke TNT and juggle dynamite; wish some screwball would start a fight.

Dollars for days and everything my wanderin' eye surveys for free; it's good to be the Chosen One, whose comin' was prophesized in holy scripture. I'm just livin' the dream, Gee, doin' it and doin' it well. Hope I die before I get old. It's a young man's world, and I carry the torch; I'm the voice of my generation.

I'm the Golden Boy! Bobby Bling Bling over here, I sport

more carats than Bugs Bunny. I'm a force of nature, that's yours truly in a nutshell. You see me comin', better step aside or you will graduate with distinction from the School of Hard Knocks. BOOYA!

The sea will crush you if you don't know how to swim, feel me? And the bottom of the ocean has a no returns policy. Ya know, you have to escape the streets to survive, and you have to survive to escape. That's just me, though. I don't need no guru, no method or no teacher. I learned more off a five-minute Tupac cut than I ever learned in school, yo. Hey, teacher, leave those kids alone!

I wake up from my dreams in a cold sweat with a ache, a kind a cold sour sorrow in my gut and a stone caught in my throat. That shit is highly toxic; it makes a motherfucker naughty by nature, homie, feel me? I'm just sayin'. These ain't tears of sadness, though. It's a cleanse; it's my process.

So, there's that; I got this. Well, don't just sit there all quiet 'n' shit. I need a hymn or a sweet Jesus song, somethin' just fittin' for the occasion. Cue the choir of angels, somebody please! I feel the Holy Ghost now; I am the rapture. Bow down!

If you got a problem with any of my shockin' saga, I don't want to hear no parts. Tell it to Oprah, motherfucker! I was raised by wolves. So, what did you expect, Buddy Boy Scout 'n' shit? College man, please!

Hey, you know me; you seen me a million times before today on the street talkin' to his lost self: the land rover over here without hope of findin' a home base to land on at long last, constantly on my way to somewhere else, another mirage on the lost horizon. No "Leave it to Beaver" experience for the likes of your humble homeboy, Jimmy G. over here, I fear. That's my heavy cross to bear. You can't blame a dude for lookin', though; just acted the part I was cast as and did it well. Your mission is to keep that strictly on the downlow. Don't be no sellout, yo!

Only the strong survive, and me, I'm still alive and kickin' up a fuss. Us original gangsters, the certified O.G.'s among us, we don't die; we just multiply, ya see. Last count, I got four little baby kids and four big booty baby mamas.

When I'm down in the dumps, I just chant my demon blues away, sayin': "I am a man among men, a hundred percent masculine, the coolest! I am bad like Jesse James. Ride, outlaw, ride! They're gainin' on you. Faster! Don't look back!"

At this time, I'd sure like to send up my props in size extra-large to my personal Lord and Savior, Jesus Christ, the ultimate superstar, who came to Planet Earth with powers way beyond those of mortal men and without who none of these blessings would be even close to possible; praise him. Amen. WOOO! Won't he do it? Hallelujah! Amazin' grace. Jesus saves! I'm livin' proof; look no farther than right here. Onward, Christian soldiers! Support my ministry. Dig down in your pocket deep! Give till it feels good to you.

Playin' myself is a load to be reckoned with sometimes, homie, but hey I still gotta be me. Heavy is the head that wears the crown, though. Mamas, don't let your babies grow up to be cowboys like me. I ain't a saint; I just play one on TV.

Ah-ight, ah-ight, ah-ight then, I feel good now! I'm in a zone, big homie. Next at bat, I see it's the ol' tried and true Advice Question. You ain't the most original motherfucker in town, are ya now? So, there's that. Hey, I ain't mad at ya, though. You're the average workin' Joe. Respect! Game recognize game. It's all good, partner. You're the strong silent type; I admire that shit in a man.

Okay, my very best heads up to the youths out there livin' out their life script on the edge in today's buyer's market, especially all my fans, and they know just who they be, too, is only this right here. So, listen good with both ears open, feel me?

Short and sweet, if you goin' through those hard hard times, keep your head to the stars, young certified-legal Americans and others not so blessed 'cause, back in the day, I was a man without, too. Yeah, I said it, and that's now in play. My life is a open book.

Chapter one: "My True Story" ... Once upon a time in that mad scary part of town that's way way off the usual tour bus route, I was so broke that the ducks threw bread at me, and the females, WHOA, they was steady loud laughin' at my down-and-out raggedy butt, too. Isn't it a pity what a town without pity can do?

The ruthless Player Haters Club, they was all steady spittin' straight hurtful words of spite at me, too, daggers like: "Oh, look! Look! Why, it's the Goodwill Kid comin' this way," and, of course, there was the time-tested: "There go Sammy Shoes or Less! Hey, Sammy, Keds are comin' back strong, yo, watch!"

Hey, my fellow soldier, I couldn't catch nothin' but a bad head cold. Battle buddy, I couldn't even pay attention. If it wasn't for bad luck, I wouldn't've had no damn luck at all, shit! My only two steady on-call friends in a pinch were the dynamic duo of Gloom and Doom, double trouble. True one!

So, cue the breakdown: I guess what I'm tryin' like a motherfucker to say right here is just this: "Hey, the game of life, it ain't no way fair, trooper, but even the champagne rich and spoiled rotten ones among us sing their blues slow and low sometimes; everybody know that tune. I used to feel like nobody loved me but my mother, and she could've been blowin' smoke up my chimney, too.

Hey, y'all, you can still score that big bad capital W, though. Proven fact that a journey of a million miles, it all commence with baby step one. Can I get a WHOOP WHOOP on that!

Now, step off on the good foot, everybody! I ain't about to

come at ya with no weak-ass shit, neither. You got my word
on that or my name ain't Jimmy Glitter aka "Kid Pleasure."

Yep, the moral of the story: life implodes on your bad self
when you least expect it to, Scoop. On top in April and put
down like a tired out old dog in May. One minute, you're
playin' nicey nicey out there with the dolphins. Next minute,
though, it's just you and Jaws doin' the wild thing like it ain't
no tomorrow.

And fans, please please please do keep on scopin' out my
hit show, "Bring da Noise," streamin' on Netflix and be advised
that my new album, it drops in a mere week; it's called
"Beware of Dog." Can I get a WOOF WOOF on that newbie!
Also, catch me live on the "Freak of the Week" tour or sure do
wish you had. If y'all snooze, y'all lose.

So, now I'm a let you go with this public service
announcement that's comin' at ya straight from my heart of
hearts, ah-ight: life in the modern world, it is all messed up,

hear what I say, but this right here right now is the only shot we get to dance on the big stage in the Land of the Living.

Suck it up, y'all. Get on the good foot and trot! Do not let nobody get you down and do not hate, congratulate! Tell that less-fortunate raggedy dude on the block, the corner kid in need of just a little somethin' somethin' to take the edge off: "You ain't heavy; you my undercover brother."

Get on the love train; it's comin'. People get ready; you don't need no ticket; you just get on board. Tell 'em that original gangsta Glitter, the dog father, sent ya. Handle your business, Soldier, ah-ight? I ain't too proud to beg, but let's not belabor the point. Enough said on that.

And so, it ends. Well, Scoop, like that's all she wrote for today's episode of "Hollywood Raw," feel me? The storybook comes to a close, as it must do. Ask anybody, it's just another hip-hop tale.

I'm just another dude from the neighborhood with a

memory to share; I walk on the wild side; no angel wings, no harp, no halo, just talent for days oozing from my every pore. Let it be known that this has been impromptu. I pulled it all, every scrap of it, right outta my ass. It's still fresh and fragrant like that, too, yo. No additives or hamburger helper.

I live the life I love, and I love the life I live. If you got a better way to go about it, then show me, and I'll follow you wherever you lead me to with a flower in my hair and a lotus leaf up my butt crack chantin' "Tinker Bell lives!"

Hey, just don't look at me like that, like you some kind a evolved evangelical motherfucker, though. You just as scared a your shadow as me 'n' the next suspect in the lineup.

Ya see, me, I been playin' tag for priceless prizes with my lemons since I was born out of wedlock; I didn't have a childhood of record, no, I'm just sayin'. I'm a bastard outta Brooklyn. Bed-Stuy ... Do or die!

That luxury cruise ship for the young and innocent comin'

up, it had already sailed off by the time I got there to the passenger loadin' dock, and it won't be comin' back, not ever, not even for yours truly, no, and I can pray on it till I turn blue in the face.

Now, ain't that a pity and ain't that just a cryin' ass shame, too? That's the price you gotta pay for bein' a soldier of fortune and pokin' a finger in John Q. Public's eye like nobody's business, and I am one eye-pokin' motherfucker, too!

Everybody and their big mama gonna know my name before my casket drop, feel me, just sayin'. I'll be gone, but not forgotten. What's not to like? It ain't nothin' but a house party up in here, homie! We got us our vintage grape; we got us our easy earth girls; we got us our song and dance. What's not to like? It ain't no party like a Hollywood party 'cause a Hollywood party don't even break for squirrels.

It's just a little somethin' somethin' oh, so special about

us outlaws, ya see. People, they just remember 'em, and me, I'm the man in black, feel me? Black hat, black horse and black leathered down, and I live for the moment and uphold the honor code to the end. Jesse James rides again!

Long ago, I traded a walk on part in the war for a leadin' role in a cage. I took the side street through life less traveled by and that has made all the difference.

Like it say on my tattoo: "Live fast, die young and leave a pretty corpse." Oh, hell, yes, and like it say on my other tattoo, words to live by: "Fuck all bitches!" Where all the nasty girls at?

Well, I'm a wrap now and put a bow on it. Gotta go. Gotta go. So, you tell everybody out there in La La Land and far beyond that, should anybody, anybody at all want a piece of me, then step right up, go for your guns and be served. You gotta kill the king to be the king. It just wouldn't do to bum rush me, neither, though. Many have tried, and many have died. But, hey, if you're fast and if you're lucky, you just might be the one. Step up!

Ah-ight then, Brother Scoop, I'm a shoot off this Money Shot at ya now 'cause I gotta call the game due to darkness. Duty calls. The Master awaits me, and I come when summoned: that's in my job description here at the Dream Factory called "Hollywood Babylon," I'm just sayin'. Everybody gotta serve somebody.

See, I pitch for Team Jesus by day, every day, yes; I do it proper, too, but night time, the night time it's the right time, Jack. That's when I be steady dirty dancin' with Mr. D. You can't touch this! I'm ain't even ashamed, though; I throw down. Few are chosen, and the competition, it is fierce!

I ride shotgun with the devil, feel me, his satanic majesty, the royal Prince of Darkness, ya heard, and I cruise the Boulevard of Broken Dreams with a mean-ass gangsta lean scoutin' for raw recruits, namely how you say your basic rookie movie star wannabe, who expected lots lots more from reality than they ever got on their best of days back in Sweet Home Cleveland.

Everything's for sale at this swap meet, feel me: their very soul for eternal youth up in here in Tinseltown, the people's playland, the happiest place on earth. Business is sure crackin'!

I sell the fantasy, feel me, and they mad swarm here in mass droves to buy in like moths to a flame. Welcome to the acade, plenty of room up in here. Bring along your alibies; tell a friend, universal soldier. Everything and everybody is plastic out here, all of it, but, yours truly, I love me some plastic, though. Good luck with all the make-believe and dress up. Theire gonna sure love you! How bad do you wanna be a star, babe?

"My risk?" you ask. Well, it's drownin' out in a bottomless cold sea of trouble, yo. So, there's that, sure, but my reward, hey, my reward is priceless; it's the bomb; it's immortality. Now and forever, let it be me. Now, you tell me somethin', Every day Joe: just how cool is that!

I'm a see my photo, just me and only me on the cover, ah-ight? The title should be "Glitter Rules," and, hey, if ya don't believe I'm leavin', you can count the days I'm gone.

It's star time! WHOOP WHOOP ... The party light is on, and I can dance just as fast as I want to. BAM! That happened. One love. Peace. See ya. I'm out. That's just the way it is. Things will never be the same. I don't have a secret; I am a secret. YEH YEH!

Made in the USA
Monee, IL
13 August 2021